The
Desert
Look

The Desert Look

Bernard Schopen

University of Nevada Press
Reno :: Las Vegas :: London

Western Literature Series

Series Editor: John H. Irsfeld
A list of books in the series appears at the end of this work.

The Desert Look by Bernard Schopen was originally
published by The Mysterious Press of New York, in 1990.
The 1995 University of Nevada Press edition reproduces
the original except for the cover design and the front
matter, which have been modified to reflect the new
publisher.

The paper used in this book meets the requirements of
American National Standard for Information Sciences—
Permanence of Paper for Printed Library Materials, ANSI
Z39.48-1984. Binding materials were selected for
strength and durability.

Library of Congress Cataloging-in-Publication Data

Schopen, Bernard, A.
  The desert look / Bernard Schopen.
    p. cm. — (Western literature series)
  ISBN 0-87417-259-4 (paper : acid free paper)
  1. Private investigators—Nevada—Fiction. 2. Mothers
and sons—Nevada—Fiction.   I. Title. II. Series.
[PS3569.C52814D4 1995]
813'.54—dc20   94-41985
CIP

University of Nevada Press, Reno, Nevada 89557 USA
Copyright © 1989 by Bernard A. Schopen
All rights reserved
Cover design by Heather Goulding
Cover photo by Peter Goin
Printed in the United States of America

9 8 7 6 5 4 3 2 1

To Joanne

Strange things are hidden in the interior of Nevada. . . .

—Molly Flagg Knudtsen
Under the Mountain

.

1

Everyone in the Nevada desert has a story to tell.

Miranda Santee came out into the desert alone to tell me a story. Several stories.

In the blustery chill silence of that late-February late afternoon, I sat on a rock beside my tarpaulin lean-to and bed of sage coals, drinking coffee and watching the shadows lengthen and listening to her coming for several minutes before her rainbow-striped Bronco dipped over the bare ridge and down to a stop beside my Wagoneer.

For a while she sat staring at the irregular ruts that had brought her to my camp. For another while she stared across the desert hillside at me.

Finally she got out of the Bronco and, in a strange stiff leaning drift, wandered toward my camp, circling the patches of crusty snow that scabbed the earth, brushing past the clumps of spiny gray sage, edging around, as if passing a still potent totem of some ancient evil ritual, the manure pile of the local mustang stallion.

She moved cautiously, almost fearfully, moved not as if she didn't know what to expect from the desert but as if she did.

Against the biting wind and the occasional snow pellets it hurled she wore lizard-skin boots, designer jeans, and a long leather jacket with a sheepskin lining and a high collar. The left jacket sleeve flapped emptily in the wind.

At my camp she put on an uncertain smile. "Jack Ross?"

I thought I knew the face: under a soft rumple of short light-brown hair the features were strongly boned, smooth, now bloodlessly pale.

1

I almost knew the voice: low, richly timbred, now weak and raspy with tension.

I knew the eyes: brown, skittery, searching everything and seeing nothing, full of trouble.

"I'm Miranda Santee. I'd . . . I have to talk to you."

I put the face and voice and name together. "Maybe. But I don't have to talk to you, Miss Santee."

"I . . . you know who I am? You've seen my show?"

Miranda Santee had been a stringer for a Reno television station for four or five years. For the last year she'd hosted a weekend show called *The Other Nevada*: news from the desert and the cow counties. But there rarely was any hard news from anywhere but Vegas, Reno, and Carson City, so mostly she did cutesy features on retired movie stars, nonagenarian ranchers, desert rats living in ghost towns, cowboy poets, and puff pieces on events staged by desert communities desperate for income.

"Powerful stuff," I said.

"Thank you, I—oh . . . you're joking. I know, it isn't . . . but that isn't what I want. . . ." A blast of wind drove snow pellets into the tarp, into her back; several settled like opals in her hair. "Could I . . . have some of that coffee?"

In her voice I could hear a quiet panic. Under her jacket I could see the outline of her left arm taped or enslung across her body. In her right pocket I could see the outline of her fist. Something was clenched in that fist.

"I'm as hospitable as the next fellow, Miss Santee, but not when there's a gun pointed at me."

"I—" In desperation or despair, she looked everywhere in the desert except at me. "I was . . . shot, I need protection."

She needed something. She was in bad shape.

"Against me?"

Her gaze skittered over me—scruffy boots, dirty jeans, heavy wool shirt over a UNR football jersey, beard—and then out over the land again.

"I know what the desert can do to . . . men. I wasn't sure what you'd be like after six months out here. Alone."

I wasn't sure what I was like either. I *was* sure that I wanted no part of Miranda Santee.

"I don't do it anymore."

"I—you don't do what?"

"Whatever it is you want me to do. Whatever brings you out here with a gunshot wound and a pistol in your pocket."

She paled even more. "You . . . have to."

"No," I said to Miranda Santee and the swirling wind, "I don't have to do anything anymore."

Her face took on a deathlike stiffness.

I tossed the dregs of my coffee into the coals and refilled the cup. "I'll trade you a cup of coffee for the gun."

Again she scattered her gaze over the desert. Then slowly she pulled out a cute little nickel-plated Colt .32 automatic, fit for pockets and purses and killing people.

"I—I won't give it to you. But I'll keep it in my pocket."

The wind whipped at her hair, her empty sleeve. The cold brought no color to her skin. Her eyes saw and didn't see.

I shrugged, held out the cup. "You'll have to drink it fast. You get caught out here at night, you'll be in deep serious."

Slowly she put the automatic back in her pocket. She moved to the mouth of the lean-to, eased stiffly down onto the foot of my sleeping bag, pulled herself into the far corner from me, pulled her long legs up in front of her body like a barricade.

She took the cup, looked over the rim at me. "The people I talked to about you, they said you were a private investigator, that you were good at it."

"Good enough," I said.

"And then you . . . just walked away from it, from what you were, from your life. I—why?"

"I got tired of looking for people and finding bodies. Or worse."

"So you . . . came out here. Alone. You came out here alone for . . ." She moved the cup in a long slow arc across what lay beyond the lean-to. "For what?"

For what.

Distant dark rugged ranges, their snow cover graying in the gathering dusk to backdrop the scattered sleet flurries that trailed from ragged clouds; a flat patch of pale playa, filled to the sky with nothing; brown desert foothills traced with ghost roads leading nowhere, dappled with snow and gray sage and dark juniper; a hillside spring a hundred yards away in a clump of willows; three rows of dead apple trees planted and tended and abandoned by some long-gone desert dreamer; a natural juniper blind behind which I'd found dozens of obsidian chips.

For what.

A calm that the flutter of the sage in the wind, the scurry of predator and prey over the sandy earth, the muffled hoofbeats of the mustangs only deepened. A silence that the rush of wind and clatter of sleet and flap of trap only enlarged.

Her disturbed voice disturbed that silence. "You really like it out here, don't you? Alone."

"Yes."

"I hate it," she said with sudden sharp feeling. "I grew up in it. My father was a miner, we lived in every ugly little town in Nevada. He was a rock hound, too, dragging my mother and me all over the desert looking for . . ."

She looked at me, as if I could tell her what her father had looked for.

"I couldn't wait to get out of it—the ugliness, the heat, the cold, the wind and dust and mud, the snakes and scorpions, the emptiness, the loneliness. Sometimes I thought I'd die of the loneliness. Now . . . it's the only place I'm safe."

"I don't do it anymore, Miranda," I said. "You'd better get out of here before it's too late."

"It's already too late," she said, looking out at the lowering scuddy sky, the darkness collecting in every swale and cut in the land.

"I don't do it anymore," I said again.

"You . . . have to."

I smiled and didn't answer.

She held out the coffee cup to be refilled. I ignored it.

She set the cup in the crusty dust beside the sage coals. From her jacket pocket she pulled out a photograph, held it out as if offering me the secret of life.

I studied it in the dying light of the day. A casino publicity shot: four men in suits thirty years out of fashion, two women in skimpy showgirl costumes never out of fashion.

I knew the tallest man. Lanky Chandler, Reno casino owner and gambler of near-legendary fame, in his trademark pearl-gray Stetson, his trademark big square-toothed grin, as he had looked in my boyhood.

I almost knew the smallest man, elegantly dressed, with a thin face and eyes that looked at the camera as if they were sighting down a gun barrel.

I didn't know the other two men.

I didn't know either of the two women. They wore bits of sequin cut to emphasize their leggy, breasty bodies. They wore masks of makeup and smiles that didn't reach their eyes.

Something in the smile of one of the women spoke to me. "The one on the left . . . ?"

"Your mother."

My mother. I didn't have a photograph of my mother, only a memory. A memory of a ghost.

I remembered only her smile, or thought I remembered it. I saw it, or thought I saw it, sometimes on my daughter's lips.

"My mother's been dead for over twenty-five years."

"I know. I think . . . she was murdered."

I remembered my grandfather's face as he listened to the call from the Nye County sheriff. His face fell apart. He never quite put it together again.

"She died in a bar in Tonopah. It was an accident. There was a brawl, she got too close, got a beer bottle in the throat."

"I think she was murdered."

I remembered my grandfather's eyes when he told me.

He looked at me, saw me, but he also looked through me. I was there, but that fact was of no consequence.

Nothing was of consequence anymore.

The desert look.

He learned to disguise it, the desert look, but he never lost it.

I had stopped looking in mirrors because the man in it looked back at me with what might have been the desert look.

But I still found something of consequence.

I reached out and took the coffee cup and refilled it and handed it to Miranda. "Tell me."

The last light had drained from the day. The wind whipped the coal bed, fanning it into flickers and flares of fire that gave no heat against the chill. From down near the spring I thought I heard the mustang stallion snort and grumble.

It was a dark and stormy night in the desert.

Miranda Santee told me a story.

2

Once upon a time in Nevada, Miranda Santee told me, a Vegas goon was murdered, another lost an eye, and two showgirls and a million dollars in skim money disappeared.

One of the showgirls, Celeste Ross, was killed three weeks later. Neither the other showgirl, Belle Smith, nor the money was ever seen again.

In the faint glow of the coals, Miranda Santee's face was ridged and shadowed like the desert at first light.

"Officially, none of it happened. The men were shot in a mob dispute. There wasn't any money. Celeste Ross was killed in an accident. Belle Smith just left town."

The desert was so dark that I couldn't see the clouds, so cold my muscles were stiffening. "How do you know it did happen?"

"The people I talked to didn't have any reason to lie."

Some people always had a reason. Others didn't need one. But it was her story. "How did you get the unofficial version?"

Her pale smile twisted bitterly. "I'm a journalist, despite what you—I dug for it. There are a lot of people in Vegas— old policemen, gamblers, newspapermen—who remember when The Boys, as they called them, ran the town."

"How did you get onto the story in the first place?"

"I . . . do you know Natty Stern?"

The small dapper man in the photograph. "By reputation."

Everyone in Nevada knew Natty Stern by reputation. Reputed mob boss, former owner of the Starlight Casino and current owner of the Gold Strike downtown. Reputed rack-

7

eteer who after forty years in Nevada had never been indicted for so much as littering, who now in the Vegas of corporations and cost accountants stood as a living symbol whose faint aura of corruption the citizenry viewed with nostalgia and the tourists with titillation.

"He just opened a small club out by Pahrump," Miranda said. "I did a Grand Opening piece on it. When I interviewed him at his place outside Las Vegas, he . . . kept looking at me. Then he had one of his men—a man with one eye . . ."

Her voice lost its feeble force, died into the night.

I waited, listened to the wind, felt sleet stinging my forehead, heard it rattle on the tarp.

"The one-eyed man," I said, "he lost the eye in the rip-off?"

"Hiram Vanca," she said, her voice as cold and empty as the playa in winter. "He . . . he brought in the picture and Stern asked me about my family. When I told him I was adopted, he told me that Belle Smith was my mother."

I felt the photograph I'd put in my shirt pocket, tried to remember what the other showgirl had looked like. All I could remember was the fine big body.

"And you want me to confirm it? I don't do that anymore."

"No," she said. "Belle Smith isn't my mother. I checked. When children are adopted, they get new birth certificates with new names but the same dates. According to Clark County records, Belle Smith didn't have a child the day I was born."

That meant nothing. She knew it.

"I could petition the court for my real birth certificate, but I—Louise Santee was my mother, in the only way that matters. I don't want to know about . . . the other. I suppose that doesn't make any sense to you, but . . ."

It made sense. "I don't care who my father was."

She didn't seem to have heard me.

"You said Louise Santee *was* your mother?"

"She died last year."

"I'm sorry."

Again she didn't seem to have heard me.

"We lived together in Reno after my . . . father died ten years ago." Her pale mouth twisted bitterly again. "He died in this desert you're so crazy about. He was rock-hunting out by Ione—alone—he fell off a ledge and broke his legs. It took him . . . a long time to die."

"I'm sorry," I said again.

She seemed sorry too. Her body sagged, her head drooped as if in fresh deep grief.

"What do you want me to do, Miranda?"

"I want you to help me stay alive."

As sleet rattled on the tarp and danced around the coal bed, she told me more of the story.

Natty Stern had made her a present of the photograph. She started identifying the people in it. One, of course, was Stern; another, Lanky Chandler. Another was a then commissioner of Clark County, the other a man from Pioche then running for Congress.

Natty Stern wouldn't or couldn't talk to her again.

One-eyed Hiram Vanca had talked to her. He'd raged obscenely against Belle Smith, detailing what he would do to her if he found her. The way Miranda's voice emptied whenever she spoke of him told me that Vanca had told her something else.

The county commissioner had died ten years before.

The candidate was back in Pioche, his dreams of political power reduced to memories of dreams. He remembered the occasion of the photograph, he remembered the two showgirls, he remembered that he'd slept with one of them. He didn't remember which one.

Lanky Chandler had known both women. He didn't know where Belle Smith had come from or where she had gone. He knew that Celeste Ross was my mother. He knew that I was in the desert.

Miranda had scared up a couple of Vegas old-timers who claimed to remember the women.

They couldn't tell her much about Celeste Ross. She was just a showgirl, down from Reno in the mid-fifties after the big action had died in the north and Vegas was becoming the playground for the mob and Hollywood that Bugsy Siegal had dreamed of. When she wasn't displaying most of her body on the Starlight stage, she ran with entertainers, gamblers, or one of The Boys.

They couldn't tell her much about Belle Smith either. She was just a showgirl, down from Reno in the early fifties. When she wasn't displaying most of her body on the Star-

light stage, she ran with entertainers, gamblers, or one of
The Boys.

In 1960 she was running with Hiram Vanca.

In 1960 The Boys were skimming huge amounts of cash
from their casino operations and hauling it back to New York
and Chicago and Miami to finance other wholesome activ-
ities.

One day in 1960, one of Natty Stern's goons was found in
the desert, slumped over the wheel of a Starlight limo, shot
in the back of the head with a .22. Vanca was in the
backseat. He'd been shot in the temple, and the slug had
angled out his eye.

Celeste Ross and Belle Smith disappeared that day.

"The word on the street was that Natty was looking for
them because they'd ripped off a million dollars, skim
money that . . . Vanca was taking back to Miami. They say
he found your mother. They say he's still looking for Belle
Smith and the money."

"How does all of that put you in danger?"

"Somebody's following me. They even followed me out
here, at least till I hit dirt, in a silver Mercedes. And there
are others—in different cars. They spy on me, they sit in
the parking lot and watch, wait. They were in my apartment. . . ."

She shuddered, violently. "They—he shot me."

I couldn't quite sort all that out.

"At first I thought Natty Stern was having his men follow
me, hoping I'd lead them to Belle Smith. Ever since I left his
place I've had this . . . feeling. It's hard to explain, it's
scary, like being haunted. I mean, I know he's there, it's not
the silver Mercedes, it's somebody else. . . ."

She shook her head. "And there's a black car, like a hot
rod, with its rear end jacked way up and loud mufflers.
There are so many . . . I got so I didn't know if I was seeing
things or not. I—I was afraid I was going crazy."

She was still afraid of it. Perhaps with reason. The Belle
Smith story had the shape and substance of myth; this story
had all the fractures and twists of paranoia.

"Tell me about the shooting."

"Three days ago I came home from another trip to Vegas
and there was a man—not really a man, a boy, younger than
I am, I mean he was in his twenties, but he acted like

a—he'd trashed my apartment, looking for something. He—I screamed, and he just . . . shot me. I got out of the hospital this morning. I came here."

Three days ago. That explained her pale weakness.

"So you don't know if he took anything?"

"No. I mean, no, I don't know."

"Did he say anything?"

"No," she lied, and hurried on. "At first I thought he was one of Stern's men, but that doesn't make sense. And he didn't look right. He was young, hairy, greasy, he looked like a street thug. He was . . . ugly."

"It sounds like an interrupted burglary, Miranda."

"No."

I let that go. "Who do you think is trying to kill you?"

"It has to be . . . whoever has the money."

"Belle Smith?"

"Or whoever was with her, helped her."

"Who would that be?"

"I don't know," she said.

"How does my mother figure into this?"

"I . . . don't know," she said. "I just know she does."

I didn't think that. But it didn't matter.

I rose, stretched some of the stiffness from my muscles.

Miranda huddled closer to the coals. "It's freezing out here. There's a sleeping bag in the Bronco. And hot soup."

The wind stirred and deepened the darkness. The two vehicles were amorphous shades of dark even when I reached them.

In the back of the Bronco I found a small Styrofoam hamper and a sleeping bag. I also found that, while Miranda Santee might hate the desert, she at least knew it. She carried shovels, a couple of six-foot two-by-twelves, a length of rope, a rolled-up tarp, a first-aid kit, and two plastic jugs of water.

When I shut the Bronco door, the darkness was so sudden and complete that I had the illusion that I was still alone.

But I wasn't alone, couldn't be. Miranda Santee's story had seen to that. It had visited ghosts on me.

Her story was ridiculous, built of speculations, guesses, rumors. Beyond that, she hadn't told all of it, and she hadn't told all the truth of what she had told. But the story was going to take me out of the desert. It was the only one that could.

Back at camp, Miranda slowly pulled off her boots and crawled halfway into her sleeping bag while I unpacked the hamper; a thermos of chicken soup, bread, cheese, apples. From my stores I added dried apricots and chocolate.

We ate and listened to the wind and the silence. Then I climbed into my bag. The lean-to was built for one. I felt Miranda jerk away from the pressure of my hip.

I was aware of her scent, faintly floral from her perfume, faintly musky from her flesh, faintly acidic from her emotions.

I was aware of my body's awareness of her body. I'd been in the desert alone too long. Or not long enough.

"How'd you like to do me a favor, Miranda?"

The silence was long and chill. "What?"

"Take the gun out of your pocket and put it where you won't roll on it in your sleep and shoot one of us."

I felt her struggling movements. "I . . . you'll have to help me get my coat off."

Her pale face floated spectrally in the darkness. I felt her shudder as my hand touched her shoulder. I helped her out of the coat, felt her shudder again as my hand brushed her blouse, felt her jerk away as our hips touched through our bags.

The hole in her shoulder wasn't the only wound she carried.

I rolled the coat up and laid it around the corner of the tarp. Then I zipped myself into my bag. "Who did it, Miranda?"

"Did . . . what?"

I listened to the wind and her breathing. Both were ragged.

After a while her breathing began to smooth. The wind seemed to be dying.

"Tell me what the man who shot you said."

"Nothing. He . . . shot me, and then he ran."

That wasn't the truth, but it didn't matter.

"Tell me what you're really up to."

"I told you. I'm trying to keep from getting killed."

"Stop looking for Belle Smith."

"I . . . can't."

"Why? Not because she might be your mother—you said you don't care about that. Is it the money?"

The wind whipped and swirled for another long time. But it was ebbing, carried no sleet. The storm was dying.

Then I heard Miranda Santee's voice, weak, disembodied in the darkness, empty in the silence.

"It's the story."

3

I was back on my rock as dawn grayed the desert, the huge cold empty sky.

I hadn't slept well. Miranda had whimpered through the night, pained by either her wound or her dreams. Even in sleep her body had violently retreated from contact with mine.

I watched the sunlight silver the frosted earth, empurple the hills and mountains, blue the sky. Then I filled the coffeepot at the spring and put it on the sage coals to cook.

I took the photograph from my pocket, tried to read the smiles of Celeste Ross and Belle Smith. The smiles were big and bright and empty, glittered like the costumes they were part of. I tried to read the eyes. The eyes were empty.

The fine big bodies were full, identical—long legs shaped sensuously as if by a desert wind, high hips draped with a strip of cloth like an aspen line rising from a grove at a hillside spring, bare midriffs like a playa to be crossed, high round breasts pushed up like desert dunes.

The resemblance between Celeste Ross and Belle Smith ended at the throat.

My mother's features were regular, conventionally pretty. Belle Smith's face, even under the masks of makeup and smile, was striking—attractive without being pretty, strong, almost fierce, the face of a woman indefatigable in pursuit of whatever she set her mind or heart on.

I looked at Miranda Santee as she stirred out of sleep. Her features were smaller, softer, but it was the same face. I didn't know what Miranda was in pursuit of.

I put the photograph back in my pocket.

Miranda eased out of her bag, out of the lean-to. Holding her arm gingerly, she stretched into the sunlight. Her body wasn't as big as those of the showgirls, but it was as fine. "I . . . need to get clean." She picked up her coat, walked slowly down to the spring.

When she came back, breakfast—a sort of scrambled-egg stew—was ready. The icy springwater had tinted her pale face with pink; the food deepened the hue.

"Thank you," she said when she finished. "I feel better."

In the crisp, still morning the sky took on a deepening blue, distant ranges floated in a pale haze like shadows or ghosts, snowcaps of the nearby ranges gleamed, the playa shimmered, sage and snow glittered with frost.

I looked at it while Miranda Santee told me why the story of Belle Smith was important to her.

"It's my ticket out of . . . all this. I'm almost thirty years old, with a degree from a third-rate journalism school, five years in the profession and no real experience. There's only one way out. The only chance I'll have at a real job is if I break a story big enough to hit the networks."

"And you think this is it? Belle Smith?"

"It is the way I'll tell it," she said grimly.

"How's that?"

Either the night of whimpering sleep or the telling of her stories had done her some good. Her eyes focused sharply, with the force of her intent. Her eyes focused on me.

"I don't care what she did, whether she shot those men or not. Belle Smith was a victim. So was your mother. Not just a victim of vicious hoods. They were victimized by Nevada, debased and destroyed the way Nevada debases and destroys all women."

"How's that?"

She caught the edge of irony in my voice, bristled. "I think you know, Mr. Ross. But if you don't, look at that picture of your mother. Look at the smile."

"I know the smile," I said.

"I know it too," she said. "I wore it, and the stupid sexist costume, carrying the tray at Harrah's while I was in school, and after. What kind of smile is that, Mr. Ross?"

"You tell me."

"It's a prostitute's smile."

"Are you blaming this on Nevada, Miranda, or on men?"

"What's the difference?"

"You don't like either, I take it."

Her face set in defiance. "Nevada is the ugliest place in the world. For a woman it's the loneliest and most dangerous. I knew about the desert. I learned about men when I worked as a cocktail waitress. My mother—she never learned, she thought all those guys, their talk and promises . . ."

Miranda didn't like Nevada, or men. She didn't, I thought, like herself much either.

But I found myself liking Miranda. I didn't agree with her—what she was raging at was there, but there were other things in Nevada—but I liked her fierceness in the face of it.

At the same time, the story of Belle Smith, regardless of how she told it, wasn't going to get her out of Nevada. That was just a story that Miranda was telling herself.

But it didn't really matter.

I rose, grabbed the small bag of garbage and a shovel. "You can help break camp, if you want."

She stared at me.

I buried the garbage and the coals, then took the dishes to the spring and cleaned them. As part of my squatter's bargain with the Paiute rancher who owned the spring, I'd cleared it of creek willows and enlarged the pool. In the stiff mud at its edge, the mustangs and Miranda Santee had left their tracks.

Back at my camp, Miranda had our sleeping bags rolled up and tied and leaning against her hamper and my large cooler.

As she watched, I hauled the tarp off the juniper poles and rolled it up, unlashed the poles and took them to the spring; the rancher would find a use for them. Then I rolled up the ground tarp, exposing the thick bed of grasses. Gathering them into a pile, I carried it to the manure mound, where I left it as part of my squatter's bargain with the mustang stallion.

I loaded my Wagoneer and her Bronco. When I finished, only tracks that the wind would erase said that I had been there.

Miranda finally spoke. "You're coming in? You're going to help me? I can't pay you right now, but—"

"No."

"But—"

"I'm no longer licensed by the state of Nevada to conduct private investigations on another's behalf."

"But you're going to help me?"

"I'm going to talk to some people about my mother. If I learn anything about Belle Smith, I'll let you know."

She shouldn't have been satisfied with that, but she was. Suddenly I knew what she really wanted of me.

That didn't matter either.

I turned to give the desert a last look, and I saw the mustang stallion.

Near the top of the brown hill above the spring, he stood glaring at us. Below him three mares and two yearlings bit and tore at dead desert plants.

"God, he's ugly," Miranda said.

He was that, a big hammer-headed gray, all bone and tendon, his hide roughly furred and scarred from battle.

"It makes me sick, the way everybody romanticizes them, makes them some kind of symbol of freedom. They're vicious stupid brutes. They maim and kill each other and control the mares with violence, they'll kill another stallion's foal while it's still in the womb, they . . . mate with their daughters."

There was more malevolence in her voice than in the mustang stallion's brutish glare.

"They aren't people, Miranda, they're horses."

"They're ugly, inbred abominations."

Almost as if he'd heard her, the stallion stiffened, shook his heavy, shaggy head. The heads of the mares and yearlings shot up from the earth, the horses wheeled and raced up and over the hillside and were gone.

"Ugly." Miranda shuddered in the bright sunlight. Then she climbed into her rainbow-striped Bronco.

We were fifty miles from Gerlach. The trip took three hours.

One-armed, twenty-four-plus hours out of a hospital bed, Miranda Santee was very good in the desert she hated. She knew the difference between ruts that led to something and ruts that didn't. She knew where alkali flat and playa were dry and safe and where they had been made treacherous by water. She knew when to follow old ruts through glutinous sand pockets and when to make her own way, when to let the land take control and when to fight it.

I followed her, admired her skill and knowledge, admired the land. The day was cold and bright, the desert empty and beautiful. In the storm-washed air, I could see for miles. In the rock and rupture of the land I could see for eons.

What I couldn't see was Miranda's past, or my own. But I was going to look for them.

We stopped at Gerlach for coffee. No silver Mercedes or "hot rod" or "other car" waited for us. Before the café, a pair of muddy pickups stood beside a dented old Oldsmobile.

In the café a thick-middled, sleek-legged waitress drifted with a coffeepot from a silent ranch couple at a small table to a silent Paiute reading a newspaper at another table to a silent duded-up young buckaroo at the counter to a pair of high school boys in letter jackets who looked at her sleek legs and grinned at each other.

The trip had taken the color from Miranda's face, the energy from her voice. She was quiet, seemed depressed.

I asked for her phone number and address. I knew the apartment complex, a newish jumble of plywood off South Virginia. I told Miranda she could reach me, for now, at the Silver Sage.

"Lanky Chandler's casino?"

I shrugged. "Good a place as any. What are you going to do?"

She looked out at the Black Rock Desert, flat and pale and empty for miles. "Try to put my apartment back together. Go back to work. I've got stories I need to edit and voice-over."

"I wouldn't push it if I were you. You need rest."

She tried to shrug, winced. "What are you going to do?"

"What you want me to. Ask questions, so that whoever is trying to kill you will try to kill me and leave you alone."

Color filtered back into her face. "That isn't what . . ."

"Of course it is, Miranda."

Her gaze scattered again.

My gaze fastened on the dudish buckaroo.

He wore denim, jacket and jeans and shirt fashionably faded to a cloudy white, cuffs embroidered with bright rainbow swirls.

He might have felt my gaze. He rose from the counter. His face was thin and pale, his eyes were blue and pale and not looking at us. He walked out, not looking at us.

I could understand him not looking at me. But the stern silent rancher, when his wife wasn't looking, looked at Miranda. The Paiute looked over his newspaper at Miranda. The high school boys looked at Miranda and grinned.

The dude didn't look at Miranda.

Miranda noticed none of this. "And you'll . . . just do it? Just let them—why?"

I didn't have an answer. I had an impulse. "Be right back."

He stood in the wind-layered winter dust of the street. He saw me, slipped behind a mask of silver-lensed sunglasses.

I smiled at him. "You driving the silver Mercedes?"

His thin jaw set into a hard silence. In the silver of his sunglasses I saw my doubled reflection. I looked as rough-furred and, despite the smile, as malevolent as the mustang stallion.

I broadened my smile. "See that girl in there?"

As she stared at us, Miranda's pale face seemed to float, as if underwater, in the shadows of the plate glass.

"She sees you. I've seen you. If either of us sees you again, I'll take you over my knee and spank you."

"That how you get off?"

He wasn't twenty-five, he wasn't a hundred and fifty pounds, and he wasn't afraid of me.

I took a step toward him. "You don't want to find out."

His lips twisted into a hard smile. His arm jerked, a spring clicked, a tiny silver gun hopped into his hand. "Back off, asshole."

I hit him as hard as I could.

He took my fist high on the forehead, spun, his arm flailing at the sky. The little silver pistol fired with a soft damp pop.

He banged into the Oldsmobile, dazed. I got to his wrist, clamped down, felt the mechanism under his jacket. Grabbing his elbow, I jerked his arm straight, then more than straight. The gun fell into the dust.

His thin face slicked with sudden sweat. His silver mask had slipped far enough that I could see the pain in his eyes.

I put more pressure on the elbow. "Move and it's finished."

He nodded rapidly, silently.

"Now you back off, easy."

I let him go, and he stumbled backward, holding his elbow.

I picked up the gun. I didn't recognize the make. It didn't look real. But it was real enough.

"I don't want to see you again."

He flexed feeling into his arm, nudged his sunglasses back over his eyes. "Don't worry, asshole. You won't."

He turned and walked up the street.

I slipped the toy gun into my pocket. The Paiute stood by the door watching me. "Pretty good."

"Pretty stupid. I could have gotten somebody shot."

"That too."

Miranda was still staring when I sat back across from her. "Who was that? Is he the one . . ."

"I think maybe he's your ghost, the one you've sensed but never seen."

"But—" Anger drove dark color into her throat. "You just let him go? You didn't even find out—"

"I found out enough. He wasn't afraid of me, and he's an arrogant little snot, which suggests that he's good at what he does. The two together suggest Natty Stern."

She looked at me. "I don't see how you can know that?"

"I don't know it, I'm guessing. But it doesn't matter. If I'm wrong, if he's an Oregon ranch hand on his way to frolic in Fun City and just happens to carry a toy gun in a spring-loaded forearm holster for protection in the wilds of Reno, then nothing has been lost. If he's not, then he knows I know about him. If I know about him, he may find that a problem. If he does, he may try to do something about it. In any case, he's thinking about me and not you. And that's sort of the point, isn't it?"

Again her gaze started to scatter. This time she managed to stop it, control it, focus. "I—I still don't know why you're just going to let . . . that happen?"

I still didn't have an answer. But I gave her one anyhow. "Why not?"

4

Cold high pressure and a temperature inversion clamped an invisible lid on the Truckee Meadows. Beneath it a greasy film hung over Reno and Sparks, tinting the light orange, fouling the air, darkening the brown desert ranges, dirtying the snow on the foothills of the Sierra.

Downtown Reno was in the throes of redevelopment—a gaudy new arch bending over Virginia Street, colored plastic strips dangling over alleys, oversized green street signs and traffic lights jutting from artsy rectangles of brown steel. Along slick brick walkways, new planters bore new shrubs already dying from exhaust fumes.

The Silver Sage was in the throes of expansion. Beside it, where a small motel had existed like a little desert in its rain shadow, a huge hole filled with dirty snow sprouted a skeleton of steel that clung to the building like a feeding parasite.

I wheeled the Wagoneer into the garage, down and around through dim concrete canyons, back up and into a space reserved for, by the faded stencil on the wall, Mr. Chandler.

In the casino, things were slow. Most of the machines were silent, most of the tables covered. Dealers costumed in jeans and Western shirts stood in stiff silence, change people and keno runners drifted like grazing animals on an alkali flat, bored bartenders ogled bored cocktail waitresses, and everyone kept an eye on the poker pit, where Lanky Chandler was dealing Hold 'Em.

From across the floor he looked, with the hat and the gray shirt under a black leather vest, with the big grin dominating his face, as he did on the billboards that lined the highways that cut through the Nevada sagelands.

As I dragged my scruff and grime into their machine-groomed lair, security men stiffened. I wasn't a tourist, I might be trouble. But I might also, in Nevada, be somebody.

In the poker pit a large blond man wearing a razor-cut and a five-bill blue suit and a smooth blank face watched me approach but didn't stiffen.

Tom Pardun was head of Silver Sage security. He knew I wasn't somebody.

When I got near, Lanky aimed his grin at me. "That you behind all that hair, Jack?"

Up close he didn't look as he did on the billboards. Up close he looked old, his squarish face seamed and sagging and stained darkly under his eyes. He looked ill.

His huge hands, bony and liver-spotted, shuffled a deck of cards. "Antes in, pot's right, everybody's a player, one's a winner." He flipped blue-backed cards over the green felt, then casually raked the ante, and grinned at me.

"Care to sit in?"

"No, thanks."

"Lucy's comin' out," he intoned, "like it or not."

The tourist on the button, a wizened woman with a smear of red lipstick, pushed a chip into the center of the table.

"She likes it," Lanky declared, "Lucy likes it a lot."

The next two players dropped. "Got'em runnin', Lucy." A young black man in a '49ers jersey called. "Carl, he ain't runnin', he's a player." The other tourists dropped.

"Let's flop 'em an' help somebody." Lanky swiftly turned over the top three cards on the deck. "Knave of hearts, seven puppy feet, hearts duck. Who's the lady smilin' on?"

The woman bet, the black raised, Lanky chanted, the woman raised, the black dropped. Lanky congratulated and commiserated, began a story about filling a boat against Bennie Binion and why the game is called Hold 'Em.

I watched for a while, and listened. Watched him deal and flop and rake, listened to him work the table and tell his stories, watched him give the tourists what they came for, give them a piece of Nevada lore, give them Lanky Chandler.

He violated every unofficial rule of casino play, commenting on the fall of the cards, speculating on hidden hands, calculating odds, cajoling, sympathizing. He grinned and told his stories as the players traded their money and he unobtrusively but inexorably raked the house percentage from each pot.

While I watched Lanky, Tom Pardun watched me, his well-fed face willfully still, his eyes steadily empty—a standard cop trick, designed to unnerve a suspect. It didn't unnerve me. It did make me wonder what he was doing watching Lanky deal.

Ex-RPD, Tom Pardun had bailed out of a lieutenancy into the security job with Lanky and was being groomed, word had it, to manage the casino end of the business. He wasn't learning much watching Lanky deal Hold 'Em.

After a few hands, Lanky glanced at me. "We need to talk?"

I nodded, and he turned to the pit boss, nodded, rose. At six-seven, he rose a long way. He grinned at the table. "Been a pleasure, folks. Good luck."

Tom Pardun watched us leave. Something struggled beneath his forced impassivity, tried to rise into his empty cop eyes. Perhaps the notion that maybe I was somebody after all.

Lanky worked his way to the elevator, joking with the help, glad-handing the tourists. His grin closed with the elevator door. He punched a button, leaned back, closed his eyes.

"Damned if I don't think the last time the medicos went into my chest they didn't hook everything back up. A couple hours takes the starch right out of me."

"Why do it?"

He didn't open his eyes. "What else is there?" What else besides being Lanky Chandler for the world.

I followed him out of the elevator and through a maze of hallways and into his office, a small, windowless room with a large desk, two heavy brown leather chairs, and white walls filled with framed photographs that recounted the myth of Lanky Chandler. In each wall a blank white door punched through the photographs like a corridor to reality.

Lanky folded himself in the chair behind the desk, leaned back, clasped his hands over a silver belt buckle in the shape of Nevada. He put on his poker face, grinned. "Been a while, Jack. You back in business?"

I'd watched Lanky Chandler play poker a few times. His grin, a flexible mask of ingenuous good-ol'-boy affability, was impenetrable, inscrutable. He'd never used it on me before.

Whatever Miranda Santee was mucking around in, Lanky Chandler owned a piece of. "I think you know why I'm here, Lanky."

"This'd be about the little TV girlie?"

I sat in one of the leather chairs. "It's about my mother."

"Celeste," he said slowly. "Good woman. I liked her."

"Did Natty Stern kill her?"

"There's a story that goes that way."

"Is it true?"

His grin didn't waver. "Nevada's full of stories, Jack, you know that. How can you ever tell which one is the truth?"

It was a curious non-answer, given the circumstances, like a check bet from a player who'd opened and hadn't been raised. I had a sudden sense that we were in a no-limit game.

That same sense structured my response. "You knew my mother. Would you put her on a robbery and murder that got her killed?"

"Nope." I looked at him until he spoke again. "Look, Jack, I don't know what your granddad told you. He—well, fathers and daughters, when it goes bad with them, things can get kind of twisted."

I had a sudden brief vision of my grandfather's face going dark and still at the mention of her name; I felt as if in a dream the depth of his silence.

"He wouldn't talk about her. Before she died, he gave me the impression that she was a tramp, if not an out-and-out whore. Afterward . . ." Afterward, the desert look.

"You know he was wrong, don't you?"

My grandmother had said so. She'd said that my grandfather and my mother hadn't gotten along, but that my mother was a good woman and that she loved me.

All I really knew about my mother was that at sixteen she'd wanted to do one thing with her life and my grandfather had wanted her to do something else, so she ran off with a small-time gambler named Virgil Ross. A couple of years later she was back in town, divorced. A couple of years later she was a Harold's Club showgirl. A couple of years later she had me and left me with my grandparents and went back to Harold's Club.

"Was he?"

"Wrong as could be," Lanky said. "Celeste was smart, funny, fu: to be around. She liked a good time, sure, liked bein' where the action was. She liked men, an' when she ran into one she liked a lot she did what anybody with a lick of sense would do, even though she never had much luck with them. . . ."

His gaze flickered, as if he were adjusting the focus of an inner lense. He started to speak, stopped.

"You knew her pretty well."

He shrugged. "It was a small town back then, everybody knew everybody. Especially downtown, the night folks, the players."

"Were you one of the men she didn't have much luck with?"

"It . . . was a long time ago, Jack. Ancient history."

"Maybe," I said, "but the story isn't over. At least Miranda Santee doesn't think so. Why'd you sic her on me?"

Lanky pushed the Stetson farther back on his forehead; his scalp glistened under strings of graying fair hair.

"Look, Jack. The girlie comes to me with a picture, tells me a story. I tell her maybe it's true and maybe it isn't. I tell her I knew Belle and your mother years ago. Celeste is dead and nobody knows where Belle is, maybe she's dead too. She wants to know about Belle's daughter, she thinks maybe Belle's her mother. I tell her the only daughter I know about is a girl named Echo, who'd be fifteen years older than her. I don't know where she is either. I tell her you're Celeste's son and you're out in the desert somewhere an' maybe you know somethin' I don't."

"Why would you think I'd know anything?"

He hesitated, grinned quickly past it. "I figured you'd seen your granddad's file."

"What file?"

"After your mom died, he showed up. He had a picture like the one the girlie's got, this one from Harold's. He didn't like the way Celeste died, asked the same questions the girlie did. I figured he'd told you about it, or he'd left a file."

My grandfather was a careful record keeper, a compulsive file-maker. "There isn't any file."

His grin broadened, as if he put me on a bluff and was about to call it. But he didn't. "Maybe not."

"What didn't he like about her death?"

"He didn't say."

"What did you tell Miranda about Belle Smith's daughter?"

"What I knew. Pretty little thing, Belle always dressed her real nice. She'd've been, what, fifteen maybe when . . ."

"Who was the girl's father?"

"Belle never said."

"Who was in the picture my grandfather had?"

"Me an' Belle an' Celeste an' this guy your mom was steppin' out with at the time; wrangled at a divorce ranch." His grin widened. "John, his name was. Everybody called him Single John."

"Did Natty Stern kill my mother?"

He looked at me. I couldn't read the look. "Maybe."

"How long ago did you talk to Miranda?"

"Couple weeks."

Miranda had known for a couple of weeks that Belle Smith had a daughter named Echo.

"Tell me about Belle Smith."

He leaned forward, clasped his big hands on the desk. I was interrogating him, and he was letting me. I didn't know why.

"Belle was . . . different," he said. "I never understood how her and your mom were friends. In their little outfits they was a prize matched pair, but—Celeste, the thing about her was she never took much real serious, you know. Especially herself. All she seemed to want out of life was to live it, maybe with a man who wasn't a total asshole. But Belle . . ."

Emotion, or the memory of it, thickened his voice.

"Belle was *intense*. She wanted what she wanted *hard*. The problem was, what she wanted kept changing. She'd decide she wanted something or somebody, and she'd flat go after it, do whatever she had to to get it. She'd get this look, sometimes, this sort of blind . . . But then it'd turn out not to be the right thing, or the right man, after all."

His voice thickened even more, like scar tissue reforming over an old wound that wouldn't stay healed. Lanky had known Belle Smith better than he'd known Celeste Ross.

"Were you one of the guys that wasn't the right one?"

"We took a turn around the dance floor," he said. He stared down at his hands, as if they enclosed a memory or a ghost. Then he leaned back in his chair, grinned his grin. "But I never was much for permanent female company. The one time I tried it didn't work out too hot. Just an old range bull."

"More like a mustang stud, from what I've heard." Lanky's luck with the ladies was part of the myth.

His grin widened. "I ran small bunches from time to time. But I wouldn't believe most of the stories I hear, Jack."

"Would you put Belle Smith on robbery and murder?"

"Not going up against Natty Stern and Hiram Vanca. Belle was intense, but she wasn't crazy. Vanca was. Still is."

"Vanca's one of Natty's goons?"

"Goon don't quite do it. Vanca . . . it's hard to say what Vanca is. Two things, I guess. One is stupid, and there isn't much you can say about that. Stupid is stupid. But the other is crazy, and there's lots of kinds of crazy and Vanca is all of them."

This time the voice didn't change, but the grin did. It tightened. Lanky Chandler was afraid of Hiram Vanca.

"He was Natty's enforcer. Most times, all he had to do was mention Vanca's name."

"Why?"

"Vanca probably killed . . . what, a hundred people? I know that sounds . . . but trust me, it's true. But it wasn't even that, it was more the way he did it. He killed a man once, the story goes, by breaking his legs. Started at the ankles, broke them all the way up."

No wonder he was afraid of Hiram Vanca. I let that go.

"What would you figure happened to Belle?"

He shrugged, grinned. "Who knows, Jack?"

I wasn't getting much out of Lanky Chandler, and what I was getting I didn't like. The sense that he, like Miranda Santee, wasn't telling me all he knew and all the truth of what he did know. The sense that he was getting something out of me.

I rose, looked over the walls of photographs, read the story of the last fifty years in Nevada. One of the stories.

They were all there. Every governor from Sawyer to Bryant, every senator from McCarran to Laxalt, every congressman and Gaming Control Board head. And the others:

Harold Smith and Bill Harrah, Amarillo Slim and Dolly Brunson, Jimmy Stewart and Barry Goldwater, Nixon and Ford, Bing and Sinatra and Elvis, Steinbeck and Jones and Mailer, both Hustons and Walt Disney. And a few thugs like Natty Stern—but only a few, for Lanky, like Smith and Harrah, was clean, a northern Nevada maverick from the mob-infested casino business in the south.

Most of the people in the photographs were dead.

And always Lanky Chandler and his grin. From the crew-cut kid in a Wolfpack uniform palming a basketball to the Stetsoned old man flicking the switch for the new Reno arch. In the photographs Lanky Chandler towered above everyone; through them he aged. After three heart operations, he wasn't quite dead.

And always women, in costumes of showgirls and waitresses, in slinky evening gowns and brief bathing suits, in bright empty smiles. Legs and breasts and teeth.

And a cute blond toddler who became a pretty blond girl who became a lovely blond woman.

"If I were in business, Lanky, would you have a job for me?"

"Nope."

The checking, betting, and raising were over. I called him. "I don't think you're telling me the truth."

He grinned, showed me his hand. "What you think doesn't matter, Jack. All that matters is what you know."

I grinned, showed him my hand.

"No. What matters is what I do."

5

One of the doors swung open. The lovely blond woman stood in it, smiled at me. "Jack. I thought it was you."

She was more than lovely.

The cut of her skirt emphasized the length and shape of her legs, the brown of her jacket deepened the glow of her brown eyes and the gloss of her bright hair, the ruffle of her pale-peach blouse draped her breasts like ribbon on a present.

"Hello, Sage."

"You look like a walking pack rat's nest." She wrinkled her nose. "And you smell like the rat died."

I laughed. I'd always laughed a lot with Sage Chandler.

She stepped in. She smelled like the desert after rain.

She turned to her father. "It's time for a pill and a nap."

"The pill, yeah, but I ain't about—"

"You're going to rest if I have to have Jack cold-cock you!"

They glared at each other with a fierceness that wasn't completely feigned. Finally Lanky sighed, rose. "Give her a little juice, first thing she does is start runnin' my life."

"Only so you can keep it," Sage said. Her eyes brightened suddenly with tears. "So I can keep you."

Lanky Chandler looked at his daughter, stepped from behind the desk and took her in his arms. Childlike, she buried her face in his chest.

His big hand gently patted her shoulder. "I'm all right. And I'll stay all right. I'll even take a nap."

She smiled at him, and he kissed her hair. He turned, opened a door. Behind him I saw part of a big room, a big bed.

"Whatever Jack needs, take care of it. My account."

She smiled. "Jack has needs that can't be taken care of."

He looked at me. He didn't grin. "Makes him just like the rest of us, don't it."

He stepped through the door and closed it.

Sage stared at the empty whiteness of the closed door. Then her expression took on a curious formal intimacy that I couldn't quite read. "Let's go to my office."

I followed her, breathing her scent and watching the soft stir of her hair and the stretch of her stride, down a hall to a frosted glass door stenciled EXECUTIVE OFFICES, into a big room filled with fine furniture so old it seemed to have grown there.

As we entered, Tom Pardun straightened out of a sprawl and rose from a chair, smoothed his face, buttoned his suit jacket over the small roll of flesh along his waist.

"Hold my calls, Opal," Sage told the middle-aged, heavily made-up receptionist. The receptionist smiled, looked at me with blue eyes hooded with blue shadow and questions.

Tom Pardun looked at me with brown eyes carefully emptied of everything. He looked at Sage the same way.

"Excuse me, Jack." She stepped over to him, he spoke softly, she spoke softly and turned back to me.

He watched her move, and again something tried to rise into his eyes. Then he looked at me and his eyes steadied, emptied.

"Come on in, Jack."

In Sage's office fewer pieces of old furniture sat on old patterned rugs on a white wool carpet, grouped so that she could be several different things in the same room.

At the large oak desk covered with neat rows of papers she could be the executive, signing her name and making decisions. At the computer terminal she could be the manager, checking revenues and expenses, personnel data and occupancy figures. At the small bar she could be the hostess, at the oval maple table the conference leader. At the two wingback chairs snuggled around a low table before a window she could be whatever she chose.

The walls bore Remington and Russell and Will James prints of sentimentally stylized horses and men, but the room was subtly arranged and lit to highlight a photograph of the Silver Sage on the night it opened in 1952 and an architect's rendering of what it would look like with a new hotel tower and a glitzy entrance.

Sage took me to the wingbacked chairs. Through the gathering twilight and slowly thickening smog I could still see the mass of the Sierra gleaming white in the distance.

She leaned forward and laid her hand on my arm. "I'm glad you're here, Jack. I was hoping he'd find a way to drag you out of the desert."

Lanky had found a way, all right. But I didn't know why.

"He—something's bothering him, but he won't tell me what it is. He's not well, he's had three heart operations, and he's not young anymore. Now he's not sleeping, he wanders around the casino at all hours of the night. . . ." Her smile was as feeble as Miranda Santee's. "I'm worried."

"Is that why you've got Tom Pardun baby-sitting him?"

"Tom and his men can keep him from drinking."

"Isn't that a sort of menial task for head of security?"

She shook her head. "As far as I'm concerned, there isn't a more important job in the organization right now. Tom agrees, he's happy to do it."

I thought about the flicker in his empty eyes when he looked at her. "I'll bet he is. But you'll have to have him help Lanky. That isn't what I'm here for. I came to ask him about my mother."

"Your mother? That's what you've been talking about?" Her voice made it a matter of no consequence. Her hand left my arm. "He didn't tell you . . ."

"No."

She looked out toward the smog and the mountains and the sky. Her profile was clean, lovely against the light, her smooth skin tinted softly by the color of her emotion.

"Your mother—what were you asking him about?"

"She was killed almost thirty years ago. We were told it was an accident. Now I've been told it was murder."

Her face blotched with color. "You think my father . . . ?"

"He knew her, Sage. I didn't. I just asked him about her."

"He—if she was murdered, who did it?"

"In the story I heard, Natty Stern."

"Who told you the story?"

"Miranda Santee."

She flushed suddenly, deeply. "She's the one who got Dad all worked up."

"She got somebody else worked up too. She took a bullet in her shoulder for it."

Her flush faded. "She . . . somebody shot her? Jack, what the hell is going on?"

I told her, briefly, the stories Miranda had told me. I showed her the photograph. She looked at it, at me. "You believe all that? I mean, it's an incredible story."

I shrugged.

She studied the photograph again, seemed to see only one person in it. "He was an attractive man, wasn't he? After he and my mother stopped living together—well, even before, if you want the truth—women fell all over him. I used to watch them watch him, they'd get this look, a sort of pure yearning. . . ."

"The same look most men give you."

She smiled. "Not all of them. Not the good ones."

"Tom Pardun isn't one of the good ones?"

"Tom is—" She bit it off, as if she weren't ready to declare what he was. "You keep bringing him up; is something going on between you two?"

I shrugged. "Not on my part. All I know is that he was a good cop who bailed out of a promising career for the job here, and that he didn't like the fact that Lanky kept me on retainer to handle . . . certain matters."

She knew the matters I meant. Delicate collection problems, sometimes, but more often sexual imbroglios—the wrong people tangling in Silver Sage bedrooms, knowledge of which could end marriages, careers, perhaps lives.

I smiled, picked up the banter again. "Now you're going to tell me that a good man is hard to find."

"More the other way around, as the joke goes." She handed me the photograph, dimmed her smile.

"I'll admit Miranda Santee looks a bit like Belle Smith, but I don't see how that validates the story. Looks are a genetic crap game. You don't look like your mother. I don't look like either of my parents. I don't see what this proves."

Something had just been proved. I hadn't identified either of the women to her.

"I'm not trying to prove anything, Sage. I'm just trying to find out how my mother died."

"Which involves you with shootings and Natty Stern and

God knows what other kinds of stuff. I—what did Miranda Santee tell my dad that got him so upset?"

"I don't know."

Sage stared for a moment at her hands, then suddenly rose and crossed the room to the bar. "Glenlivet rocks, wasn't it?"

She brought back two drinks, placed them on the table. Pale colors that took their hue from her blood and their urgency from her emotions washed over her throat.

Sage Chandler, unlike her father, had no poker face. What she felt spoke in her lovely skin. I had a sudden sharp memory of that skin, dappled and glowing, under my hands, lips.

"So, what do you think?" She waved her hand abruptly, vaguely at the room. "Not bad for a runner-up, huh?"

"You'll never forget that, will you?"

"That and catching my husband with a pair of bimbos and getting a 'B' in cost accounting and being dumped by a sleaze-ball private eye. I need things like that, keeps me humble."

At seventeen Sage had been runner-up in the Miss Nevada Pageant, at eighteen the wife of a San Francisco Giant 20-game winner, at nineteen a divorced mother, at twenty-two a graduate of Cornell and assistant hotel manager. Now, nudging thirty, she was vice-president of hotel operations for the Silver Sage.

"The air must be a little thin up here on top," I said. "You seem to have confused the dumper with the dumpee."

"You were the one who slunk out with his shoes in his hand."

"And you were the one who was lying awake watching me."

"I thought you were going out for Danish."

We laughed. We had been joking about our encounter nearly from the night it occurred. It was either joke or decide what that remarkable experience might have meant, what consequences it could have. Neither of us was ready to do that. So we laughed.

Sage looked at me for a moment, looked away, sipped her drink in nervous uncertainty. Her gaze fixed on the photograph and drawing of the Silver Sage. "What do you think?"

I thought she was stalling, that she wanted something but

didn't know how to ask for it. I thought I knew what she
wanted.

"It ought to impress the tourists."

She smiled grimly. "It better, with all the work it's taking.
My social life is nonexistent these days."

"The price of success."

"It's higher than that. I haven't been laid in six months."

"It's lonely at the top."

She grinned. "I cancel a meeting just to talk to an old
friend, to tell him all my troubles, and this is what I get?"

"Life is hard."

"That's about the only thing."

I laughed. She started to speak, put her drink to her mouth
instead. In my glass, melting ice turned the liquid into a
smear of brown like the air hanging outside the window.

In a sudden, nervous rush, Sage began talking business.
She had plans. The hotel expansion was just the beginning.
She had plans for moving into Vegas and Laughlin, maybe
Atlantic City. She had building plans, marketing and pro-
motional schemes. What she didn't have, or didn't mention,
was financing plans.

I listened to her, looked at her, enjoyed looking at her as
much as I enjoyed looking at the desert.

Something in my look slowly silenced her. After a moment
she rose abruptly. "Do you have clothes fit to be seen in?"

"In my rig."

"Give me your keys."

I rose and gave her my keys, watched as she long-strided
her way to the door and opened it. She spoke and the
receptionist was beside her. She spoke and handed the
woman my keys, turned back toward her desk.

The receptionist looked at me. No questions lurked in her
hooded eyes now. Now blue lids shadowed a smirk.

Sage sat behind the desk and took out a checkbook. As
she began to write, I studied the framed snapshots on her
desk.

In one, her father held on the back of a pony a small boy
I knew to be her son. In another, a fair-haired woman I
knew to be her mother gazed wanly as if at nothing. In the
third, a youthful Sage Chandler in a strapless formal and
bleak artificial smile stood stiffly beside another girl simi-

larly attired but for the smile. Her smile was real, wonderful.

"Your clothes will be in your room in five minutes. Take a shower and leave the rags for the laundry. You've got an appointment with the barber in forty-five minutes." She ripped the check from the book. "Here. You're on the payroll again."

"No."

"Jack, goddammit—"

"I don't do that anymore."

Color like pale flame licked at her face. "Like hell you don't. You've been doing it since you got here."

"I just came here to ask—"

"Dammit, Jack. Miranda Santee started asking questions and all hell broke loose. Now you're going to ask the same kind of questions. Some of them are about your mother, but some are about my father. He hasn't been the same since Miranda Santee sashayed into his office. Whatever upset him is the same thing that dragged you out of the desert."

"Maybe."

"Maybe, my sweet ass."

I laughed. She didn't. She waved the check at me. "Here."

"I couldn't take it if I wanted to. I can't conduct investigations on behalf of another party in this state anymore."

"Are you still an attorney? I need one. Here."

"I've never practiced law. I won't pretend to now."

"I don't care what you pretend. Pretend you're my fancy man, if you want. Just take the check!"

Color played on her face like light on the desert during a storm. She wasn't used to not getting what she wanted.

What she wanted now was what everyone wanted when they held out money. She wanted control of the situation. Of me.

"Good-bye, Sage."

I was halfway to the door when she called my name. Softly.

I turned, watched as she moved around the desk toward me. She put her hand on my arm. I could smell her hair, her scent.

"I'm sorry, Jack. That's no way to treat a friend."

"It doesn't matter."

"Yes, it does. I—we are friends, aren't we?"

I'd never been sure what we were. "Yes."

"Is there anything you can do to help me? As a friend?"

I told her the same thing I'd told Miranda Santee. "I'm going to ask some questions about my mother's death. If I learn anything that will help you, I'll let you know."

"I—if you won't take my money, will you take this?" She held out a room key. As I reached for it, she added, "I've got people to meet, but I'll be through about nine. Dinner?"

"Sure." I was opening the door when she called my name again. She stood in the center of the room. Among her various sets for her various roles, she looked very alone.

"What is it that you really want to find out? If your mother was murdered?"

"No. What I really want to know is if she was a murderer."

6

I negotiated the door and the maze of halls to my room. When I stepped inside, I understood the receptionist's smirk.

There was a large sitting room with a bar and desk and TV, a large bedroom. My bag sat beside the bed, my keys on a bedside table. An open closet held women's clothes, shoes. The vanity off the bathroom was covered with cosmetics. To everything clung a hint of Sage Chandler's damp-desert scent.

I sat on the bed and picked up the phone. My ex-wife told me that my daughter was in San Francisco on a biology field trip. Miranda Santee didn't answer. The clerk at the mini-warehouse where my belongings were stored told me he'd leave a key for me.

I did what Sage Chandler had ordered, and an hour later I was clean, had my hair cut and my beard trimmed, and wore good boots, clean jeans, a blue shirt, and an old Harris Tweed jacket.

In the silent gloom of the parking garage, I discovered that the Wagoneer had been washed and vacuumed. I climbed in and, although there was no reason I should have, unlocked the glove compartment and discovered that the toy pistol wasn't there.

I started to get out, then heard footsteps chunking on the concrete. Echoes spread like ripples on water.

Tom Pardun adjusted his jacket, and his face, as he came up. "You just buy the place, Ross? I only asked because of where you parked. And the way you corner Lanky and Sage, stroll around like you owned the place."

His voice wasn't especially deep, but it reverberated through the garage impressively. He seemed impressed by it.

"I'll try to do this civilly, Ross. Do you possess any information that might be important to me as head of security?"

I considered it, him. Tom Pardun was my age, fit if a bit overfed, from all reports good at what he did, and from my own observation something else. I'd never quite got a handle on that something else. My sense of him was finally that he wanted more—of what I didn't know.

"Not to my knowledge."

"You lost your PI license."

"It expired."

"Same difference. So if you were working for either of the Chandlers you'd be breaking the law."

"Not necessarily. I'm still an attorney. But it's moot, since I'm not working for either of them. But you are, and since you're so conveniently and coincidentally here, I'd like to report a breach of security. A small object has been stolen from my glove compartment."

He didn't so much as blink. "What kind of object?"

"A dangerous kind. You'll note that the door lock hasn't been tampered with, nor the lock on the glove box. The keys were out of my possession for about fifteen minutes. I saw them go from Sage Chandler to her receptionist. I assume they then went to a bellman or other functionary."

"You want to go up and file an official report?"

"No, I—"

"I didn't think so. Scumbags never do. Why is that, Ross?"

"I'm certain you're about to tell me."

He didn't. He told me something else. "Be careful, Ross. It only takes one mistake."

He wheeled and walked off, again sending the sound of footsteps reverberating off the concrete walls.

I'd already made one mistake. I hadn't wiped my fingerprints off the toy gun.

I drove through downtown, through the thickening smog and deepening darkness to a mini-warehouse out on West Fourth Street.

I opened the small metal rectangle, flicked on the light, and stood in the door, stunned. It was nearly empty.

I'd spent the winter in the desert, surrounded by the deep space charted by the stars in the huge sky, the deep time etched into the land. In that vast and silent emptiness, life reduces to a breath and a heartbeat. All else—memory, dream, desire—becomes of no consequence.

The metal shed seemed emptier than the desert.

What had been my life was in cardboard cartons stacked on and around a few pieces of furniture. Fewer than two dozen cartons, like cardboard cubes processed by some contraption whose function was to establish uniformity and meaninglessness.

The boxes were neatly labeled, in my daughter's pubescently tentative hand. The thought of her laboring over the detritus of my life touched me.

I sorted through the cartons, separated four of them, opened the two labeled BUSINESS PAPERS. Two hours later I closed them. I had kept my grandfather's files—closets full of skeletons—for reference. What I was looking for wasn't there.

I tried the box marked PERSONAL. It had been opened and resealed. The first thing I saw was a small teakwood box.

My grandfather's .38 Smith & Wesson lay snugly in the indentations time had worn in the green felt. The last time I'd seen the gun it was lying on the bottom of a swimming pool whose clear water was stained by the blood of a man I'd just killed. I thought I knew how the gun got back in the box.

Everything else in the box was paper. School and military records, diplomas and certificates, financial records and tax statements, and bundles of letters organized, I slowly perceived, both by year and by gender of the author.

The fourth box was labeled "Family." Under the word my daughter had drawn a Kilroy face, a happy face, and a heart with an arrow through it and surrounded by Xs.

More paper. Certificates of birth, marriage, death. My grandparents' memorabilia. Photograph albums, and loose photos my daughter had arranged in groups.

I knew what was in the albums. My grandmother as a young woman just over from Switzerland. My grandfather in uniform as a high school football player and then a deputy sheriff. Courtship and marriage, my mother as an infant. My grandfather in the gray suit he'd worn for years as the uniform of a bail bondsman and private investigator. The three of them growing older, smiling. And then, when my mother was sixteen, suddenly just two again. Then several years later, another infant. The three of us growing older, but my grandfather rarely smiling.

I didn't look at the albums. I looked at the loose photos bound in rubber bands.

A group showing people my daughter apparently hadn't been able to identify. I couldn't either.

A group showing old houses, apartment buildings, alleys, mostly Reno locations. Pictures my grandfather had taken on cases but didn't need for his records.

A group of casino publicity shots, interspersed with post-cards showing the same thing: bright light from sun or neon, swimming pools and gambling tables, bright empty smiles.

One of the smiles belonged to my mother.

She was younger than in the photo I had in my pocket, wore a Harold's Club costume, stood nestled in the crook of Lanky Chandler's arm. Beside them, Belle Smith stood with her arm draped over the shoulders of a man four inches shorter than she was, a handsome fair-haired man with a strange smile.

I felt something swelling in me, something I hadn't felt for months. Anger.

My life was such that in the desert I hadn't recognized a photograph of my mother. I'd given that life to my daughter. She hadn't recognized a photograph of her grandmother.

I put the photograph in my pocket, put the boxes back on the stack, turned out the light, and locked the metal door.

Night had fallen, and the temperature. The cold bit into my hands, stung my forehead. The air smelled of wood smoke, hung heavily in the reflected neon light.

When I pulled the Wagoneer into the street, I tugged a pair of headlights out of the adjacent motel lot. I got angrier.

I hauled the headlights up onto the interstate, east, toward Sparks, off at Rock Boulevard, into the sprawl of warehouses and light manufacturing plants around the railroad tracks. Whoever it was wasn't very good. In the labyrinth of streets and alleys he stayed so close he was obvious, so close that when I hung a hard right and slammed to a stop, he was around the corner and on me before he knew I was there.

He swerved, skidded, accelerated, the taillights diminished, disappeared. I hadn't seen his face, but it didn't matter. I'd seen the silver Mercedes. I'd seen the license plate: SAGE 7.

Tom Pardun wasn't that bad. A rookie wasn't that bad. He wanted me to know Lanky had put him on me. And on Miranda Santee.

I drove back downtown. In the cheerless smear of neon light, tourists huddled into their coats. Across the river, South Virginia seemed deserted, a neon channel leading, eventually, to nothing. Through the murk, the huge Peppermill Casino sign flashed like a confused rainbow uncertain of its promise.

Miranda Santee's apartment complex stood alone in the middle of dead fields, a two-story box of plywood boxes. I pulled into the parking spot, got out, felt the cold, smelled the smoke, heard the hum of traffic on South Virginia, heard something else. The grumble of an engine filtered through custom mufflers.

I moved toward the sound. Near the corner of the complex an old black TransAm, its rear end elevated, lights off, shuddered in the cold. A dark figure sat in the passenger seat. Three spaces away sat Miranda's rainbow-striped Bronco.

Pretending to scan the building, I stopped, made a mental note of the TransAm's license, moved to the side.

The man inside showed me a wary, middle-aged face. I tapped on the window. After a moment he rolled it down, releasing a cloud of warm air and cigarette smoke.

"Can you help me out, pal?" I said. "I'm supposed to pick up a broad lives here, I forgot her apartment number."

"I, uh, I don't live here. I don't know—I'm just waiting for a friend."

He'd been a big man once, not bad-looking. The lined looseness of his face, the worn looseness of his topcoat suggested that he had been reduced by illness or dissipation. Or maybe he hadn't been big. His voice held a perhaps congenital whine.

"Damn," I said. "A guy'll freeze wandering around out

here. I—you been here awhile, maybe you seen her. You'd recognize her—Miranda Santee? The TV broad?"

Confusion and panic tightened his mouth. He fumbled in his coat pocket. I tensed, but with a hand full of stiff, twisted fingers he brought out a cigarette, and I relaxed as he stuffed it into his face. "I ain't seen nobody."

He sounded like a man who'd spent much of his life denying accusations that hadn't been made.

"Yeah," I said, "well, she's in there somewhere; I guess I'll just have to bang on a few doors."

I moved toward the Bronco. The TransAm's grumble deepened. I turned to see it backing out. Lights flashed on, gears ground, it jerked forward, caught itself, rolled toward the street.

A dirty frost coated the Bronco's hood and grayed its windshield. Miranda hadn't driven it in several hours.

I followed the walk into the rectangular "garden"—small empty pool, dead grass, stunted shrubbery. Behind the undraped windows of a few apartments glowed the pale-lavender nimbus from television screens; from somewhere came the wail of a country guitar, from somewhere else a sudden squeal of female laughter.

Miranda's second-floor apartment was dark. I climbed the rickety steel stairway to the narrow balcony, knocked softly on her door. After a long silence, I knocked again.

I tried the door. The knob turned brokenly in my hand.

Flattening myself against the wall, I cursed in a silent despairing rage. I was sick of opening doors like this, sick to death.

I shoved on the door. It swung inward. Nothing happened.

I dropped to my knees, frog-jumped around and through the door, rolled twice into the darkness.

Into a lump of bone and flesh.

My body involuntarily jerked back. I rolled back farther.

Nothing happened.

Darkness. Silence.

After a while, I got to my feet, felt the wall for a switch, turned on the light.

It wasn't Miranda.

7

The body lay on its side, a small dark hole in its skull just behind the ear. In the beige carpet around the shaggy head dark blood had spread like a ragged halo.

He'd been in his mid-twenties. His brown hair was long and greasy, his face cratered and lumped with old acne scars that a scraggly beard couldn't mask. His blank blue eyes didn't see the .38 Colt Diamondback that lay a foot from his nose.

The room was small, homey, old-fashioned: stuffed furniture covered and skirted with faded chintz, worn old rugs, ferns and spider plants in clay pots on tables and dangling from ceiling hooks.

Stepping carefully around the body, I moved quietly across to an alcove that held a scarred old rolltop desk, its top lined with quartzy rocks and three photographs.

In one, a smiling teenaged Miranda Santee stood before a Joshua tree, her arm draped over the shoulder of a small, pretty, fortyish woman. In another, a slender balding man held up two chunks of quartz like trophies. In the third, Miranda and the small woman, in identical casino uniforms, stood before a long restaurant counter; Miranda's arm was again draped over the woman's shoulders, now protectively. Miranda wasn't smiling.

I looked back at the dead man, at the room. I listened. The only sound inside the apartment was my own breathing. From outside drifted in the muted cackle of a TV laugh-track, a ragged wail of guitar, the hum of traffic on South Virginia.

I stepped through an arch into a neat kitchen from which

led a short hall with three closed doors. Behind the first was
a neat bathroom, behind the second a room with a desk
chair and filing cabinet surrounded by a riot of papers and
folders and videotape cans from which snarls of tape trailed
like razor wire.

The third door was locked. I knocked softly. "Miranda?"

A muffled pop, wood splintering just below my hand, a
soft tug at my jacket sleeve.

I slammed myself against the wall. It shuddered, Sheetrock that would give me less protection than the plywood
door. I dropped to my knees again.

"Miranda, it's Jack Ross. It's all right."

Silence.

"It's all right, Miranda. He can't hurt you."

More silence.

"It's over, Miranda."

Nothing.

I needed help. I needed, suddenly, to get out of there.

"I'm going to call the police, Miranda. It's all right."

I found the phone in the kitchen, dialed. Frank Calvetti's
wife answered. "Jack? How are you? When did you get
back?"

"Today. I need to talk to Frank, Sheila."

"Yes." She'd been a cop's wife for years. "Here he is."

"The return of the prodigal," Frank rumbled. "I wish you'd
let me know, I'm all out of fatted calves at the moment."

"I've got a body, and a girl with a gun locked in a
bedroom." I told him where, and something else. "I won't be
here. This call is anonymous."

"Jack, goddammit—"

"Shut up and listen." I described the black TransAm, the
man driving it. I gave him the license number.

"Good," he said. "I'll be there in five minutes. You'll be
there too, if you know—"

I hung up and went back to the locked door.

"Miranda? The police are on their way. I have to go now,
but you're safe, it's over."

I heard something that might have been a moan.

"Are you all right? Miranda?"

Nothing. Then, maybe, something. Something moving.
The doorknob jiggled and clicked, the door cracked open.
The nickel plate of the .32 glittered in the light. On her left

shoulder, blood soaked into her white cotton blouse; her left arm dangled limply at her side. The gun trembled in her right hand.

"They . . . where . . . ?"

"There's no one here, Miranda."

"I heard them. I—he shot—I . . . did I shoot him?"

"Yes."

Something went out of her. She stumbled through the door and sagged into me. I pried the gun from her fingers, then half-led, half-carried her into the bedroom, flicked on the light, and sat her on the bed. I sat beside her and held her.

Miranda lay heavily against me, silent, still. Then her body convulsed in sharp shudders and she was crying, softly at first, then, as more shudders racked her body, violently, her whimpers swelling into ragged wails.

I held her.

There was no way I was going to get out of there.

The room was small, strange. The walls were festooned with posters of rock stars whose vogue had passed years before. Worn children's books filled a case next to an old stereo system. Stuffed animals sat in corners and in a row at the foot of the bed. On the bedspread a stylized horse bore an eyeless young girl with streaming hair in an endless circle.

Miranda's sobs subsided. Her face was streaked with tears, her eyes with bleakness. "Why did he want . . . to kill me?"

"I don't know. But he won't be trying it again."

"He's . . . dead? I—I killed him?"

"He won't be bothering you anymore."

"Oh God." Her body began to tremble. I held her closer.

"He's the one who shot you before, isn't he?"

The trembling grew stronger, more violent.

"It's all right, Miranda. It's over."

Pain and fear and despair settled into her face, stiffened the flesh into a mask of momentary madness. Her mouth opened, but no sound issued from it.

"It's all right, Miranda," I said again.

The words finally came, like a cry of a dying animal alone in the desert. "He's . . . my brother!"

Twenty minutes later Miranda was in the bathroom with a

policewoman, the living room was filled with policemen, and I was in the kitchen with a homicide lieutenant and still trying to get out of there.

"That's quite a story," Frank Calvetti said, leaning his loose-limbed frame against the sink. "The DA will love it."

I'd given him an abbreviated account of my meeting with Miranda Santee, a severely edited version of her tale of Belle Smith. I hadn't mentioned Lanky Chandler or my mother. I hadn't told him how Miranda had identified the dead man.

"I don't see how you figure into this. You were just in the neighborhood, thought you'd drop in?"

"I told you, Frank, she wasn't in great shape when I left her, she said she was going home. I called to see how she was and got no answer. I thought I'd better check."

That was all true, but it wasn't all the truth. Frank knew me well enough to know it.

"You gonna stick with that story? Even though everything in this place is wrong?"

"Like what?"

"Like, to start with, the place itself? Chintz? Rocks? Rick Springfield and ABBA? This look like the apartment of a young telejournalist career-person and aspiring yuppie?"

"Her father died ten years ago. She and her mother shared the apartment until her mother died last year. You don't need a psychologist to explain this place."

"She has psychological problems?"

"She has pain, for Chrissake! Grief! Loneliness!"

I didn't know why I was shouting. Frank gave me a long steady look.

"Maybe," he said. He continued to look at me, to watch me. "How about what's wrong with the body?"

Frank looked his usual disheveled self. He also looked weary, hollow-eyed. "You perhaps didn't train your investigative powers on the evidence of the crime scene."

"The only crime I saw any evidence was B and E."

"You perhaps didn't notice the geometry—the position of the body, angle of the wound, that sort of stuff. And the powder burns on the not very clean skin just behind the not very clean ear of the deceased. They tell an interesting story too."

"Like what?"

"Like the young lady heard him working the door, stood behind it, let him step inside, then stuck her little popgun behind his ear and pulled the trigger."

"Before he pulled the trigger. Look, Frank, he shot her a few days ago. She was supposed to let him do it again?"

"James. Dalton James, he was, of the Las Vegas Jameses, by his wallet. By his pockets he was a patron of the Cattail Club and Tawny's Fillie Ranch and a smoker of unfiltered Camels, seedy grass, and crack. By the amazingly prescient tattoo on his arm, he was 'Born to Lose.' But you probably knew that."

"No."

"You probably also know why a sleaze bag like that is terrorizing a television reporter."

"No." I hesitated. Frank's scenario was playing in my mind. I didn't like who'd been put in the starring role.

"He'd been following her. Others were too." I told him about Tom Pardun, about the denim ghost and the toy gun.

"You're telling me that either a Natty Stern goon or Tom Pardun may have witnessed this, or done it?" He scowled. "You can't be worried about a setup. That gun isn't here."

"I'm just telling you what I know."

"We'll see what your little girlfriend has to say."

"Leave her alone. In the last week she's been shot, probably raped, and shot at again. Leave her alone." I was shouting again.

"What rape?"

"If you don't call an ambulance, I'll take her myself."

Frank pushed away from the sink. "It's on the way."

"Good," I said. "So am I."

Frank followed me out past the photographs and rocks, past the men examining and photographing the body, past the young uniform at the door, along the narrow balcony to the stairs.

"Wait a minute, Jack."

I stopped, stared down at the people staring up, pale faces like dying flowers. Into the miasmic air drifted the harmonies of the Beatles and "Eleanor Rigby" and an unanswerable question.

Frank had a different question. "Where are you going?"

"Right now, to bed. Tomorrow, Tonopah."

"Who probably raped Miranda Santee?"

"I don't know."

"Why are you going to Tonopah?"

"Family business."

Frank Calvetti was part of my family. He was no longer my brother-in-law, but he was still my daughter's godfather. And still my friend. "Then what?"

"I don't know."

"Back to the desert?"

I stared down at the pale faces staring up at me. I looked at them and saw a truth about myself.

"No."

8

The Silver Sage was bright, quiet, strange as only a Nevada casino on a slow winter night can be strange, an eerie glittering cavern of shadowless solitude. The few tourists only deepened its emptiness and intensified their own isolation.

Solitary gamblers hunched over cards or handles or buttons. Solitary drinkers hunched over glasses at the long bar.

One of the drinkers was Lanky Chandler.

On the elevated television screen, Larry Bird and Magic Johnson were doing silent and magnificent battle, but Lanky wasn't watching. He was staring into the mirror behind the bar, doing battle with his reflected and reflective self.

He saw my reflection, took a long swallow from the glass in his hand, refilled the glass from a bottle of Wild Turkey. Tom Pardun wasn't around to stop him.

I eased onto a stool, took one of the photographs from my pocket, and slid it into his line of sight. He picked it up, peered at it blearily. The photograph trembled in his hand.

"Them two were a pair to draw to, weren't they?"

When I didn't answer, he turned to me. "Don't get old, Jack. You won't like it. Just reminds you how alone you are."

I tried to determine how drunk he was.

"Smith," he said.

"Belle? What about her?"

"No. John. I 'membered his name. John Smith. Like hers. Single John, they called him." His head swiveled loosely as he looked back at the photograph. "Only man I ever met who

49

really and truly didn't give a shit. He purely did not care. I never knew how anybody could do that. Never knew why the girls went so crazy over it. I . . ."

He drifted off for a moment, jerked himself back. He took a long pull from his glass. "Lots of things I never . . . knew."

"What does he have to do with what happened?"

He looked at the picture of his earlier self, then at his reflection in the mirror; he frowned, as if he didn't understand the significance of his two faces.

"Nothin, I guess. He was just . . . a guy. He was in town for a while and . . . then he wasn't. That's all."

In his reflection he seemed to see something that frightened him. To ward off the vision, he raised the photograph to eye level. "I—you found the file."

"There isn't any file. Just this."

"No file," he echoed solemnly.

"What did you think would be in that file?"

His body trembled, as if in the grip of an alcoholic seizure or deep emotion. "I . . . let it alone, son."

"No."

"She's dead." The photograph fluttered from his fingers. "She's been dead a long time." The words were raspy, like winter sage rattling in a cold wind. "We'll all be dead a long time."

His face was damp and flushed, his eyes watery and vague.

"You'll be dead quick if you don't lay off that stuff."

"You soun' like my daughter." He raised his glass, slopped liquid in and around his mouth. Setting the glass on the bar, he shoved it over the slick wood; at the edge it tipped, vanished, hit the floor with a cracking crash.

The bartender moved toward us with willfully dead eyes.

"Couple glasses," Lanky said with a sudden expansive grin. "A drink for me, drink for my friend. Tired a drinkin' alone."

I warned the bartender off. "I don't want a drink, Lanky. I want to know—"

"No. You don' wanna know. Leave it alone."

"Tell me the truth."

"Truth," he echoed. He addressed the Lanky Chandler

who looked back at him from the mirror. "Truth he wants. Dumb shit. Already got the truth. He just can't see it."

"Show it to me."

"Already got . . ." His big hand rose, flopped at the end of his arm. "Gimme the other one, picture."

I took out the other photograph and placed it beside the one on the bar. "Look at 'em, whad'ya see? What happened to 'em?"

"You tell me."

His eyes blurred with booze and emotion. "They got old."

I got angry. "Goddammit, Lanky—"

"Too old. Over thirty. They got loose . . . it wasn't like now, with the unions and all, biddies struttin' in outfits that don't show nothin' but flab and varicose veins. Belle, Celeste, they got old, younger broads coming all the time. . . ."

I looked at the women. Neither looked old or ugly to me. "What are you trying to tell me, Lanky?"

"You wanted truth, you got it. You had it all the time."

"The story Miranda told me is true?"

"Of course it's true." His eyes suddenly cleared. "They set up Vanca and that other goon, blew them away, took the money and ran. Goddamned Vanca. Only man I ever hated. Hurt people for fun, hurt 'em all kinds of ways. . . . But they made mistakes, one each. Belle didn't kill Vanca. Celeste didn't run fast enough."

I didn't know if he was telling me the truth, telling me a lie, or telling me a fantasy woven of memory and melancholy. "Why didn't you tell Miranda Santee this?"

"Why the hell should I? What do I care about her goddamn TV stories? Besides, Natty Stern never caught up with Belle. He never will, if you and the girlie leave it alone."

"What about the police, Lanky? Belle murdered a man."

"Who gives a shit? You? One of Natty's goons gets taken out and you gonna get all bent out of shape? Nobody else did. Not the cops. There ain't no warrant out for Belle, even though everybody knew what happened. Not even Natty gives a shit, not about that. He only cares that somebody took something of his. This is Nevada, Jack. Nobody cares. It just doesn't matter."

He was right. I didn't care if Belle Smith had killed a man. But I did care if my mother had.

"Tell me one more thing, Lanky. Why?"

"What would you rather be, Jack—a killer or a whore?"

"Those couldn't have been their only choices."

He looked at me, laughed. "Grow up, Jack. What else was there? Put the dazzle on Joe Tourist from Altoona, fuck him till he's brain-dead and haul him off to a wedding chapel and back to the tract house and keep fucking him as long as he keeps paying the bills? Women been doing it for centuries, do it now, but what's the difference between that and hooking?"

I didn't say anything.

"It's over," Lanky said quietly. "Leave it be."

"Why should I?"

"People will get hurt. Innocent people."

"People are already getting hurt. Miranda Santee has a bullet hole in her shoulder and God knows what kind of damage to her soul. She just shot and killed a guy named Dalton James."

He sagged, grew smaller.

"Who is he, Lanky?"

He shook his head.

"Why did you have Miranda followed?"

He shook his head, poured bourbon into the glass the bartender had brought him, drank it all.

"Why did you have me followed?"

He started to shake his head, stopped. "What?"

"Tell your troops that they shouldn't do surveillance work in casino vehicles."

Lanky shook his head again, now as if trying to clear it.

"I don't know what you're talking about. I—why can't you just leave it alone? Your granddad did. Why can't you?"

"Did you lie to him, too?"

His broad face twisted, paled. He got big again. His hand slashed across my face.

"Goddamm street rat! Who do you think you're talking to!"

The backhand slap hadn't hurt me, but I could feel the patch of ragged flesh in my mouth, taste my blood.

Two young, uncertain security men appeared. I put the photographs in my pocket, rose slowly from the stool, stepped carefully away from him. "See you around, Lanky."

"Jack . . ." A drunken distress replaced the anger in his

face. Whatever had been pumping the adrenaline into him, clearing his eyes and voice, had suddenly stopped working. "Jesus, Jack . . . I . . ."

He got off the stool, took a step, tottered. One of the security men grabbed his arm. Violently Lanky flung the hand off his arm and himself off his feet, stumbled, wheeled, lost his hat, fell through the grasping hands of the security men, thudded on the floor.

For a moment all motion seemed to cease, all eyes fixed on the long length of Lanky Chandler crumpled on the floor of his casino.

Then Sage Chandler was there, and Tom Pardun.

Sage's face was ugly. "Jack, you bastard!"

She knelt over her father. Lanky had rolled onto his shoulder and was struggling to get up. "Are you all right?"

Slurred syllables trickled from his mouth.

Sage turned on Tom Pardun. "Get out. You're fired."

He didn't move.

"Get the fuck out of here!"

He backed away from her, but his blank eyes fixed on me. "Jack, help me get him up!"

We hoisted Lanky to his feet. He wasn't dead weight, but he was close. We handed him to the two security men.

"Get him to his room," Sage ordered, and they half-carried, half-dragged Lanky toward the elevator.

Sage followed them, I followed her. The few gamblers glanced at us, found nothing of consequence, looked back to their games.

The security men loaded Lanky into the elevator and braced him against the wall. His head flopped on his neck like a hanged man's. Sage looked at him, her face filled with fear and anger.

She turned on me. "You can get the fuck out of here too."

It was the most sensible thing anyone had told me all day.

The elevator door closed on them. I punched for another car, waited, took it up and went to my room. Sage Chandler's room.

For a while I stood looking out at the thickening night, the glitter and gleam of Reno wavering in the foul air.

I had to get out of it. But where I was going wouldn't be any better.

I grabbed my bag, tossed the room key on the bed, and went back to the elevator. The doors opened.

Sage Chandler stood inside, alone, looking at me.

9

Alone.

Forlorn. Deserted. Abandoned. Destitute. Hopeless.

Sage looked at me, stepped out of the elevator. My arms rose, spread. She stepped into them.

Her hair was soft against my mouth, her breath warm against my throat. "I'm sorry," she said. "I don't want you to leave."

I felt the softness of her breasts against my chest, the weight of her hip against my groin. "I won't."

She pressed closer. I felt myself pressing toward her.

She leaned back, smiled. "You were alone in the desert too long." Her eyes changed. "What's the matter with your mouth? There's blood."

"I'll survive."

Sage wet the tip of her finger on the tip of her tongue, pressed the fingertip to the corner of my mouth, then to her lips. Her eyes fixed on mine, deepened.

She stepped out of my arms. "Let's put your bag back."

In her room, she went to the bar. "He's all right. His pulse is steady, and his blood pressure is reasonable. He's sleeping—that's what he needs more than anything."

She gave me a small penitent smile. "I—I saw him lying there and got scared. They told me he was drunk before you got there. Somehow, everybody got confused about who was supposed to watch him. I—I'm sorry I turned on you."

I eased onto a stool as she mixed two drinks. She handed me one, took more than a sip from the other.

"I—why does he do it, Jack? He knows what the doctor said. Is he deliberately trying to kill himself?"

"I don't know."

"He's going to die, I know that. I've accepted it. But it doesn't have to be now. He could live another five, maybe even ten years. But . . . what was he talking about to you tonight?"

"About getting old. He told me not to."

She smiled grimly. "Beats the hell out of the alternative." She went at her drink. "You don't have any idea why he's . . .?"

I considered it. "Something Miranda Santee told him jarred his memory, set free all his ghosts. He's angry, and he's afraid. And he's feeling guilty."

Her grip whitened on her glass. "Guilty about what? Something to do with Belle Smith and those preposterous stories?"

"I don't know."

She drained her drink. I watched the alcohol tint the smooth flesh of her face, brighten her dark eyes, as she fixed another.

She looked at my glass. "You didn't drink the one this afternoon either. Are you on the wagon?"

"I only drink now when I have a good reason."

"Well, here's one." She tried to grin her way through a sudden embarrassment. "How about drinking with me so that I don't have to stand here feeling like a sot?"

"That's a good reason," I said, grabbing the glass with exaggerated haste. Her grin spread.

The Scotch burned into the torn flesh in my mouth, warmed my chest. "Sot?"

Sage laughed, stepped from behind the bar to a couch before a window. As I followed, she slipped out of her jacket and shoes, sat with a long sigh. I started to take a chair, heard her pat the cushion. "Not there. Here."

I sat beside her. Through the window the neon of downtown Reno pinked the smoggy night like a thin smear of blood.

"Jack, who is Belle Smith? I know she was a showgirl, but . . . who is she really?"

I tasted my drink again. "I thought you might tell me."

"Me?" Her gaze went blank, empty, reminded me of Tom Pardun's. "How would I know?"

"This afternoon, when I showed you the picture, you knew which one she was."

"I . . ." She gave me another blank, empty-eyed look, then looked out into the pink-smeared darkness. "Damn. I'm sitting here sorting through lies, and I don't even know why I want to lie in the first place."

She tried to smile, couldn't quite manage it. "I've seen her picture before, when I was small. Dad kept a snapshot of her, in his desk drawer. All his other pictures were on his wall, all except that one. I . . . when you showed me the picture I just somehow knew which one was Belle Smith."

She leaned back, lifted her long, slim legs onto the low table in front of us, stretched her elegantly arched feet.

"I used to sneak in his office to look at her. I worked up an elaborate fantasy that she was a wicked witch who had made my mother unhappy, and my parents not love each other, and my mother not like me or my dad."

Sage sipped at her drink. "After my mother finally decided to . . . stay away, I realized that she didn't like us because she didn't like herself." She held up her glass. "The only thing she liked was this."

I knew the story of Sybil Chandler's drunks. My grandfather had tracked her down several times; the last time he found her shacked up with two winos in an abandoned sheep wagon by the dump in Ely. Lanky put her in a Vegas hospital, then in an apartment there when she got out. She slowed but couldn't stop the slide into dissolution and despair. Along the way she lost her looks and, for periods, her mind. The last ten years she'd been in and out of institutions. Lanky paid the bills and never divorced her.

"I know it can't be fun growing up when your mother has died, Jack, but there are worse things."

I nodded. One of the reasons I'd quit the investigation business was that I'd seen those worse things too many times.

Sage's face was as pink as the square of night outside the window, her expression as somber as the darkness beyond it.

Then she smiled. "Speaking of mothers, I'd best act like one."

She rose and moved toward the bedroom. I sipped my

drink and looked into the night. I realized that I wanted to be out in it. I didn't know why.

Sage came out of the bedroom, her stockinged feet hissing on the carpet. At the bar, she filled her glass with Scotch and drank deeply. Her face was flushed but expressionless, deadened.

She refilled her glass. I got up and went to the bar and took the glass from her hand and set it down.

"He was already asleep. I haven't seen him in three days."

"Go home. You can see him in the morning."

"I've got an early meeting. I'd be gone before he got up." Something—grief, guilt, self-pity—darkened her gaze, turned it inward. "I'm doing it to my son, the same thing my mother did to me."

"Stop doing it."

Her lips quivered. She bit them. "I've tried. I keep trying to spend more time with him, quality time. I make plans. And then something comes up, problems, questions. . . ."

She picked up her drink. "Are we really friends, Jack?"

I knew what I was supposed to say. I resisted. "I don't know, Sage. Friends are supposed to trust each other."

"You . . . you think I don't trust you?"

"I think you had Tom Purdun follow me."

Her eyes went blank again. "I . . . was concerned about you. Miranda Santee got shot doing what you're doing."

"Were you concerned about her too? You had her followed."

Her eyes filled with anger, her face with blood. "I wanted to know what's going on! Is that so terrible? She came waltzing in here and did something to my father and I want to know what it was! You're damned right I had her followed! So what?"

"Miranda shot and killed a man tonight."

Her flush deepened. "So fucking what! You think it's my fault, that I'm responsible?"

I didn't think Sage was responsible. I thought she was nearly hysterical. I didn't know why.

"You son of a bitch! Don't look at me like that!"

She threw her glass at me. It flashed past my head, splattering me with Scotch, and shattered on the wall behind me.

Her lovely features twisted grotesquely in something

closer to madness than anger. Then with a childlike wail she threw herself around the bar and ran into the bedroom.

It was my cue, or excuse, to leave.

I wanted to leave, even more than I'd wanted to leave Miranda's apartment. I couldn't.

I went into the bedroom. Sage lay sprawled on the bed, her head buried in her arms. Her body shook rhythmically, silently.

I sat on the bed, put my hand on her shoulder. She shrugged it off violently. I put my hand back on her shoulder, my other hand on her waist, gently pulled her up through her wordless resistance until she sat on the edge of the bed.

I held her as I had Miranda Santee a few hours before.

Her body slowly stilled. She showed me her face. Her makeup was streaked and smeared like the playa after a thunderstorm. Her brown eyes were muddied with emotion.

"I—sometimes I think I'm going insane."

"You're not."

"I think I'm going to end up like my mother, with the alcohol and . . . everything."

"Don't drink so much."

"I've got everything I want, but I'm still not happy. Just like my mother. Why can't I be happy?"

She didn't expect an answer. She didn't think there was one.

"You can," I said.

"No." Then, as if she'd just caught some profound message in the timbre of my voice, she said, "How?"

"Heed the words of the philosopher Roger Miller."

She stared at me. "Roger . . . ?"

"You can't roller-skate in a buffalo herd, Sage, but you can be happy—if you've a mind to."

Her smile came like a desert sunrise, slowly, inevitably, completely. She became beautiful. "You're the one who's insane."

"Probably."

She stood up, brushed at her eyes. "And I must be a mess. I've got to clean myself up."

She smiled, stepped toward the bathroom. At the door she stopped. "We are friends, aren't we?"

"Yes."

"And you're going to stay with me tonight, aren't you?" As a friend, she meant.

I didn't want to stay with her. I didn't know why. Nor did I know why I said, "If you want me to."

"I don't want to be alone tonight."

"I'll stay."

As the bathroom door closed, I went out to the bar, found my drink, freshened it. I found myself thinking of Miranda Santee. I wondered how she was, where she was, what would happen to her.

I told myself it didn't matter.

I finished my drink, flicked off the lights, went into the bedroom and undressed to my shorts and switched off the lights. Then I opened the draperies and looked out into the night.

The smoggy streets were quiet, the buildings vague and soft-edged. Every patch of light had a particulate-laden nimbus. The pinkish sky seemed an elemental brew in which dead matter drifted in search of the impossible connection that would create life.

The sound of the shower stopped. I got into bed, blessed the crisp cleanness of the sheets. I discovered that I was exhausted.

From the window pale pink light spread like a deadly mist. I turned at the sound of the bathroom door opening. In her white nightgown Sage seemed to float, ghostlike, toward the bed.

I turned back the covers, and she slipped into the crook of my arm. Her arms folded chastely across her chest, she snuggled against me. She smelled of soap and shampoo, toothpaste and Scotch, and still, somehow, of the desert after rain. She felt soft against my arm and chest and hip.

"You don't mind if we don't . . ."

I realized that I was erect. I shifted my hip away from her, so that she wouldn't realize it. "It doesn't matter."

She snuggled, sighed.

I closed my eyes. I was very tired.

I was nearly asleep when she spoke. "I'm sorry."

I didn't know how to answer, or if I was supposed to.

"About Miranda Santee. I'm sorry she got shot, and I'm sorry she . . . shot somebody. Is she in jail?"

"The hospital."

"Will she need help? An attorney? I'll help if I can."
I didn't know why she would do that. It didn't matter.
"You're concerned about her, aren't you, Jack?"
"Yes."
"Are you in love with her?"
"No."
"Are you . . . concerned about me?"
"Yes."
Her voice drifted into my mind from far away. "Good."

Blankness. The desert. The playa spread emptily before
me, the sky emptily above. The earth shuddered, rolled. A
deep pool appeared at my feet. I bent to drink, saw the
water bubble, felt the steam dampen and warm my face.
From the surface of the water my reflected face stared back
at me. Beneath it floated another face, a woman's face. The
water was pink with blood, spread over the sand from the
pool that was a woman . . .
    I was erect in Sage's hand. Her face hovered pale and
ghostlike over mine. "I changed my mind."
    Her voice was thick, her nightgown was gone, her breasts
were brushing my chest. Her face lowered, her lips touched
mine, softly. Then not softly. Her hand tightened on me.
    Her mouth and hands moved on me. I drifted, floated,
seemed somehow submerged.
    She rolled away from me, fumbled in the drawer of the
lamp table, rolled back. Struggling toward complete consciousness, I came up onto my side to meet her. She pushed
me onto my back, rose to her knees beside me.
    Her hands were at my hips, my shorts were gone. She fit
me with a condom, swung astride me and fit us together.
    She leaned forward and kissed me, rocked back, rocked.
    My hands were miles away from me on her breasts.
    Her breathing deepened, her skin warmed, dampened,
her knees and thighs gripped hard. Flesh and flesh, wave
and trough, soar and dive . . .
    "Ah," she said. "My good horse."
    "What?"
    "Horse."
    Her skin glistening in the pale-pink light, her face a grim
and shadowed mask, darkness spreading like rainwater on
white sand over her throat, shoulders, chest, her back

stiffening, straightening, she rose up over me and with a savage shake of her bright head began to come and ground herself into me and with a sharp series of grunts kept coming and then began to sag slowly back onto my chest, her breasts crushed slick against me, her own chest heaving, her breath hot and ragged on my throat.

Slowly she separated us, rolled onto her back. "Now you."

Her arms, her legs invited. I entered and got lost.

I was somewhere else. Noises, scurry in the brush, slap and splat, sighs of death, cries of pain and yearning.

Then I was back, coming, hard, painfully.

Sage pushed her way out from under me, edged away. "Jesus . . . what was that? You hurt me."

I didn't answer.

"You . . . really were in the desert too long."

I awoke in darkness, remembered where I was, knew I had to get out of there.

I sat up on the edge of the bed, found my shorts and stood up and put them on. The condom was gone. I was sheathed by a crust of Sage Chandler and semen.

I found my clothes and boots and put them on.

Sage was awake.

I went to the bedroom door. "I've got to go."

"You really are a bastard, Jack. A real bastard."

Out of the eternal brightness of the casino into the grim concrete grayness of the parking garage. In the black shadow of a pillar, Tom Pardun stood hardly hiding.

He hadn't been there long. He'd known where I was, what I'd been doing. He wanted me to know he was there. As he'd wanted me to know he had followed me the evening before.

I ignored him, climbed in the rig and fired it up.

He stepped out of the shadow, walked over. His suit was rumpled, his shirt unbuttoned over the roll of flesh at his waist. Fair stubble on his chin glittered in the pale light.

"We have to stop meeting this way," I said.

He scowled at me.

"Such dedication to duty," I said. "I'd commend you to your employer, if you had one anymore."

He spat on the concrete. "Sage Chandler doesn't fire me."

He told me that for a reason. I didn't know what it was.

"She put you on me."

He shrugged. "Stupid. Wasn't worth the effort."

"So you blew it quick and got out. You blew it with Miranda Santee too. Did you also blow Dalton James away?"

"I haven't blown anything, Ross. But you have. You've blown it all."

He turned and walked away through the gray garage, his heels on the concrete again sending echoes through the air like the ripples of a rock dropping into a pool.

10

At sunrise I had driven a hundred miles south of Reno, was finishing breakfast in a small café in Yerington. No one had followed me.

I had tried to understand what had happened with Sage. I couldn't. I quit trying. It didn't matter.

I went out into the still, crisp air. From fireplaces and wood stoves, smoke rose to flatten at the invisible line of the inversion, to spread and thin and vanish in the pale light.

An hour later, after the ranches and farms that trailed the Walker River to Schurz and on to Walker Lake and Hawthorne, the desert began to change.

Beneath the snowy mountains, haze lurked in pools and streams at the edges of the long valleys. The land lost its brown fur of vegetation; the valley floors were playa and salt flat, the sage shrunken to widely spaced nubs of growth. The ranges grew rockier, below the snow line were stratified and streaked like a painter's mixing palette—dull reds and pale violets, muddy yellows and dirty whites.

Diggings old and new littered the land with piles of rock like monuments of some obscure religious ceremony. Few cattle, fewer fences. In the few tiny towns, battered mobile homes and old frame houses, a few mostly abandoned businesses, an always open brothel, a few people. Nothing else but the barren land and the empty highway.

And an hour after that, Tonopah, spread haphazardly over a sandy hillside, a main street painted and neoned in a desperate meretriciousness, more small houses and mobile homes scoured by the sand-laden wind and standing in lawnless yards beneath tired trees. Nothing grew easily in

Tonopah but the old ore derricks that rose up in the brittle sunshine above abandoned diggings.

Tonopah was above the inversion. The morning sun warmed the chill air as I walked into the Nye County Courthouse. The noon sun warmed the back of my neck as I walked out of it.

I'd been in most of the offices—the sheriff, the coroner, the DA, the Justice of the Peace. Records? Almost thirty years ago? Accident? Mutters and mumbles about storage and microfiche and two or three days. Everybody involved had either moved, died, or disappeared.

Everybody except, finally, James Bacigalupilaga.

His Main Street storefront office was locked.

The Nye County Library was open. I found an account of the incident in the local weekly. It didn't tell me much.

My mother had been killed on a Saturday night, the biggest and wildest night of Jim Butler Days, the local celebration of the discovery of the Tonopah silver strike by a desert rat or his mule, depending on which story you believed.

The police log for that week was three and a half columns long: public intoxication, DUI, resisting arrest, assault, indecent exposure. Party time, Nevada-style. Nothing in the list interested me. Something in one of the ads did.

The partying at the Waterhole Saloon had taken place to the Western swing rhythms of Cletus James and the James Boys. The band was being held over indefinitely.

Dalton James, Cletus James. James was as common a name as Smith, there could be no connection. And I could be Bob Wills.

Walking up the street, in the middle of a block of old sandstone buildings, I came to the Waterhole, a dive whose dark windows glowed with swirls of neon. I stopped, then walked on.

James Bacigalupilaga's office was still locked. As I tried to decide what to do, a muddy Ford pickup pulled up to the curb.

The driver was a broad, powerful Basque of mid-height in his mid-fifties, with large black eyes under a broad-domed forehead shadowed by a sweat-stained old Stetson. His hands were smeared with grease, his jeans with dirt, his bootheels with cowshit.

The woman was ten years younger, thin, in designer denim and incongruous black heels. Under faded blond hair her thin face was worn by desert weather to the color of the desert earth. She had been pretty once; now she looked empty, somehow used up.

"Mr. Bacigalupilaga?" He smiled when I pronounced his name correctly. "I'd like to talk to you about the death of my mother, Celeste Ross."

The smile faded, telling me that he knew who I was talking about. After nearly thirty years. I didn't know what that meant.

The woman smiled, a strange savage smile, full of bright teeth and hatred. Her blue eyes looked at me and didn't see me.

"It was a long time ago, Mr. Ross," he said.

"Yes."

He looked at the woman. Her smile didn't quiver, her gaze didn't flicker.

"I only open the office three days a week. I just came in to get some papers, and my wife's got some shopping to do." He glanced at his hands. "I've got a baler scattered over half an acre I've got to get back to."

His hands were battered and scarred by work he hadn't done in an office. "That much law business you can do it part time?"

He smiled. "I only lawyer as much as I have to to keep the ranch going. I run a couple hundred head and breed a few horses over in the Big Smoky."

"I don't need a lawyer," I said. "Just information. You seemed to be the only one in town I can get it from."

He looked at me for a moment, then at his wife. "I'll see you in a few minutes, Lois."

She still hadn't moved.

He put a thick hand on her shoulder. "Meet me at the Iron Horse. I'll buy you lunch."

She continued to stare at me.

He opened the door and led me through a standard outer office into a room like a ranch-house den—dark paneling, large leather chairs, bright woven rugs on polished hardwood floors.

I turned to shut the door and discovered that his wife had

followed us. She stood just beyond the doorway, still smiling that fierce smile, still silent.

I stepped aside. She didn't move.

Then her husband was beside me, speaking softly, steadily.

"Lois, I'll be through in a few minutes. Then it'll be over. Do your shopping and I'll meet you for lunch."

She looked at him, saw something else, something old, evil, painful. "I told you she wasn't dead."

"She's dead, Lois. She's been dead for years."

"She's not dead. She'll never die."

"Lois . . ."

His voice thickened with pain; the pain was his, but it was also hers. "I'll see you in a little while."

Gently he closed the door on her smile, her eyes.

He turned to me. "I'm sorry, Mr. Ross. I—I thought she was well enough to . . ."

"I'm sorry too, Mr. Bacigalupilaga. I didn't mean to disturb her. But I can't help wondering why I did. Or why the mention of my mother did."

He moved behind the desk. "It's not that. She's all right out at the ranch, alone, it's just around people . . ."

"Why did she say that my mother wasn't dead?"

He shook his heavy head. "She wasn't talking about your mother. She was talking about the child we lost. She's never . . . Postpartum Syndrome, they call it."

He shifted back suddenly in his chair, changed the subject. "About Celeste Ross. I was deputy DA at the time. The coroner's verdict was accidental death. The verdict wasn't satisfactory, for a number of reasons, but we had no evidence to refute it."

"What happened?"

"Apparently, it was a celebration fracas that got out of hand. A couple of drunken miners got into it in the Waterhole. As is occasionally their wont, the rest of the crowd joined the fun. By the time the sheriff arrived on the scene, everyone capable of running had. Two men were unconscious, and several others were in various stages of shock from alcohol and injuries. And your mother."

"Why didn't anybody like accidental death?"

Under his broad forehead his eyes were like dark caves. "As we reconstructed it from the pattern of wounds, the bottle hit her in the temple, broke, slashed down across her jugular. From the bruise on her temple, it appeared that the bottle had been in somebody's hand. It appeared that it might have been deliberate. Her body—"

Something caught in his throat; he cleared it. "The body was curled in a corner behind the bandstand. It might have been stuffed there. There was so much blood that it was difficult to be certain."

"And nobody saw anything?"

He shrugged. "You know how it is."

I did. "Who was she there with?"

"A local prospector named Jude Bascomb. They were staying at the Shoshone Lodge."

"Doing what?"

His dark eyes steadied. He leaned forward in the chair, folded his thick-fingered, grease-coated hands gently, as if he were cradling a small animal. "Whatever a man and a woman do in a motel, Mr. Ross."

He was not, if I read him right, an insensitive man. He was, in the oblique desert way, sizing me up.

"I don't meant that. I mean why were they here, in Tonopah."

"Jude had come in from the desert with an ore sample he wanted assayed. He planned to sell the claim. Then he was going to take her back into the desert."

"Was there anything unusual about that?"

"The way you ask the question," he said with deliberation, "suggests that you have an answer in mind."

I smiled. "I know that a lawyer never asks a question that he doesn't know the answer to, at least in court. I used to be a private investigator. An investigator never asks a question he does know the answer to."

"Used to be?"

"My license expired. I'm just a citizen."

"You'd be the Jack Ross who . . . ?" He let the question hang. I had a sense that he already knew the answer to it.

He silently studied me. "I've been trying to think of who you reminded me of. Your grandfather, I guess. I met him when he came to identify the body. He asked the same questions you are."

"What answers did he get?"

"What there was. Like Jude, part of it was usual and part

of it wasn't. Jude Bascomb had been finding good rock in this country for a long time. Nobody'd see him for months, maybe longer, then he'd be in filing claims and getting what he could for them. The mining industry was pretty much bust, so he never got much, but he'd grab it and light out for the Bimbo City. A week or so later he'd be back in the desert."

It wasn't an attorney who told me the story of Jude Bascomb. He spoke like a tired rancher having coffee around the stove after a long jaunt in the desert.

"What was different this time?"

"This time he came into town with your mother. This time he wasn't going to Vegas, he was going back to the desert with her."

"Why?"

He shrugged. "He already had what he went to Vegas for?"

I was getting a funny schizoid sense of him. Sometimes he was a lawyer and sometimes he wasn't. His face was stained by the desert sun and wind, but his skin was smooth, soft, well cared for. His hands looked strong enough to snap fence posts, but they still lay folded as if protecting something helpless. His black eyes looked steadily out-ward, but seemed to be watching his responses rather than mine.

"Where did they meet?"

"Vegas. His story was she'd picked him up. Not that you could believe Jude about women. The only action he got around here he paid for, but he always came back from the Big Sandbox with tales of his sexual prowess. Celeste was his living proof."

"If he was in Vegas," I said, "how did he locate the claim he was trying to sell?"

"That's a good question, Mr. Ross." He was being slow and deliberate again. "I don't know the answer."

"You mean nobody asked for it?"

"He wasn't a suspect, he was a witness. We questioned him, but we didn't interrogate him."

He was no longer the grimy-handed rancher telling sto-ries around the stove. Now he was an attorney, and something else.

"He told you a story that didn't make any sense and you didn't call him on it."

"You might say that we saw no relevance to that line of questioning."

"You might say that you fucked up."

"You might say that, if you were vulgar enough."

Or irritated enough. James Bacigalupilaga was irritating me. He was playing games with me.

"I beg your pardon. You erred. You perhaps erred again in not asking him where the claim was located?"

"We didn't have to. It was recorded. All we had to do was look it up. We had no reason to."

I did. And I would. "Did Bascomb say where in the desert they were planning to go?"

"No." He unfolded his hands, looked at them as if surprised that they were empty.

"I know she was your mother, Mr. Ross, but I'm not sure I understand your interest, after all these years."

"I'm not sure I do either. What happened to Bascomb?"

He glanced out at the bare earth, the skeletal derricks breaking the horizon, the empty sky. "The desert got him."

"He's dead?"

"No. He's out there. But it got him." He looked at me to see if I understood what that meant. "Last I heard, he was out in Sand Creek Canyon." His dark, shadowy gaze settled on me again. "I wouldn't bother to look him up, though. He's . . . gone."

I would look up Jude Bascomb. But not yet.

"What can you tell me about the brawl?"

He was silent for a moment. "This is a mining town, full of hard people living a hard life. The life breeds frustration, anger, loneliness, and it doesn't take much to set things off, especially during the celebration. As far as we could tell, it was just a fight. There's one in town every Friday and Saturday night, and one every couple of hours during Jim Butler Days."

"Lot of women get killed in them, do they?"

Even more his eyes reminded me of dark caves in a granite ledge. I didn't know what lived in those caves.

I took out the two photographs and placed them before him.

"She—" Again something stuck in his throat. "She was a fine-looking woman, Mr. Ross."

"How many of these people do you know, Mr. Bacigalupilaga?"

"I don't know any of them, Mr. Ross. I recognize Lanky Chandler, of course, and Natty Stern. I—are you suggesting that there's a connection between these people and your mother's death? If you have information that would bring into question the coroner's verdict, as a member of the bar you're bound to report it. Would you like me to call the DA's office for you?"

"All I have are questions, Mr. Bacigalupilaga." Including how he knew I was a member of the bar.

He sat back in his chair and looked at me. I asked him another question.

"Do you know a man named Dalton James?"

"No."

"A country musician named Cletus James?"

He picked up the two photographs, handed them to me. "I think I will phone the DA."

"He'll tell you that last night in Reno a young woman named Miranda Santee shot and killed a man named Dalton James."

He looked at me for a while. "You said that your private investigator license had expired."

"Correct."

"You are here as a private citizen to inquire into the accidental death of your mother nearly thirty years ago."

"Correct."

He stood up. "I don't believe you, Mr. Ross."

I stood up. "That is your prerogative."

His big hands became fists. "I too am a private citizen, Mr. Ross. I suggest you take your inquiry to the official representative of Nye County, if in fact you can with impunity, for I have nothing further to say to you."

I looked at him and saw that he meant it.

I shrugged, turned, went to the door, opened it.

Lois Bacigalupilaga hadn't moved. Her smile was still savage. Her eyes were still bright and unseeing.

11

Two days after my mother died, Jude Bascomb had filed a claim in the Willow Creek region a few miles north of the Clark County line, less than an hour from Las Vegas.

I wasn't going to Willow Creek. I was going to Las Vegas. But first I was going to find Jude Bascomb.

An hour after I left the courthouse I was in his territory.

Sand Creek was an inch of water six inches wide running in a bare channel six inches wider. It trickled under the highway through a narrow culvert and wandered down to the alkali flat in the middle of a narrow empty desert valley.

I turned off the other way, followed the creek and a pair of rocky ruts up an alluvial slope studded with spiny forked Joshua trees standing like sentinels in the silence.

Near the mouth of a small canyon, four wild burros froze at the edge of the creek as if in a photograph. They glared, spread their front legs, bared their teeth. They were old studs who'd lost their mares but not their lives in battle. Their challenge was pointless, driven by vestigial instinct or memory or dream. When I kept coming, they fled in a stiff-legged lope.

Inside the canyon an abandoned mine littered the steep hillside—a few old sagging sheds, gutted machines and broken tools slowly rusting in the desert air, a huge tailing pile.

To the west, I knew, over a series of snowy ridges and the sheer wall of the Sierra, lay Death Valley. To the east, covering miles of emptiness, was the Nuclear Test Site.

Halfway up the steep, rock- and snow- and sage-strewn hill, an old twenty-foot Airstream sat like a silvery mutant growth on the land. Halfway up the tailing pile, a man stood watching me.

The head was small and thin, the body grotesquely broad, bloated, and lumpy. Then I realized that the body was small and thin too, that it was cloaked in ragged layers of heavy clothing.

He watched as I got out of the Wagoneer. Then, as if he'd seen nothing, he turned and climbed slowly up the pile.

When he had slipped over the top, I stepped across the trickle of water, punched through a thin line of creek willows, and climbed up to his shack.

The Airstream sat on tires flat so long I couldn't tell where they stopped and the earth began. The windows were covered with rotted cardboard, the door shielded by a hut of mismatched boards. From a jumble of wood at the end of the trailer rose a crooked stovepipe propped up by rocks and rusting wire. Beyond it, a garbage dump trailed its tin and rot down the hillside.

A power line, nearly bare in spots, ran over the tailing pile to the trailer, through a crack in a window, and vanished.

I went inside. It was like stepping into a diseased brain.

The room reeked of flesh and rot. The floor was covered with garbage—empty food cans and boxes, the bones of small animals, crushed paper sacks and wadded-up newspapers and, lying over and under everything, pornographic magazines. Photographs. Grainy, black-and-white shots on pulpy paper. Slick four-color poses. Fucking and sucking of every conceivable description—the images scattered through the garbage made it seem as if some insane revel had been destroyed by a more insane god.

The garbage stirred at my feet. I nudged a beaver rag and a scorpion, tiny, deadly, stiffened his tiny deadly tail.

A rutlike path through the garbage ran to a mattress stuffed into a cavelike indentation in a wall; another twisted to a wall where a jagged hole exposed a blackened wood stove.

The power cord was wired to a color TV and VCR. On the screen, in a silent frozen frame, a glazed-eyed young woman wearing only bridal white stockings and garters opened her arms and thighs to a young man with an erection the length of an ax handle and the shape of the scorpion's stinger.

I got out, dragged in deep gulps of clean, dust- and sage-scented air. It wasn't enough. My body revolted, cramped, bent me double, and I retched into the dust.

I went back to the Wagoneer, rinsed my sour mouth with water. Then I climbed back up to the Airstream, sat on a rock and watched the light play on the desert, listened to the windless silence.

I was about to give up when he stepped around the corner of the shack.

As ragged as his clothing, his small-featured desert face was seamed and scoured by the sun and wind. In one bloody hand he held the body of a small lizard from which he'd torn the head. He walked past me as if I weren't there, into the trailer.

I waited for a few minutes. He didn't come back out. I sucked up air and followed him.

On the TV screen, the bride of quietness was being ravished by the young man and his impossible erection. Jude Bascomb sat before the screen on a stool, several layers of pants at his knees, stroking his semi-erect penis with his bloody hand in a slow rhythm of his own creation.

I stepped past him and switched off the set. He continued to stare at it, to masturbate.

Something in me snapped.

I kicked the chair from under him.

He toppled into the garbage, looked up at me like an animal looking at its death.

His body convulsed, squirmed, tried to dig itself into the filth and rot. He clutched his penis as if it were life itself.

I went back outside, sat and stared at nothing.

A few minutes later he came out, looked at me as if he'd never seen me. I took a picture from my pocket and held it up.

He sidled closer, snatched the picture.

Slowly he began to smile. Despite his ragged teeth and ruined face, it was a smile of impossible sweetness, filled with love, yearning. "Virgin Mary."

I didn't know what that meant. "Who killed her?"

His face didn't change, but somehow the smile was gone.

He looked into the empty sky. "She said she'd have my baby too."

"Who killed her, Jude?"

He stared into the emptiness of the sky.

I stood up, into his line of vision. He didn't seem to see me, or to notice when I took the photograph from his hand. On Belle Smith's face he had left a bloody thumbprint.

Slowly the magical smile rehumanized his face. "She said we was gonna lay on the bank beside the creek and be naked together and fuck and eat chokecherries all day."

"Where?"

"Fuck all day. Chokecherry. She said she loved me."

Again the inner illumination of his smile died. "She lied. Fucking whore. They're all whores."

He turned, seemed to see me for the first time, grinned in a lascivious shrewdness. "Big guy like you, hung like a horse I bet. Me too."

Then he stepped past me as if I weren't there. He began climbing the tailing pile.

Jude Bascomb had been named for the appropriate saint. He was a lost cause.

12

The long descent to Las Vegas.

Down the twisting canyon to Beatty, down onto the Amargosa Desert, its huge dunes bunched against a distant range, down.

The air warmed, dried. The land shriveled, buckled, seemed to force out of itself busted-back ranges and solitary cinder cones, stubby yucca and stringy greasewood, broken rock.

Near Indian Springs a road left the highway, meandered into the desert toward Willow Creek and, eventually, Death Valley. Across the highway, a half-dozen vehicles sat in a gravel parking lot before a square of mobile homes that was Tawny's Fillie Ranch. Pink neon flickered like a smile of halfhearted seduction, dull white paint tried to gleam in the pale sunlight.

Dalton James had frolicked within those tinny walls. I braked, turned around, and pulled into the lot.

For a moment I sat there. I knew what was likely to happen if I went in. I realized that I was looking forward to it.

I got out, opened the back of the Wagoneer, took out a bottle of Glenlivet, jerked the cork, took a big pull, let part of it dribble from my mouth over my chin and onto my shirt. Then I stuffed the bottle back in the box and shut the door.

The six other cars carried California plates, nosed like packhorses to the rail fence that was supposed to simulate a corral. As I approached the door, it opened, and a pair of small, short-haired, wide-grinning young men stepped out, punching and elbowing their way toward me. One winked at me. "Try the redhead. Buck ya every way but loose."

The "parlor" was poorly lit, decorated in a phony desert art nouveau—potted cacti and palm, drawings of stylized nude women frolicking in grassy meadows. From a huge jukebox lit up like a Day-Glo rainbow came the nostalgic rhythms of Western swing and Randy Travis's promise to love somebody forever and ever, Amen.

The redhead—more a strawberry roan—was occupied. Or about to be. At a small table near the jukebox, she sat wedged between two burly middle-aged men in baseball caps and down vests, haggling over love and money.

A pair of palominos in hot pants and halters rose from a couch and gave me the smile. At the five-stool bar, a long-limbed bay left an obese thirtyish man in a short-sleeved shirt and tie brooding over his pony bottle of beer, came up with a look that would calculate my alcohol consumption to the ounce, my height to the inch, my weight to the pound, my erect penis to the centimeter, and the contents of my wallet to the penny.

"Hi, welcome to Tawny's."

She slipped her hand inside my elbow. "I'm Tammy, darlin', and this is Jodie and Sunny. What's your name?"

"Jackie."

"Hi, Jackie," Tammy said. "You want a drink first, or you want to get right to the party?"

The blondes were mares rather than fillies, their halters stuffed with maternal-looking flesh and cut to emphasize heft. They had pale skin, faces stained a shade darker with makeup, bright mouths, dull eyes.

Tammy was almost skinny, her face small, her features sharp. Something—greed, uppers, intelligence—brightened her eyes. I slipped my arm around her insubstantial waist. "I got me a powerful appetite, but only one spoon. You'd do me just fine."

Tammy smiled, moved so that my hand slid onto her haunch. The palominos moseyed back to the couch. The music ended.

"I might could use a whistle-wetter," I said, nudging her to the bar. "Barkeep, set up a pair of them monster brewskis."

In his pearl-buttoned Western shirt, the bartender looked like a scrawny old bronc buster who'd been thrown once too often. As he set two tiny bottles of beer on the bar, his silence told me he didn't buy either my buckaroo patois or drunken slurring.

Tammy did, or didn't care. She slipped her hand onto my thigh. "A long piece of dust between waterholes, huh?"

"Clean from Reno. Speaking of that, I run into a guy up there last night, said he'd meet me here, treat me on account of it's my birthday. He here? James, his name is, Dalton James."

I took a small swallow of beer, using the motion to watch the bartender do something under the bar.

Tammy ignored the name. "A birthday boy? We'll have to fix somethin' real special nice for you. What you got in mind?"

The strawberry roan and the down-vested men rose from the table and disappeared through a heavily draped doorway. Now more bovine than equine, the blondes ruminated on the couch. The fat man stared glumly at his beer.

"Oh, I'm just a meat-and-potatoes fella," I said. "But I'd hate to pay for a prime piece when I can get it free. You gotta know Dalton, he tells me he practically lives here. Young guy, long sort of brownish hair, drives an old black Trans-Am?"

"Darlin', he could drive a one-horse shay for all I'd know." She moved her hand higher up my thigh, leaned forward to show me her nubby breasts. "The thing is, honey, I got responsibilities, I can't be spending my time chatting."

She gave me a smile of moronic salacity, while on my jeans an insistent fingernail traced the shape of my penis. "Besides, you're workin' up a powerful appetite in me."

The draperies in the doorway moved. A big-bellied man with perhaps the last ducktailed crew cut in America came in. The police stick pressed to his thigh was as scarred as his floridly alcoholic face.

No scars marred the woman who followed him.

Her long hair was smooth and hard-looking, layered with lacquer, the color of buckskin. Tawny.

Her eyes were dark and hard-looking.

Her face was heavily, carefully made up, so smooth and hard-looking it seemed a mask.

Her body, under a smooth and soft-looking pale-green

knitted outfit that clung to her flesh, was smooth and hard-looking.

Her hard face and body said she was thirty-five. The seams at her throat added ten hard years.

She stepped past the pussel-gutted goon, moved to the jukebox, dropped in a coin and punched buttons. A guitar chord slammed, the room filled with the growling wail of the old Troggs song about a wild thing and the possibility of love.

"What do you want?" Her voice was as devoid of emotion as the desert is of promise.

Tammy looked at her, gave me a look of pure hatred, jerked her hand from my crotch, slid from the stool, and moved over beside the obese man hunched over his beer.

I abandoned my act. "Information about Dalton James."

"Who's he?"

"A young man who was shot to death last night."

I didn't get a reaction. "Who are you?"

"My name's Ross."

"What are you?"

What indeed? "I'm an attorney-at-law."

"You're trouble," she said in that same empty voice. "We don't like trouble here. You'd better go, while you can."

What she actually said was, "You're not a cop so you're not a threat." I wanted to disabuse her of that second notion.

"After we talk. And if your man there comes at me with the stick he'll eat it. If the bartender's hands leave the bar he won't ever pour a drink again."

I didn't know if I could carry out either of those threats. I did know I'd love to try.

Not a trace of emotion stirred in her face, flickered in her eyes, quivered in her voice. "Let's see."

I grabbed the bartender's collars and jerked his head down onto the bar, heard his skull hit the wood and felt his sudden weight and let go and smashed the pony beer bottle on the edge of the bar and stood up and flourished the jagged glass at the goon.

Adrenaline lit his veiny face like neon.

He smiled, came at me slowly, cradling the heavy battered stick in his heavy battered hands. The way he held it told me he was an ex-cop, told me too that he knew how to use it.

We did a slow shuffling circling waltz. His face slicked with sudden sweat as he feinted with the stick, small, playful feints. His smile was small and not at all playful.

I didn't feint. I had only one chance against the stick.

I held the broken beer bottle in front of his face, turning it with a slow movement of my wrist. The light from the jukebox collected in the glass, broke into bands of color on the bevel of its edges, swirled as I turned the bottle.

He tried not to focus on it, tried to watch my eyes, my shoulders. The sharpness of the glass, the revolving rainbow of color tugged at his gaze.

I shoved it at his eyes.

Even before his arms came up to parry my thrust I'd stopped it, continued with my leg, and drove the point of my boot into the pit of his stomach. He sagged, gagged, and as he doubled over I hit him as hard as I could with my left hand. He fell as if in slow motion, like a rock from the edge of a cliff.

He lay on the floor, still clutching the stick. His face was blotched with pale patches like alkali flats; his eyes were open but glazed with pain.

Tammy and the man at the bar, the pair on the couch hadn't moved. The woman with the buckskin-colored hair looked down at the goon, up at me, over at the bar. I turned and found myself looking into the small empty eye of a large revolver.

The bartender's forehead was knotted and turning purple, his face angry, his hand shaking. There was no reason in the world that I could think of to prevent him from shooting me.

I realized that I didn't care if he fired or not. The spurt of violence had drained me of what I recognized had been a minor madness. Now I felt nothing.

I looked into the eye of the revolver and smiled.

The Troggs ended their desperate wail. The jukebox whirred, clicked, and Grace Slick began to shriek over shrieking guitars that she wanted somebody to love, needed somebody to love.

"That was cute, especially for a lawyer," the woman said.

"If he's going to use that thing, tell him to do it."

"You don't care?" She didn't.

I dropped the broken bottle to the floor, shrugged.

Nothing changed in her face, her eyes. I had the sense that nothing ever did. "Put it away," she said to the bartender, "Mr. Ross won't cause any more trouble."

I wondered how she knew.

"Why don't we talk about all this in my office. Take care of Bruce, will you, girls?" She stepped over to the drapery and pulled it open. "Mr. Ross?"

Cautiously, alertly, I followed her through the door, down a narrow hall lined with closed doorways. From behind a couple of them came the muted sounds of music and coupling.

Her office was a small room with a desk and filing cabinet and two hard-looking chairs. The walls were bare. The desk held a telephone and an intercom and a framed photograph.

The man in the photograph was darkly handsome, his face at once well-fed and fit, his smile broad and cruel. Something about the photograph told me it wasn't recent.

Even old hookers needed somebody to love.

She sat behind the desk. I remained standing, where I could see the door. "You'd be Tawny."

"That's what they call me."

"Dalton James is dead."

Nothing moved in her hard eyes, smooth face. Yet in the light of the office, her face was somehow subtly different. "That makes it pretty stupid of you to be asking for him here."

"I was just tossing a rock into a cesspool to see what kind of slimy creatures come scurrying out."

"You're sweet. All you got was me."

"And something else. I mention Dalton James and the barkeep hits the panic button and you show up sporting a goon. Why?"

Her eyes were like agate, deep brown and polished by old pain. The gloss was so hard now that nothing could penetrate it.

"It wasn't the name, it was that it was a man's name. You might have noticed this is a whorehouse. Men don't come here looking for other men. When they do, they're either seriously confused or they're cops. Either way, they're trouble."

"You're telling me you didn't know Dalton James?"

"We don't have our clients sign a guest book," she said. Then she said, "Why are you asking about a dead man?"

That was a mistake. It wasn't much, just a question. But she shouldn't have asked it.

I pulled up one of the chairs, placed it where I could see the door, straddled it. "Let's talk."

"You start. Who are you working for?"

"Myself."

"Lawyers don't work for themselves. If you are a lawyer. You don't handle yourself like one, you don't talk like one, and you don't look like one. You look like a cop. Or a killer."

"Known a lot of killers in your time, have you?"

"The best. What do you want?"

"Dalton James was killed last night trying to kill a friend of mine, a girl named Miranda Santee. You know her?"

"No."

"A long time ago a woman was killed in a bar in Tonopah. Her name was Celeste Ross. You know her?"

"No."

"The band playing the night she died was Cletus James and the James Boys. You probably don't know him either. But I'm fascinated by what I doubt is a coincidence."

"So what?"

"The woman who got killed was my mother."

"So what?"

She seemed to be what all hookers try to be or pretend to be, hard to the core. After years of penetration by organs and appendages, she seemed impenetrable. After years of absorbing semen, she seemed impregnable. After years of being handled and mauled and grabbed and stroked, she seemed untouchable.

And there was her face. In the light her makeup seemed excessively heavy, even for an old hooker—thick, stiff, like an expanse of frozen snow over a slope that contained sharp rocks and treacherous holes. She was hiding, or protecting, something.

"So I want to know who killed her."

She looked at me for a while. Something might have been stirring inside her. Or not.

"I knew Dalton James," she said. "I knew his father better. He worked here for a while when he got out of the joint.

Relief bartender, once in a while he'd pick up a girl or a john at the airport for me. Cletus."

I'd given her no reason to give me any information.

"A big guy who looks small, crippled hand?"

She nodded. "Are you going to kill him?"

"Should I?"

Her smile was strange, eloquent. It said that she didn't care if I killed Cletus James. It said that she didn't care about anything. I'd seen that smile before.

"What's your real name?"

"Who cares?" Her expression and voice were as blank, as empty as the walls of her office.

"I do, darlin'. I'm falling for your charm, your wit and intelligence, your sparkling personality. I want to know all about you—your favorite color and song, what you do on rainy evenings. Do you like sushi? What's your sign? Your name?"

She almost smiled. "Linda. Linda Goshgarian."

"You don't look Armenian."

"You don't look stupid."

"Where do I know you from?"

"Do you? Maybe we partied once."

"I'd remember that."

She did smile this time.

Something in her smile spoke to me.

She stood up, and something finally came into her hard eyes, her smooth hard face. With that fierce self-lacerating pride so many hookers have, she showed me her body.

It was a fine body, the shoulders broad enough to bear the weight of her heavy breasts, the waist narrow, the flair of hips smooth, the legs strong and sleek.

"You better believe you'd remember."

13

In the softening afternoon light, I drove through the barren land.

In Sage Chandler's bed I had been mindlessly brutal. In Jude Bascomb's trailer I had been inexplicably outraged. In the whorehouse I had been eagerly violent, brandishing the same weapon that had killed my mother.

I should have stayed in the desert.

I should have been an old impervious hooker. . . .

Las Vegas was ugly.

At the ragged edges of the city, random squares of housing developments patched the desert like fields of dead crops. Condo complexes in artificial Spanish style—sprayed-on stucco walls, fiberglass roof tiles—enclosed golf courses the insistent green of counterfeit bills. In older areas, houses huddled under dust-choked trees and scraggly imported palms.

Concrete, asphalt, plywood, grass. Yet everywhere rose the desert that Vegas would deny—curbs duning up with drifting sand, empty lots tufted with weeds and spiny brush, lawns dying into dust at the edge of the sprinkler's arc.

Downtown was bright lights that paled the waning winter sun, casino neon splashing over more neon that advertised palm readers and pawn shops, wedding chapels and adult book stores, seedy motels, small stores selling junk jewelry and T-shirts.

The exterior of the Gold Strike was new, ersatz brick and flashy neon. The interior was old, worn carpet and dingy paint, old dreams and old scams. Under the din of voices and machines, the air conditioner labored to wash away the odor of smoke and booze, sweat and anxiety, the fetid rankness of dead promises.

The pert, pretty young desk clerk didn't seem to notice. She gave me a pert, pretty young smile as she took my money and I filled in the registration card. "Where are you from?"

"Reno."

"Welcome to Nevada."

"Thanks."

She handed me a key. "Good luck."

I'd need it. I'd registered as Hiram Vanca.

I went to my room, changed, and went out for a run.

I ran through downtown, out to the Strip, to the end of it.

The day's heat clung to the cooling earth. A soft southerly breeze ruffled my hair and cooled my sweat.

The air was clear and golden in the setting sun. In that air everything was sharp detail and vivid color and crisp shadow and uniformly ugly.

None of it mattered.

I ran back in the neon-lighted, neon-shadowed darkness.

No one waited in my room, although someone had been there.

After I showered, I sat on the edge of the bed, ignored my body's clamor for rest, and tried to figure out what to do.

I'd tossed a rock into a bigger cesspool, but nothing had scurried out. Forcing the issue with Vanca didn't seem wise.

Besides talking to Vanca, which probably would get me only bruises, what I had to do in Vegas I had to do in the Clark County Courthouse, which wouldn't be open till the next morning.

I decided to let things take me where they seemed to want me to go. I looked in the phone book. Cletus James lived on Lone Star Lane.

No one answered my call. I got dressed and left.

Someone had been in the Wagoneer too. The lock on the front door was scratched, the new dust on the dash smudged.

I started the Wagoneer and drove out into the garish night.

The Strip pulsed with artificial light that cast eerily vague shadows. Casinos announced shows featuring impressionists, female impersonators, chimps that acted like humans. Soft-edged, shadowy, somehow insubstantial figures drifted like ghosts along the sidewalks, lounged on corners and in doorways. On marquees neon champagne glasses bubbled, neon legs flashed. At The Dunes, the monolithic orange sign that was supposed to suggest Byzantine towers pulsated like a huge, hard-pumping phallus.

Unreal city.

I turned off on Desert Inn Road, followed it past shopping centers and apartment rows and tract houses, turned on Lone Star Lane. Small, '50s-style ranch houses cast faded yellow light through tiny windows onto lawns more sand than grass, onto broken toys on broken concrete sidewalks.

The house I wanted was dark. It was better kept than most of the others, its paint fresh, its lawn neatly cut and bordered with carefully tended flower beds.

I drove past, turned, and coasted to a stop a block away. Cracking my window, I let the cool night air brush over my face.

The authorities would have notified Dalton James's family of his death. If there was more to the family than his father, they would be making arrangements or seeking solace from their grief.

Dalton James's family. Miranda had told me that he was her brother. I still didn't know what that meant.

I leaned back and willed my mind into blankness and looked up at the emptiness of the neon-muddied sky and the flicker of the neon-dimmed stars. . . .

Lights glared on my face, a taxi pulled away from the house.

A light inside flicked on, then another flared pale yellow over the small concrete pad before the door.

I got out and walked over to the house. Through the thin walls I heard the smooth baritone of Jim Reeves and his old lament about city lights and a woman, a moth and a flame.

At my feet lay a small white card. I picked it up. Over her name a metro detective sergeant had scrawled a message in pencil. "Please call me as soon as you can."

Dalton James's family didn't know of his death. I put the card in my pocket and knocked on the door.

The music died.

The door was opened by a slave girl.

Under a cap of soft blond hair, the face that should have been pretty was ravaged by old acne scars that her heavy makeup couldn't hide. The deep lines around her nose and mouth resulted not from disease but from life.

Her slender body looked younger than her face, with breasts just large enough to maintain the plunge cut into the front of her pseudo-classical slave-girl outfit.

"Yes?"

"Good evening. I'm sorry to disturb you. I—would you be Mrs. James. Mrs. Cletus James?"

"I'm Cleo James." Her eyes were large, dark, fine. They began to muddy in their depths.

"My name's Ross, Mrs. James. I'm an attorney. I wonder if I might come in and speak with you for a moment."

What slowly swirled up into her eyes was close to despair.

"It's nothing serious, Mrs. James. I'm investigating an accident your husband witnessed. There's no problem."

Her eyes suggested that there was always a problem.

"He's not here. At least I don't think he is. I just got home. Let me check." She stepped aside.

The small living room was carpeted in inexpensive but clean and well-kept beige. The two chairs and sectional piece in one corner were covered in a bright floral pattern. A few framed prints of New England villages and European churches and Oregon beaches graced the walls, a few magazines and books lay in a neat scatter on the gleaming surfaces of tables and TV set and sound system.

The room looked as if it had been copied from a magazine or a dream.

Cleo James motioned me toward a covered chair. "I'm going to change, too, Mr. Ross, and make myself a drink. Can I get you a . . . libation?"

The last word came out with a queer shy pride. I smiled. "Whatever you're having. Thank you."

While she was gone, I examined the room.

The magazines were slick women's publications proffering advice on room decoration and homemaking and love, the record albums country, the books slim tomes of psychobabble and self-help directed at unhappy women. The one on the coffee table was titled *Love and Loneliness: Marriage in the Eighties.*

Everyone in Nevada seemed to have three framed photographs in prominent display. Cleo James's sat atop the TV set: in an old black-and-white shot, an elderly couple stood unsmiling before a large barn—Desert American Gothic; in the most recent, Dalton James grinned colorfully from inside his TransAm.

Between them was a tinted wedding portrait—another bride of quietness, a youthful, hopeful Cleo James gazed up at a large, not-quite handsome man with a large, not-quite-confident smile, the man who had withered into the whiner I'd talked to outside Miranda's apartment. One hand hid behind his hip.

Cleo James returned in a heavy-napped pink robe and pink tasseled mules. Her face shone cleanly, her scars were sharply etched in her skin. Her face looked like the desert after a violent rain. Strangely, she was almost lovely now.

She had two glasses of ice and dark liquid in her hands. "I hope you like crème de menthe, it's sweet, but—"

"That's great."

She handed me a glass, sat on the sectional.

"I never used to drink. After serving it for eight hours, the last thing I wanted when I got home was alcohol. But lately I've come to like it more. It's an excellent . . . soporific."

I smiled. "I take it that your husband isn't home?"

"No. He and our son went off a couple of days ago. It doesn't look like they've been back."

"Did he say where he was going?"

"They . . . I think they went off to . . ." She gave me a naked, steady look. "Are you sure he's all right?"

She was afraid of something. She'd been afraid of something for a long time.

"As far as I know, Mrs. James. I—I understand that your husband is a musician?"

"Not for years." The lines around her mouth deepened. "It's hard to make music with a handful of broken fingers."

"I'm sorry," I said, and tried to look it. "What happened?"

"He got mixed up with the wrong people." She looked at me to see if I understood what, in Las Vegas, that meant. Then she looked away, at nothing, her past, her life.

"He was good, real—really . . . accomplished, almost

good enough to—but that's the story of Vegas, isn't it? Everybody here is almost good enough or smart enough or talented or beautiful enough. Almost City."

She smiled a small, rueful smile. "I was lucky. I was never almost anything." The smile brightened, went false. "But I do pride myself on my . . . veracity. You aren't being very . . . veracious with me, are you, Mr. Ross?"

Before I could answer, she smiled again, more brightly.

"Don't you wonder why I let you in? A strange man appears at my doorstep in the middle of the night, I'm a woman alone in a city . . . rife with rape and assault, and yet I invite you into my home, offer you alcohol. Don't you wonder why, Mr. Ross?"

I didn't wonder. She'd let me in because she was lonely.

The smile increased in brightness, falseness.

"Men have appeared on my doorstep in the middle of the night before. Men like you. They were always policemen."

"I see."

"No," she said, "I don't think you do. I'm not sure that I do. I try, but . . . I know you want something, Mr. Ross. I'll give it to you, if I can. But I want you to tell me something."

"If I can."

"Does this have anything to do with a television reporter named Miranda Santee?"

"Yes."

Her fine dark eyes brimmed with sudden tears. "I knew it. Ever since she talked to Cletus, he and Dalton have been . . ."

"What did they talk about, Mrs. James?"

"I don't know. I—are you working for her?"

"I'm not working for anyone." I went on, in the face of her disbelief. "Mrs. James, I'll tell you the simple truth. Miranda Santee told me a story, and part of it had to do with my mother. Many years ago my mother was killed in a bar, and Miranda told me that she was murdered. I'm trying to find out if that's true. Your husband and his band were playing in the bar that night. I want to ask him about it."

"A bar in Tonopah?"

"Yes."

Through tears she looked over at her wedding photograph, wistfully, as if at the image of a child who had died.

"It always comes back to that bar in Tonopah. Every-thing."

More and more, it was looking that way.

"Miranda Santee told you a story, Mr. Ross, but we all have stories. Let me tell you mine."

Cleo James had grown up on a hardscrabble ranch in the desert north of Searchlight, the only child of middle-aged parents. At twelve she was pretty, at thirteen purulent, her face erupting from within and her skin flaming and cratered like some volcanic wasteland. At fourteen she met Cletus James at a high school dance.

In the pretty white dress her mother had made for her, the white dress that deepened the inflamed red of her skin, she stood before the bandstand with the others, the pretty girls, and he looked at her. He looked at her and made her feel beautiful.

In the break before the last set, in the backseat of a '54 Buick, because he had that night given her something she had despaired of ever having, she gave herself to him.

He came back, several times. He told her that he loved her, and she knew it was true. He told her that when she finished high school, she should come to Vegas and they would be married.

When she was a senior, he stopped coming. His band was playing all over the state, so she wasn't concerned. She was concerned that he'd stopped writing, but she wasn't fright-ened; she knew he loved her. When she graduated she went to Vegas and found him with no band and a broken hand and a pregnant girl.

Three years later he walked into the bar where she was waiting tables, looked at her and asked her to marry him.

She did.

He couldn't play the guitar anymore, but he could still sing. He tried. He didn't get anywhere. It was the fault of the people who ran the music business.

She bore him a son, then went back to work. He gave up music, took up gambling. He didn't get anywhere. It was the fault of the casinos.

He gave up gambling and took up drinking. He got to the drunk tank. It was the fault of the booze.

He gave up drinking and took up dreaming, concocting surefire schemes that slowly took him to the other side of the law. He got to prison, a short stint for burglary, a long one for armed robbery. It was the fault of the police and the court system and society.

Their son inherited his mother's skin and reacted with rage. He inherited his father's fast-buck scheming. He'd been in and out of juvenile hall since he was thirteen.

His father had been out of prison for two years, tending a little bar and cashing a lot of unemployment checks, when Miranda Santee came to talk to him.

Cleo James had hardly seen her husband or son since.

I'd heard the story before. The details vary, the language derives from Harlequin romances or counselors or the street, but the stories told by women with ex-con men are always the same.

"Why did they break his fingers, Mrs. James?"

She spoke slowly, carefully. "Some people were looking for a woman. He saw her and called them. She died before they got there, and they broke his fingers."

"Who broke his fingers?"

"You know you don't mention those names, Mr. Ross."

"I do. It was Natty Stern, wasn't it?"

She might have nodded.

I realized that I was exhausted. I didn't know how well my mind was working, how clear my perceptions might be. I was feeling a great deal of sympathy for Cleo James, even though I knew that she might be running one of the sympathy cons at which the women of cons are often so good.

I didn't care. I asked the next question as kindly as I could. "Did Cletus get his fingers broken because he killed her before they could talk to her?"

Cleo James began to wither, to shrink. "Go away."

"Mrs. James, officially my mother's death was an accident, and officially it will stay that way. I don't want revenge. I just want to know. Did Cletus kill my mother?"

"I don't know." She didn't want to know.

She sat shrinking in her neat little room in her neat little house. Nothing—not by-the-book understanding, not by-the-magazine homemaking, not by-the-dream love—could keep out the pain.

I had more questions, but not the heart to ask them. I rose. "I'm sorry to have troubled you, Mrs. James."

She sat silently crying.

At the door, I slipped the policewoman's card from my pocket and dropped it to the floor. Then I thought of a question I had the heart to ask.

"What happened to the girl you found him with?"

"She . . . ran off, he said."

"What was her name?"

She was silent so long I thought she wasn't going to answer.

"She was beautiful. Her name was beautiful too. Her name was Echo."

14

I should have gone to bed, but the promise of connections, the irrational sense of inevitablility that often came over me as a case took shape, tugged me back downtown, over into North Vegas, to a neighborhood of run-down gas stations and one-man used-car lots and seedy bars, to a low block building flashing phallic cattails in red neon.

The parking lot was full—pickups, older sporty coupes, an occasional slumming or dealing newer Mercedes or Cadillac or BMW.

As I walked toward the entrance, I could hear the charged rumble of male voices rising to answer the bellowing assertion of Joan Jett and the Blackhearts that love is pain.

Heavy doors of studded leather spread before a grimy hallway leading to a flimsy door traced with obscene comments and smears and spatters of blood. I pushed into a dim cavern filled with the damp heat of bodies charged with booze and testosterone, the raucous clamor of voices and music, the miasmic swirl of smoke.

The room was lit only by the bar lights and the red neon cattails flashing on the walls and at the base of the three small floodlit stages that seemed to float, isolated and attached to nothing, in the dimness.

On one stage a young pony-tailed blonde in what looked like a satin maxi-pad pranced like a confused cheerleader. A high-haunched and nearly breastless black girl in a phosphorescent G-string undulated coitally on another. The girl on the third stage was statuesque and apparently entranced, or stoned; with her eyes closed, she moved her sequin-splattered hips with slow sinuousness to music that existed only in her mind.

The men in the audience encouraged, cajoled, commented, or sat silent. All looked at the dancers the way a coyote looks at a rabbit just out of his killing range.

I pushed my way through bodies to the bar as the record ended. Almost immediately Mick Jagger began to complain about getting no satisfaction.

Wedging in at a station, I held up a twenty and asked for a draft. The bartender slid a glass of beer and fifteen dollars back at me. I slid the change back at him. He took the change, stuffed it in his shirt pocket.

"I'm looking for Cletus or Dalton James."

"Don't know a Cletus. Ain't seen Dalton. He usually comes around in the afternoon, when Wes is on duty."

"Wes who?"

"James. His uncle."

I left the glass of beer on the bar, pushed my way out of the room and down the dim hall and into the night.

On the floor of my room lay a white card the size and shape of the one I'd found outside Cleo James's door. It bore only a message in ink in a script so neat it seemed stamped by machine: "Be at Marci's after one."

It was already after one.

It was after two by the time I found out what and where Marci's was, ran the gauntlet of sense- and psyche-assaulting lights on the Strip, turned off on Spring Mountain Road, and came in sight of the stucco-and-tile building sitting like a fortress or a prison within a square marked off by a hedge of pyracantha.

I nosed the Wagoneer around the circular drive before the entrance. A young Hispanic in a white attendant's jacket took my keys as if I were handing him feces.

The tiled entry was brilliantly lit—too brilliantly. I looked over the heavy double doors, found the blank electronic eye that was looking me over. Bowing, I did Jackie Gleason's Away-We-Go shtick, bowed again at the door, and stepped inside.

The walls of the hallway I entered were hung with what looked like carved masks from a Latin American voodoo ritual, on the right broken by two closed doors. The hall led to a curtained door, before which stood a small thin man in a tuxedo who watched my approach with stony disdain.

Even before I reached the doorway, he had blocked it with his not very intimidating presence. He looked at me—my boots and jeans and old tweed—as if I were feces.

"I'm sorry, gentlemen are not admitted without a tie."

"Fine, lend me yours."

The flesh under his eye twitched. "In any event, no one is seated without a reservation."

His eyes widened with apprehension as I reached into my coat pocket, stayed wide as I pulled out the white card and handed it to him. "I think maybe I have one."

He looked at the card, and his entire face began to twitch. As I watched the flesh jerk and quiver, I heard the closing of a door, the soft step of hard heels on the tile floor.

She was exquisite, tall and slender in an orange sheath with a floppy decorative bow at the throat; she had fine features, flawless opalescent skin, pale-brown eyes, soft brown hair.

She was smiling the purest, most human smile I'd seen since leaving the desert.

She was also somehow familiar, although I knew I'd never met her, knew she would be impossible to forget.

The maître d' was sputtering. "Miss Howe—this . . ."

"I'll handle it, Jason, thank you." She held out a slim, lovely hand. "Hello, Mr. Ross. I'm Marci Howe. Why don't we see if we can find a suitable article of neckwear in my office?"

I didn't know what was happening, didn't much care. She smelled faintly, wonderfully, of musk and smoldering autumn leaves and earth.

More Latin masks decorated the stucco walls of her office; a particularly crude and savage-visaged pair bracketed a built-in television monitor that showed the emptiness of the tiled court.

She ignored the desk, its phone and small panel of switches, and led me to a white love seat and low table on which stood a crystal decanter and brandy glasses. "May I offer you a drink?"

"You betcha."

She laughed, sat, half filled the glasses. The brandy

smelled almost as good as she did. I sipped it, wondered if Marci Howe would taste as good.

"How did you know who I was?"

"I was given a description—a large man in boots and beard behaving bizarrely. Although I found your little dance at the door quite charming."

I found all of Marci Howe charming. "I have many talents."

"No doubt. I also have a message for you."

"From Hiram Vanca?"

She sipped her brandy, then smiled. "From Sage Chandler."

"Uh—I . . ." I finally managed to get out, stupidly, "You know Sage?"

"We were in a contest once. We've been friends since."

"The only contest that I know about, Sage lost. You—" That's why she was familiar. She was the other girl in the photograph on Sage's desk. "You won."

She smiled. "Sage says that she's sorry. And thanks."

"For what?"

"That she didn't say." Her smile was wonderful, full of warmth and care and fun. "Are we having a lover's spat?"

I didn't know what we were having. "How did she know I'd be seeing you?"

"She knew Hiram Vanca spends time here. She knew you were going to talk to him."

That didn't do it, but I let it pass, fortified myself with brandy. "I take it he's here. I'd best get with it."

"Not quite yet." She rose, still smiling. "Jason will be beside himself if you're not properly attired."

I stood as she went to a closet door and swung it open. On a wooden rack hung a couple of dozen neckties. "See anything that strikes your fancy?"

"Only you."

She smiled again. "You have no idea how fanciful that is."

"Probably." But I wasn't under the sway of fancy. More like giddiness. The giddiness of exhaustion and confusion and not a little fear. I'd been giddy most of the night. I got giddier.

"My sense of style cries for the one you're wearing."

"I see what Sage meant by 'bizarre.'" Then she smiled. "It turns out I have something of a taste for the bizarre myself." She tugged at the orange bow at her throat, moved to the desk and took out a letter knife and sawed until the cloth came free. "It's not going to go around your neck and into a bow both."

I tied it in a loose cowboy knot. "How's that?"

She laughed. "What are you going to talk to Hiram about?"

"I'm going to ask him if he had my mother killed."

"'Bizarre' doesn't begin to describe your behavior, does it? Suicidal, perhaps." Her smile restructured itself. "But I can tell you the answer. No."

"Do you know who my mother was?"

"It doesn't matter," she said. "Hiram Vanca has never had anybody killed. He's never had the authority or the inclination. If there's killing to be done, he does it himself." She smiled again. "If you're not careful, he may do it to you."

She knew a lot about Hiram Vanca. "As a great American philosopher once observed, so it goes."

She laughed. "So it doesn't go all over my restaurant, let me perform the introduction."

She ushered me out, past the visibly outraged maître d' and into a big room out of a '30s movie. Around a square dance floor, booths and tables were arranged to create the illusion of privacy while ensuring that everyone in the room had none. The goal of everyone in the room, over their meals and drinks and chitchat, seemed to be to be looked at.

The men were mostly middle-aged and older, in dinner jackets or suits, mostly attempting to exude an aura of wealth and power and virility. Some succeeded. The women were mostly young, in outfits ranging from high-slink to low-down, mostly attempting to exude an aura of sexual availability. All succeeded.

Everyone watched Marci Howe lead me across the room toward a large curved booth against the far wall, in the center of which sat the only man in the room who looked like a pirate.

He too was familiar, but not strangely. That afternoon I'd seen his hard handsome face, minus thirty years and a wicked white scar at his temple and a black patch over one eye, smiling from the photograph on the desk of Linda Goshgarian.

Beside him sat a vacant-eyed and very young woman in too much makeup and too little clothing. She was so still she seemed to have willed herself into an oblivion approaching catatonia. One of Vanca's hands was under the table, on her.

Two men flanked the pair. One was dark, forty, fit; his steady gaze suggested the shadowed darkness of deadly alleys. The other was fair, younger, larger, and, my guess was, less dangerous. Goon and Apprentice.

Marci Howe took my elbow. "This is Jack Ross, Hiram. He wants to know if you had his mother killed."

His eye focused on me with sudden raptorial intensity. "Celeste. She was a dumb cunt."

In a thin, reedy voice he spoke with the syllable-slurring rush that comes with crack. But he wasn't stoned. He was one of those near-manic psychos whose system generates its own powerful amphetamines.

"A cunt, maybe," I said calmly, "but smart enough to rip you off and give you that cute little eye patch."

Marci Howe's fingers clamped down on my arm, Goon and Apprentice stiffened. Vanca did something under the table and the eyes of the young girl went even blanker.

His eye twitched and rolled in his unmoving head, settled on Marci Howe. "What's the story on this asshole?"

Her fingers left my arm. "You know as much as we do."

"You used my name at the Gold Strike."

"I thought it might get me a decent room. I was wrong."

Again the absence in the young girl's eyes deepened. Again Hiram Vanca's eye found Marci Howe, as if he expected her to translate the remarks.

"Who killed my mother, Vanca?"

His face tightened, the girl's empty gaze deepened again. His eye pulsed with the mindless brute intensity with which the mustang stallion had glared at Miranda and me two days before.

I didn't know what he was doing to the girl under the table. I did know it wasn't pleasant.

"I'll tell you who killed your precious fucking mother. Her goddamn cunt-sucking girlfriend killed her. A pair of lesbos, wasn't even worth fucking."

He smiled then, as if he had triumphed in some gladiatorial battle, but the smile that had seemed cruel in the photograph in the brothel now seemed idiotic.

I was wasting my time with him. "Thanks. See you around." I turned to Marci. "Thanks for—

"Wait a minute, asshole."

Apprentice was out of his seat and Goon was right behind him. Vanca leaned forward. "What you gonna do?"

"I'm going to find Belle Smith."

"You can't," he said. "Nobody can."

"That just means you can't. It doesn't mean I can't."

He thought about that. I knew he was thinking. His eye dimmed as if something were drawing current from it.

"I want her," he said finally. He turned his eye on the girl and began a long, graphic, obscene account of what he would do to Belle Smith when he had her. The girl looked at him with eyes as blue and unseeing as Dalton James's.

I felt as I had in Jude Bascomb's trailer. I turned again.

"Wait a minute, asshole. I ain't finished with you yet."

Marci Howe put her hand back on my arm, protectively now. "He's not worth it, Hiram. You might kill him, and there'd be trouble. Let him go."

"Let him go, my ass—"

"Remember what Mr. Stern said the last time?"

The whole scene had been unreal from the start. Now it was surreal. She spoke to this stupid psycho killer as if to a child.

Vanca sputtered. His face reddened as he tried to form words. The young girl's face paled to a ghostly white.

Marci Howe gave Goon a nod, and he and Apprentice each took one of my elbows. "Now," she told them quietly.

Goon gave me a nudge. "After you, jerk."

I didn't argue. I was glad to be getting out of there alive.

Across the door, past the now gloating maître d', down the hall lined with ugly masks, out the door and into the brightly lit court, onto the circular drive. The white-coated attendant came running.

Apprentice stopped him with a word. "Keys."

Goon gave me three words. "This way, jerk." He tugged me onto a strip of asphalt that led to the back of the building.

The large parking lot was filled with large cars whose waxy surfaces reflected the gleam of lot-lights and stars. And one dusty, slightly beat-up Wagoneer. Goon shoved me toward it. "Real class, jerk."

For a brief moment I thought they were going to let me go. I reached for the door handle.

"Not a chance," Goon said.

That's about what I'd have against them. Apprentice alone wouldn't be too bad, but Goon alone would. Together, they would be very bad.

I got myself squared, leaned back against the door for a little leverage. They moved farther apart. Then they stopped moving. It was their move.

Nothing happened.

The attendant ran across the lot and handed Goon my keys. Then he ran back.

We stood there. Goon looked at me, at the sky, the stars. Under Apprentice's jacket, muscles moved in barely perceptible motion, as if he were doing isometric exercises.

Then Marci Howe came walking across the parking lot.

Goon gave her my keys, me a smile. "So long, jerk."

They walked back toward the building. I turned to Marci Howe. "That's the message? So long?"

"Don't forget the jerk part." She smiled, handed me the keys.

I slumped back against the door. "I don't suppose you'd like to tell me what's going on?"

"Any friend of Sage Chandler's is a friend of mine. I'll be happy to tell you anything you want to know."

"That stuff with Vanca, was all that for real?"

The air was thirty degrees warmer than in Reno, nearly balmy. Marci Howe shivered, hugged herself against it. "As real as it gets with Hiram anymore."

I was beginning to see it. "Goon and Apprentice, they aren't his bodyguards, they're his keepers. They work for Natty Stern."

She smiled, shivered. "Goon, Apprentice—they'll enjoy that. They work for me."

"And you work for Natty."

"I'm but a simple innkeeper, Mr. Ross." She shivered again.

Something clunked into place in the back of my mind. "Where were they when Vanca raped a TV reporter named Miranda Santee?"

She didn't smile. "I don't know, because I don't know when or if it happened. Are you sure it did?"

"Reasonably."

"Does it matter to you?"

It seemed a curious question, given the circumstances. But then many things about Marci Howe seemed curious. "Yes."

"Then I suspect they were there." She shuddered again, hugged herself again. "Is there anything else I can tell you?"

"Do you know who killed my mother?"

"No."

I opened the door and climbed in the Wagoneer, shut the door, and had another thought. I rolled down the window.

"The girl with Vanca, she can't be fifteen."

"So?"

"She shouldn't be in there."

"Does it matter to you?"

"Yes."

"Enough that you'll go in and take her away from him?"

I thought about it. "Not right now, it wouldn't be—"

"I didn't think so."

Her smile deepened, became a mask, seemed to detach itself from her flesh and float into the space between us.

Then she hugged herself again, spun on her heel and went striding across the lot.

15

My own system seemed to be producing amphetamines. My body and mind tossed each other around for a
long time before I fell into a fitful sleep. I awoke exhausted.

After a quick breakfast, I found a phone booth on a
Fremont Street corner and called Frank Calvetti.

He was his surly morning self, his always ironic self. "So
how are things in Tonopah? Assuming there are things in
Tonopah besides rocks."

"I'm in Vegas. I need a favor."

"Jack needs a favor. What an incredible surprise. No."

"I've got some names. You have a pen handy?"

"Read my lips. No."

"Come on, Frank, I need help."

"Help with what? Family business? That certainly must be
it. Since you're no longer a snoop, it can't be anything
connected with the killing of Dalton James, or you would be
in violation of the law. Unfortunately, I am not authorized to
assist private citizens with private matters."

"Frank, I'm trying to find out if my mother was murdered."

When he finally spoke, no trace of irony remained in his
voice. "Jesus Christ, Jack—why?"

"The truth?"

"That would be a refreshing change."

"I don't know why. I just am."

As the silence stretched over the five hundred miles of
desert between us, I found myself watching a tall balding
man in torn black sneakers, muddied old brown suit-pants,
and a tattered Air Force dress jacket from which sergeant
stripes had been torn. To some silent military drum he

marched down the sidewalk. His eyes were bright with madness and tilted toward the empty sky; his mouth was open in song. The tourists and the street scum, the casino hustlers and the dreamers, the losers and the lost gave him brief startled looks and then paid him no mind.

Finally Frank spoke again. "What do you want?"

"All the information in the Clark County criminal files on the following people: Belle—"

"You're in Vegas, get it yourself."

"They wouldn't give it to me, I don't have any connections down here. All I've got are my bar credentials, and for what I want that isn't enough. They'll want writs and stuff."

"What makes you think they'll give it to me?"

The mad songster disappeared around the corner. "You've got connections."

"Not for something like this. I've got to give them a more or less reasonable story."

"Tell them it's part of the Miranda Santee–Dalton James investigation."

"Is it?"

"The man in the TransAm the other night was Cletus James, Dalton's father. Cletus was playing guitar in the bar my mother was killed in. Cletus doesn't play guitar anymore, because Natty Stern broke his fingers."

"Natty Stern. That's just wonderful, Jack. You wouldn't know where we might locate Cletus James?"

"He hasn't been home. If he's running, he'd probably run here. But he wasn't running when I saw him, he was waiting, probably for Dalton. I think he left because I spooked him, he figured me for a cop. It's conceivable that he doesn't even know Dalton is dead. He could still be in Reno."

"He knows as of an hour ago, if he listens to the news."

"Maybe. But I don't know where he is."

Another silence.

"Listen to me carefully, Mr. Ross. Are you in possession of any information relevant, material, or in any way germane to an investigation being conducted by RPD?"

"Not to my knowledge."

"I'll accept that, as the word of an officer of the court," Frank said. "and I'll take the names as leads on the James killing. They'll become part of the official file."

"Whatever."

He got a pen and I gave him the names. Belle Smith, Echo Smith or Echo James, Cletus James, Wes James, Celeste Ross, Jude Bascomb, Linda Goshgarian, Marci Howe, and James Bacigalupilaga.

"Thank God for the Basco and the Armenian. With all the Smiths and Jameses, this could take a year. Where can I get in touch with you?"

"I'm at the Gold Strike, but if you call, just leave a message and I'll call back."

"You're at Natty Stern's place? Are you out of your mind?"

"Probably." Just another mad song-singer. The crazy man appeared at a different corner. He'd marched around the block. "How's Miranda?"

"Miss Santee is quite well, thank you. She's out of the hospital, and she has not been charged with a crime."

"Why not? I thought you—"

"We have another consideration at this point."

"What consideration?"

"The political consideration of the considerable political clout of Mr. Lanky Chandler, as exercised by his daughter. She's hired a lawyer, who has made it clear that should RPD make even the slightest misstep in its handling of this matter we will all find ourselves up to our ears in shit."

I didn't know what to make of that.

"Did you get anything from her—from Miranda?"

"Her story is that there was somebody with James, although there is not an iota of physical evidence to support it. She says she fired from the archway, fired at James and his shadow as he came toward her. He of course was shot from behind at close range. She said these things after talking to her lawyer."

"You don't believe her?"

"I'm retaining my incredulity until I see a ballistics report."

"Which way are you going on it now?"

"Looking for witnesses. The entire apartment building seems to have been inhabited by monkeys."

I knew what he meant. See no evil. . . .

"Do you have anything that might help us in this pursuit, Mr. Ross?"

I did, but I wasn't ready to give it to him. "Not really."

"Then stop wasting my time and the taxpayers' money."
He hung up.

I stepped out of the phone booth just as the mad marcher
passed. To a stiff rhythm of metronomic precision, he was
singing a Paul Simon song.

He was, he declared, a rock. He was an island. He felt no
pain. He never cried.

I spent the rest of the day in the Clark County Courthouse,
the night in my room at the Gold Strike waiting for something that didn't happen, the next morning back in the
courthouse.

I spent it intimidating, flattering, and bribing my way
through red tape and regulations.

I found something. Maybe.

Even in Nevada, where so many people drift like ghosts,
pretending to be who and what they wish to be, living lies
and dreams that become more real than reality and truer
than truth, even in Nevada they leave a trail of paper.

The trail may be disguised and gapped, buried here
under a pile of other paper like a mound of dead leaves,
brushed away there by money and power, but if you're good
and lucky you can trace it.

I was good at it, and lucky. I didn't find where the trail of
Belle Smith ended. I did find where it had begun. Maybe.

I found other things too.

I found a birth certificate of a girl named Mabel Margaret
James. The girl's parents were Echo Smith and Cletus
James.

As I was growing certain Miranda had, I checked the
records of the births in Clark County on the same day Mabel
Margaret James was born. I found a certificate of the birth of
Miranda Santee.

Miranda was not Belle Smith's daughter. She was her
granddaughter, the daughter of Cletus James and Echo
Smith. She was also the half-sister of Dalton James. Probably.

I found that Marci's was owned by Deep Desert Enterprises, which was owned by a holding company. That was
as far as I could go in the Clark County records, but I
thought I knew where that trail would end.

Deep Desert Enterprises owned several other businesses,

from an answering service that was probably a call-girl operation to an auto-body shop that was probably a hot-car barn.

Nowhere on these papers appeared the name Nathaniel Stern.

I found nothing with the name Celeste Ross.

I found nothing with the name Belle Smith.

Then, on a whim, I checked Lawrence Albert "Lanky" Chandler. That's when I got lucky. I found a marriage license issued to Lawrence Albert Chandler and Mabel Margaret Madigan.

Mabel Margaret Madigan, Mabel Margaret James. Echo naming her daughter after her mother?

Mabel. Belle. Maybe.

It wasn't much, but it might be enough.

Then I got luckier. I found a bored supervisor who had heard of me, who delighted in the notion that he could justify breaking the regulations of the job he hated by assuming that he was involved in a virtuous righting of bureaucratic wrongs, and who took me on his lunch hour to a warehouse a couple of miles away, led me through labyrinthine tunnels of files and cabinets, and stood beside me with gleeful anticipation as I pulled out the original application for the marriage license of Lawrence Albert Chandler and Mabel Margaret Madigan and discovered that Mabel Margaret Madigan had been born in Chokecherry, Nevada.

16

In the brightness of midday, the Cattail Club hunched along the dismal street like a dissipated woman ashamed to be seen in the unforgiving sunlight.

The parking lot held a couple dozen cars, some nearly junkers, a few looking as if they had been abandoned there.

Through the open leather doors drifted the Pointer Sisters' plea for a man with slow hands and an easy touch. The inside door sported a new smear of brownish blood.

The men scattered around the room sat in the pained and surly silence of the hung-over. They stared angrily at the lone dancer on the platform floating in the center of the room.

It was the same statuesque and bespangled girl who had moved to her own tune the night before. She still moved to it, her eyes open now but seeing nothing, her hips and heavy breasts swaying in what seemed to be perpetual self-seduction.

The bartender looked nothing like Cletus James. He was of mid-height and barrel shape, with an oddly ugly low-browed and lantern-jawed face, and heavy thick-fingered hands.

At one end of the bar, three young men in touristy duds perched on stools like hawks on fence posts and stared as if transfixed and transfixing at the dancer. I took a stool at the other end and dropped a twenty on the bar. The bartender rolled toward me, stopped, looked at it. "What'll it be?"

"I'm looking for Wes James."

He nudged the twenty back at me. "You found him. But I already told the other detectives, I don't know nothing about

Dalton getting himself killed and I don't know where Cletus is."

I nudged the twenty toward him. "I'm not a cop."

"Then you're the guy who talked to Cleo last night. I don't know nothing about what happened in Tonopah."

"How is she? The news about Dalton must have . . ."

His ugly face filled with a mixture of emotions I couldn't quite read. Suffering, resignation, something else.

"She's hurting. I wanted to go to Reno with her, but she . . . said it was Cletus's place, not—you lookin' for him?"

"Yes."

"If you find him, tell him I'm gonna kick the livin' shit out of him." He made his thick-fingered right hand a fist, held it in his left hand, looked down at it.

I took a guess. "Make any difference before?"

"Not much," he said. "The stupid son of a bitch."

I identified the other emotion in his face. "She's an unhappy woman. I'd guess she's been unhappy for a long time."

He glared, and for a moment I thought I'd overdone it. Then he dropped his glare.

"He put her through hell, with the booze and broads, in an' out of prison, pretty much ruined Dalton at the same time. All 'cause he can't play the guitar anymore. I don't play the bass anymore, neither, but that don't mean . . ."

"You were there that night in Tonopah, weren't you, Wes?"

He put his hands flat on the bar. "I don't know nothin' about that. Now, you want something or not? No loiterin'."

"A beer."

He drew one quickly, set it before me, rang it up and gave me the change.

If I had him figured, only one thing was going to work with this man. It was also the only thing I really had.

"She was my mother, Wes."

Without looking at me he turned and moved down to the other end of the bar.

I sipped the beer, waited.

The Pointer Sisters finished their sultry song. The dancer continued to dance in the silence. The mutter and mumble of the men watching her faded. The silence deepened, grew strange.

Then the rhythm of her body began to change, to slow. Her feet and hands and hips rotated in slower and smaller arcs, the ripples and quivers of her flesh weakening, as if the life were draining from her body, until she stood unmoving in the center of the platform. She stared out into the dimness above her audience, seemed to see, to feel, nothing.

There was no movement in the room, no sound.

Then she turned and stepped out of the light and like a ghost stepped down through the dimness and disappeared.

Again there was movement, sound, in the room.

Wes James watched as the three young men walked out. He dropped their glasses in a sudsy tank, wiped the bar, came back to where I sat.

"I seen her, your . . . mother," he said slowly. "We was in the Mizpah, she came up looking for Cletus an' this girl he was with. We had adjoining rooms, me and Sammy in one an' Cletus an' the girl in the other. Then she came to see Cletus at the bar that afternoon. Then I seen her that night, after she . . ."

He again laid his hands flat on the bar. "I never seen that much blood. I—she was stuffed in a corner behind the stage, I thought she was hiding, getting out of the way of everything. I mean, we'd hit the deck, trying to cover our instruments, bottles flying, ashtrays, chairs, everybody screaming and slugging, half the lights got knocked out—it wasn't just a fight, it was like a whole roomful of people just went crazy at the same time."

His eyes met mine, seeking not understanding so much as confirmation. Did human beings really do things like that?

"You found her?"

He nodded. "Everybody heard the sirens and started running. Me and Sammy waited till most everybody had lit out, then we started to haul our stuff out. An' we seen her."

"Where was Cletus?"

His eyes left mine just long enough to tell me he was going to lie. For some reason that saddened me. "He . . . was still on the stage."

The room echoed with the sounds of male voices, the scrape of chairs, footsteps. A man drifted to the bar, a waitress in a halter like those of the blondes in the brothel rested her breasts on the bar and ordered drinks in an empty monotone.

I sat and sipped my beer, watching Wes James work. He was silent and efficient, moved with surprising economy and grace.

A guitar chord slammed dramatically. Onto the center platform stepped a small young woman with bright blond hair, a doll-like painted face, small sloping breasts, wearing a gauzy white bikini bottom that looked like a bandage over a savage wound.

I'd never heard the song before, found myself listening to a raw female voice screaming over the clash of guitars:

> Give me your hatred
> Give me your heat
> Give me your anger
> Give me your meat
> Give me your kick and your bite and your slap
> Give me your mind and your soul and your sap
> I want it all
> I want it now
> I'll make it love

The guitars screamed, a drum crashed. The girl with the doll's face thrust her pelvis at the pale angry silent faces of the men staring up at her.

Wes James came back. I took a swallow from my beer and asked over the clamor, "Did you see my mother come in that night?"

For a moment he didn't answer. He was still back in the bar in Tonopah, still seeing a dead woman splashed with blood and stuffed into a corner. Then he nodded. "She come in alone."

"Why did she come to the hotel?"

"I—to see this girl, I guess. Cletus said she was a friend of the girl's mother or something."

"The girl was Echo Smith."

"Yeah. Cletus got her pregnant, they was gonna get married but her mom was against it, so she'd run off with him. She—your mom—Cletus said she was trying to get Echo to go back."

That didn't make any sense, but I didn't pursue it. We were nearly shouting over the obscene howling of the music. "What happened to the baby?"

"They gave it up." He looked at me, still disbelieving, still dismayed. "To welfare. Cletus—his own baby."

"What happened to Echo?"

He shrugged, as if in pain. "She took off."

With another crash of chords, the masochistic music ended. Yet somehow it lingered in the stale air, stained to a dark and malevolent hue the seduction of the song that followed, a new version of the Doors' "Light My Fire."

"If Cletus was in trouble, where would he go?"

"Here. He always comes to me. Like a fool, I always help."

"He hasn't been here?"

"No." He looked down at his hands. He seemed to be wondering if they were capable of helping his brother any more. "Is he in trouble?"

"I don't know, Wes. Not from me." I finished my beer and slid off the stool. "Who would want to kill Dalton?"

His face took on that same stoic acceptance of suffering and love that it had when he spoke of Cleo James. "Nobody. He—he wasn't worth killing."

"Why not?"

"He—I tried to help him, but . . . nothing ever stuck with him. He was always too mad. At everything. He never figured anything out. He got like Cletus, got these crazy schemes. Jesus, the last time he was gonna go out to Willow Creek and make some kind of deal, he thinks he can just walk in there an' . . ."

"What's out at Willow Creek, Wes?"

"Everybody knows what's out there. Natty Stern's what's out there."

17

Twenty desert miles from the highway and Tawny's Fillie Ranch, the dirt road edged a dry creekbed that curled through low rocky hills spattered with greasewood and yucca. The road was in better condition than a desert dirt road should be, carefully bladed, shored at curves, culverted at low spots. At that, as I crawled toward the distant snowy loom of the Sierra, I raised a dust plume that announced my presence to anyone within miles.

The creek bottom dampened, began to pool brackish-looking water. Soon there was a flow. The road bent around a rocky corner and entered a narrow valley blocked by a gate in a chainlink fence bordered at the top with curls of razor wire and at the bottom with dead tumbleweeds and matted, wind-driven trash.

The water spilled from a large, steaming hot spring bordered by reeds so dark a green they seemed black. An engine sucked water and pumped it up to a large two-story house built of rock inset with varnished wood that gleamed in the pale sunlight.

Two smaller rock-and-wood buildings flanked the house; one was a garage, before which stood a long gold Mercedes limousine, a white BMW, and a dusty old gray Pinto; the other, from the look of the satellite dish beside it, was a bunkhouse for goons.

I stopped before the chained and padlocked gate, climbed out and stretched and hopped up on the fender and waited.

In the sudden silence I could hear only the dull grinding groan of the water pump, in the stillness see the slow swirl of steam over the pool of hot water. The thick stench of sulfur soaked into the desolate hills, the dead land.

I had a couple of options. One was to assemble the .30.30 in a case in back and see how many windows I could shoot out with it. I liked that option, but I didn't take it. I sat, waited.

Not long. Goon stepped from the smaller house. He took a pair of shades from his pocket and put them on. From inside his blue blazer he took what looked like a .45.

He strolled down the dusty road. When he neared the gate, I slid off the fender and he pointed the .45 at my gut. "Goon?"

I pinched the lapels of my jacket and pulled them apart to let him see I had no gun. "We were never properly introduced."

"Let's leave it at Goon. What do you want?"

"I want to talk to Natty Stern."

"You want to ask *him* if he had your mother killed?"

"You got it."

He nudged his dark glasses up on his forehead, tried to give me a look of amused condescension. "You're crazy, Ross."

"So they tell me. How 'bout it? You gonna open the gate?"

"I was told to." He took out a key, unlocked the heavy padlock, released the chain, backed away from the gate.

I pushed through it.

"Lock it." I did. Before I could turn to face him he had the .45 pressed hard against my spine. "The position."

I spread-eagled myself against the fence as he patted me down. The pressure of the .45 left my back and I turned and my consciousness fragmented into tiny points of brilliant light and snaky swirls of darkness.

Vaguely, as if from some immense distance, I was aware of blows and pain. Then I wasn't aware of anything.

Then I was aware of dirt. It was in my mouth. I heard a groan, became aware that it was mine.

I grew aware of pain in my back and sides, my face, my head. I was sprawled face-down in the dirt. I slowly sat up, realized my eyes were shut, opened them.

The sun was lower in the western sky. Silence, stillness, steam wisping over the dark pool.

I was still inside the fence.

I climbed to my feet, fought the pain in my skull, cleared my head and eyes.

Goon was strolling toward me again. He didn't have the .45 in his hand now. He had a can of beer. He smiled, shook his head. "You weren't much, Ross."

"Sorry," I said. I ran my tongue around my mouth, felt for loose teeth, collected dirt, spat out a mess of blood and dirt and mucus. "I'll do better next time."

"Fat chance." He stepped aside. "Let's go."

After a few woozy steps, I got my legs back. After a few more I got part of my brain back, stopped, checked myself over.

My jeans were dirty at the knees, my shirt was splattered with blood. I could feel a small trickle of dried blood from above my eye, another from my nose.

"Who told you to work me over, Vanca or Stern?"

"Move."

I didn't move. "Speaking of Vanca, where is he? I thought you were one of his keepers."

"He's . . . busy." His face settled into a smirk.

I remembered the young girl with the dead eyes. I got angry, at myself as much as anyone. "And you're not there watching the show?"

He turned to face me, and again lifted his sunglasses. Slowly his hand squeezed the beer can; froth and fluid bubbled and spurted through its tiny opening. "You want more?"

"Sorry," I grinned. "I'm just confused. You're his guardian angel, right, making sure he doesn't embarrass the boss, litter or park overtime or kill somebody? But that doesn't include rape, or you wouldn't have let him go at Miranda Santee."

He lowered his sunglasses again. "She belong to you?"

"No."

He shrugged. "She asked for it."

"Don't they always."

He picked up the ironic edge in my voice. "She came here looking for Vanca. She knew what he is. He did what he does. You play with scorpions, you get stung. She brought it on herself."

"Right."

The door of the big old house opened before we got to it,

and Marci Howe filled the dim emptiness with her lovely length. She wore a lime-green lounging suit and her wonderful smile.

"Mr. Ross, what a pleasant surprise."

"The pleasure's all mine. I came to return your tie."

"How thoughtful of you."

"Not thoughtful enough. I forgot it. But since I'm here, I'd like to have a word with Mr. Stern."

Her smile deepened. "You seem to have had a minor accident. That didn't dissuade you?"

"I'm a slow learner."

"To your eventual and deep regret, I suspect. What makes you think Mr. Stern has any interest in having a word with you?"

"The fact that I'm standing here at the door rather than lying in a bloody heap on the other side of the fence."

She laughed. "Not that slow a learner. Perhaps you've learned enough to be extremely careful what you say and do."

She stepped into an antechamber, off which led three closed doors. We went through one, down a hall, through another door into a large glass-roofed square at the center of the house.

In the damp warmth a garden of desert plants—delicately leaved ephemerals, small cacti and shell-like succulents, sprays of rice grass and sprawls of sage and one Joshua tree—surrounded a small tiled square pool filled with steaming water.

On either side of an empty wheelchair, two men sat in deck chairs—a well-muscled young man in wet swimming trunks and a white T-shirt, and the faded-denim ghost I'd braced in Gerlach. In the water a well-muscled young woman in a one-piece bathing suit attended a very old man.

Only his sweating, sparsely haired head showed above the dark water. His face had collapsed in on itself.

Marci Howe again performed the introductions. "Mr. Stern, this is Ross."

Age hadn't changed his eyes. He looked up at me as he had looked at the camera in the picture in my pocket, as if he were sighting down the barrel of a gun.

"Why do you pester, Mr. Ross? Disturb my business,

bother my people. Why?" His voice creaked like an old house in the wind.

"I want to talk to you about my mother."

"Celeste, yes. I knew her well. She was a nice girl."

The water, with its gentle churning and hovering steam, beckoned my aching body. I winced my way out of my jacket and handed it to Marci Howe. She looked at me with arch-browed incredulity. I unbuttoned my shirt. "Did you have her killed?"

Natty Stern stared at me.

"I told you he was strange," Marci Howe said. Goon took a step toward me, but she stopped him with a hand, shook her head at the ghost as he started to rise.

I grinned at Natty Stern, struggled out of my shirt. "You don't mind if I join you, do you? I've had a hard day."

Something scraped in his throat. A laugh. "You have no diseases? No AIDS, like that? Terrible disease, that AIDS."

"No diseases." I tossed my shirt on a deck chair, sat and pulled off my boots and socks, stood and pulled off my jeans.

"My goodness." Marci Howe smiled. "Don't stop now."

Goon smiled, the ghost studied my scars, the man and woman with muscles tried to ignore me. I shrugged, slipped out of my shorts, and eased into the pool.

The water was so hot that I immediately broke into a sweat, so hot that I almost forgot my aches and pains.

"So, Mr. Stern, did you have my mother killed in Tonopah?"

His laugh scraped again. "Mr. Ross, you have much of your mother in you. She too had a sense of humor that was sometimes hard to understand. Especially in the bedroom."

"I often get laughed at in the bedroom," I said. "Did you have her killed?"

"I was distressed to learn of her death. Very distressed."

"She died before you could grill her about Belle Smith?"

"That is correct."

"So what's the story? Why did you want to talk to her?"

He sighed his gaze on me. In his creaky voice and stiff syntax he told me essentially what Miranda Santee had. A few of the details were new. Belle and Vanca had left this house together. Several hours later one of Stern's goons had found the limousine nose-down in the creekbed five miles downstream. They found my mother's car ten miles down the highway toward Vegas.

"What did Vanca say happened?"

"He of course said nothing for some time. He later said Belle distracted him with her charms, then shot him. She then obviously shot the driver, and the car went off the road. We saw where she had climbed back up. Then your mother apparently arrived and they fled. The car broke down—it had a damaged fuel pump. They disappeared. Then your mother reappeared."

"In Tonopah." I struggled against the sucking, sapping heat of the water, the mind-emptying pleasure. "Cletus James told you where she was."

"A very foolish man, Cletus James. We told him to make sure she stayed there. He took matters into his own hands. We made certain he could not take matters into his own hands again."

I let that mingle with the foul steam for a while. "Are you telling me, Mr. Stern, that he killed her?"

"He said no. Other people said yes. They said Celeste was trying to get his girlfriend to leave him, so he killed her."

"You have no doubt that my mother conspired with Belle Smith to kill Vanca and your driver and steal your million bucks."

"None." His sagging face folded itself into a faint smile. "But hardly a million. People exaggerate, stories grow."

At the moment I had a half-dozen stories growing in my mind. Growing more and more confusing. "Did it surprise you that she would conspire against you? You knew her pretty well."

"Reasonably well. I would not have thought she would betray me. But then I long ago ceased to be surprised by what women do."

That wasn't much help. "Vanca told me that Belle Smith killed my mother."

"Hiram is not always reliable. In this case, he may be correct. Or not."

I sank deeper into the heat of the water, sank until I too was just a talking head.

"You looked for Belle?"

He smiled broadly. In his crumpled face his teeth were bright, strong, looked as if they belonged to a younger man.

"The other night I saw a Humphrey Bogart movie. He played the detective Sam Spade. Spade gave his lover to the police because he had a code. Do you have a code, Mr. Ross?"

"I'm not a detective anymore."

"Everybody needs a code. We have one. It says that when someone steals from you, you punish them so that no one else will steal from you."

"If you can find them."

He smiled again. "You told Hiram that you can find Belle. That is why you have been allowed into my home. Can you?"

"Maybe. Did you get anywhere at all?"

His head bobbed sideways. "She was curious, Belle. Always with people yet always alone. She could not be alone, she had to have people constantly, yet she was alone even then. So everyone knew her, but no one really knew her. Except your mother. But as soon as Celeste appeared, she died. We got nowhere."

"What about Belle's daughter, Echo?"

"She does not know where her mother is."

"I'd like to talk to her. Where is she?"

He smiled again. "If you can't find Echo Smith, Mr. Ross, you are not good enough to find her mother."

I let that go, asked a question that had been lurking in my mind since the night Miranda Santee first told me her stories.

"What about Belle's other daughter, the daughter you thought Miranda Santee was." Without knowing how it happened, I found myself staring into Marci Howe's wonderful smile.

"There was an infant, yes. She disappeared with Belle."

I kept looking at Marci Howe. "Who was the father?"

The old man scraped out a laugh. "Hiram was her father. Hiram fathered many children. Many."

I turned back to Natty Stern. "God help us all."

He laughed again. "Like your mother again, Mr. Ross. You talk just like her."

The muscle man in white rose, stepped down a small ladder into the pool. "It's time, Mr. Stern."

He and the muscle woman flanked Natty Stern, braced his elbows and guided him to the ladder. Stern grabbed the rails with clawlike hands, the man pulled himself from the pool and grabbed him gently under the shoulder, the young woman placed her hands on his hips, and slowly the old man rose from the water.

For a moment he stood naked on the tile. His calves were lumped and veiny, his thighs thin and loosely fleshed; his testicles drooped low beneath his shriveled penis; his belly was as distended as that of a starving child, his chest flabby with duglike breasts, his arms skin over fleshless bone.

He smiled at me. "Not pretty, is that right?"

"Nature can be cruel, Mr. Stern."

The denim ghost came up behind him with a robe. The old man covered himself with it. He smiled again at me.

The muscle man helped him ease into the wheelchair. "I was going to warn you, Mr. Ross. I was going to tell you not to get old. But I don't think you will."

He could have been right. But I had a couple more questions. Rocks into the pond. "Why did Belle Smith do what she did?"

"It doesn't matter. It only matters that she did it."

"I think it does matter."

He sighted down his nose at me. "I don't know why she stole from me. Because she thought she could, maybe."

"Why would she try to kill Vanca? Wasn't she his lover?"

He laughed a creaky laugh. "Hiram had no lovers. He had what he took. For a while he took her. I expect that she took delight in shooting him, since he killed one of her other lovers."

"Who would that be?"

"A man called Single John Smith. Hiram beat him to death and left him in the desert."

That was new.

"Speaking of dead men, did you do a deal with Dalton James?"

Stern shook his head. "A foolish young man, like his father. He proposed that Miranda Santee knew where Belle was and that he could force her to tell him. I gave nothing, we did no deal."

"Will you call your dogs off Miranda?"

The denim-bedecked ghost stiffened behind his shades.

"I have had her watched. That is all."

I let my gaze fasten on the ghost. "Closely enough to know who killed Dalton James?"

"You bring me Belle Smith, I may tell you what I know."

"Fine," I said. "In the meantime, you can have the ghost there stop haunting Miranda. Put him on me. I'm the one looking for Belle Smith now."

"I thought you were not a detective any longer, Mr. Ross."

"So did I, Mr. Stern. But I guess I was wrong."

18

I closed my eyes, drifted in the heat. After Natty Stern was wheeled off, I heard nothing but the slap and gurgle and slush of water.

Then I heard Marci Howe. "Too much can kill you. The heat places a huge burden on the cardiovascular system."

She stood above me, in her pale-green jumpsuit as lovely as a spring shoot sprouting in the desert earth.

I hadn't gotten much by tossing the rock of myself into Natty's Stern's steamy sump. I decided to dump a few pebbles into her pond. "So, what's your story, Miss Howe?"

"I have no story, Mr. Ross."

"All God's chillun got stories. But let me rephrase it. How'd a nice girl like you end up in a place like this?"

"My father worked for Mr. Stern, who took an interest in me. The rest, since we're employing clichés, is history."

"Your father. Would you be one of Vanca's many whelps?"

"You've an unreinable urge to speculation, haven't you?"

"But this accounts for so much. Why you've convinced Natty to keep Vanca alive, for example. We don't want to do dear old daddy, now do we?"

"And I suppose you think I'm Belle Smith's daughter?"

"The possibility occurred to me, briefly. But if you were, Vanca and Natty would know it, and Natty wouldn't have suggested to Miranda Santee that she was."

"My, my. Logical too."

"It also accounts for your rise to the airy climes of High Thuggery."

"Again, I'm but a simple innkeeper, Mr. Ross."

"And a scorpion is but a simple arachnid."

"Arachnid?" She smiled her wonderful smile.

I bounced a pebble off a different wall. "Does Sage know the nature of your business?"

"She knows I own and manage a restaurant."

I was thinking about Sage's ambitious plans for expansion. "Any possible joint ventures?"

Something not quite wonderful filtered into her smile. "I don't discuss my business, Mr. Ross."

"Natty Stern is an old man, apparently not in the best of health. If he croaks, who takes over?"

"That decision has not been made."

"Despite your youth and gender, would those people who will make that decision consider you a candidate?"

She shook her head. "The world I live in is still fairly primitive, Mr. Ross. That wouldn't be possible. But I expect to be in a position of some influence."

"You must be as tough as you are lovely."

"So I've been told."

"Who killed Dalton James?"

She laughed again. "I'm beginning to understand your method of interrogation. If it can be called a method. You just open your mouth and let whatever's in it fall out, don't you?"

"Essentially. I—" Suddenly I was back outside Jude Bascomb's hideous home, listening to his insane ramblings.

She said she'd have my baby too. Too?

"You'd better get out. You're about to have a stroke."

I came back from the desert, realized that she was right. I could feel the blood swelling in my veins, my heart banging hard in my chest, the strength oozing from my muscles.

"I don't suppose you have a robe, or a towel?"

"You're suffering a sudden attack of modesty?"

"I was thinking more about drying off," I said.

She smiled again. I struggled out of the pool. My arms felt weightless. My legs quivered like those of a newborn colt.

Marci Howe examined me with dispassion. Her eyes

finally reached mine. "You're proud of your body, aren't you?"

"I try to keep it in good working order."

She shook her head. "Not that, it's not your body itself you're proud of. Most nude men move so that attention is drawn to their muscles, if they have any, or their genitals, if they have any of consequence. You move to draw attention to your scars."

"Poor things, but mine own."

"Machismo rampant, more likely. What story do *they* tell?"

I shrugged, moved to the chair my clothes were piled on, grabbed my jeans and began toweling myself off.

"You need a shower," she said. "We can't have a friend of Sage's smelling like he's been splashing in the River Styx."

I grabbed my clothes and boots and followed her through the desert flora to a long hallway, down it to a large and intensely female bedroom—gossamer and lace, satin-covered and -skirted furniture, all in shades of red from the pale rose of transparent membrane to the bright crimson of arterial blood.

The room was dominated by a huge bed surrounded by mirrors that reflected red satin sheets and various images of the prone naked body of a sleeping young girl.

Marci Howe smiled her wonderful smile. "You have more of your questions, Mr. Ross?"

"How did you manage to get her away from Vanca? Goon said he was even now taking his pleasures. You make a trade with him?"

"You don't approve of this manner of sexual expression?"

"Hey, different strokes. But not with my children."

She smiled again. "You're naive. Amy has lived on the streets for three years. She's older than you'll ever be."

"And now she's yours?"

"One doesn't possess lovers, Mr. Ross, but briefly. One simply enjoys them. Regardless of their age or gender."

"Lucky you."

"Yes. But perhaps you have another question about the nature of my relationship with Sage Chandler?"

I didn't answer.

Marci Howe laughed. "My goodness, there is a way to shut the man up. The shower's over there."

I showered, patched my face with a Band-Aid, and dressed. The bedroom was empty. I went out the way I'd come in.

The sun sat like a flaming rock on the distant rim of the Sierra.

The BMW was gone. Beside the Mercedes, Marci Howe stood watching the young girl as she drifted, in a childlike dance, through the scattered brush toward the middle of the barren desert valley.

"I hope Amy doesn't get too close to the pool. Animals do, occasionally. The water is much hotter there. So hot that death is relatively painless—instant shock, and so forth. But the bones dissolve slowly. Sometimes, while they're in a glutinous state, they get sucked into the pump. It makes quite a mess."

"What kind of animals?"

"Small ones, usually, lizards and things." She smiled her wonderful smile. "Sometimes larger ones."

"You're a sweetheart, Miss Howe."

Her wonderful smile got more wonderful. "And you, I think, are a dangerous man, Mr. Ross. Mostly to yourself, but also to those you come in contact with. You kill people, don't you?"

"I have."

"You probably feel guilty about it."

"Sometimes."

"A very dangerous man. I'm afraid I may have made a—"

She saw something, stopped. I followed her gaze.

A woman walked toward us. She wore silver two-inch stiletto heels that stabbed into the earth, a flame-red microskirt as short as the heels were long, a diaphanous red blouse cut to the navel and studded with sequins.

It was a costume of strange savage self-parody. Her makeup continued it: lipstick so thick her mouth seemed made of plastic, rouge-spots drawn on her cheeks like targets, silver swoops of eye shadow in which metallic glints flashed in the feeble sun.

Somewhere under that mask hid the face of Linda Goshgarian.

Marci Howe and I silently watched her approach. Through the blouse her breasts swayed gently; they were the only thing about her that seemed real. They seemed somehow forlorn.

She noticed my look, caught my eye with hers, shot me a look of pristine hatred.

As she climbed into the gray Pinto, Apprentice came out of the bunkhouse and headed toward the gate. Linda Goshgarian started the Pinto and backed away from the house.

"She has Vanca's picture on her office desk," I said.

Marci Howe smiled again. "You do get around, don't you? True love, they say, for years. Despite what he's done to her."

"What's that?"

"Years ago, Hiram ran a small stable, mostly for the use of men Mr. Stern wished to impress. Linda was one of them, till Mr. Stern had to put a stop to it—too many of the girls beaten to death in the desert, or clogging the pump. But Linda stayed with him. So he turned her out, on the street, in brothels around the state. But whenever he calls, she comes running." She smiled. "Maybe he loves her too, in his fashion. Over the years he's only broken a half dozen of her bones."

"And he lets her run Tawny's."

"Your naïveté is bottomless, it seems. Hiram Vanca hasn't the authority to let anyone do anything. I put her in charge."

"So she can be near her heart's desire, no doubt."

"A romantic as well. Linda knows the life, she knows the job, and she knows who the boss is."

"You'll go far in your profession, Miss Howe."

She smiled. "Yes. Somehow I doubt that you'll go far in yours. Or long."

"Who's in the BMW? The denim ghost?"

She laughed. "I'm beginning to understand why Sage finds you appealing. Your naive, sentimental, romantic, bumpkinish charm. Too bad you're also stupid."

"Where'd he go?"

"Not far, Mr. Ross. Not far." She smiled, then turned and walked out toward the young girl who was twirling her way slowly across the shadowing desert.

Apprentice waited for me at the gate. I walked through it, heard it shut behind me, heard his soft, raspy call. "Hey."

I turned into his bright young grin. "I didn't watch Vanca do Miranda Santee. I helped."

I climbed in the Wagoneer, watched as he locked the gate and started back toward the house, watched as Marci Howe slipped her arm around the waist of the young girl.

I had a sudden powerful impulse to assemble my .30.30 and fill it with shells and fire a bullet into his brain and fire a bullet into the brain of Marci Howe, and maybe the brain of the young girl and certainly the brain of Natty Stern and Goon and anyone else within that fenced-off piece of dead land who looked like he or she needed it.

I didn't yield to the impulse. I knew that one didn't. I didn't know why one didn't.

I drove back to the highway.

In the gathering darkness, the rear of the battered old gray Pinto extended from behind the back of Tawny's Fillie Ranch as if in sexual presentation.

I drove into the night, north.

Somewhere in the darkness I thought once more about Jude Bascomb. I thought of trying to talk to him. I wasn't up to it.

I drove slowly, changed speeds a few times, stopped once at a roadside trash barrel. Three cars passed me, none a white BMW.

Still, I knew it was out there.

I got to Tonopah late, checked in at the Mizpah, had a meal, went to the bar and ordered a beer and stuck my change in a poker machine and lost it.

I ordered another beer and watched the Vegas news.

Little was new. The governor said there wasn't enough money, everyone else said there ought to be. The city council said there wasn't enough money, everyone else said there ought to be. People were abusing each other. The UNLV Runnin' Rebels won, the UNR Wolfpack lost. Vegas was clear and warm. Reno was still in the grip of the temperature inversion; the elderly, the young, and those with respiratory conditions were urged to stay indoors. Three people had died.

Then on the screen, amid a mass of hovering and solicitous faces, appeared the face of Cleo James, the ravages of youthful disease nearly obliterated by the ruin visited by grief.

In tones at once somber, unctuous, and fatuous, the news reader read that a double tragedy had struck a Las Vegas woman, who returned from Reno after identifying the body of her son, shot to death in an apparent burglary, only to be informed that a body discovered in the desert at mid-morning was that of her husband.

Cletus James too had been shot to death.

19

The next morning I tried to shower and stretch the ache out of my body, got breakfast in the coffee shop and some information and directions and curious looks in the sheriff's office, gassed up the Wagoneer, and drove out of Tonopah, east.

Once past the whorehouse and the shacks and trailers and hay sheds and corrals that trickled down a gulley to the local fairgrounds, past the airport, past the turnoff to the not-very-secret government installation where the military was testing Stealth aircraft, past the turnoff to the Big Smokey Valley, the highway cut a course through a land of marvelous desolation.

Under a pale empty sky, the pale empty earth buckled and swelled into huge alkali-centered bowls and yawning valleys; rock and patches of cheat grass and stubby gnarled sage lay scattered as if flung down by the hand of some disgusted god.

Miles and miles of moonscape, space, time.

And to the north, massive mountain ranges—drab bases, dark flanks, bright white crests under the pale-yellow sun, the pale-blue sky. Mountains split from each other by wide desert valleys, mountains somehow alone, detached from the land itself.

Human beings lived in this land, traced it with twisting rutted dirt roads, fenced it here and there in geometrical shapes that would ignore and thus dominate the physics of the earth, staked it with white plastic tubes that promised minerals, drilled it for water, drilled it for oil.

Human beings lived in his land, but not many: at the base

of a distant mountain, a ranch huddling against a row of spring-fed poplars; halfway up a slope, a shack oozing smoke into the still air; at a turnoff, a sudden flowering of silver mailboxes.

Crazy people lived in this land.

I felt right at home.

I drove and looked at the land and, for the first time since Miranda Santee had brought her wounds and stories and gun into my desert camp, tried to understand what the hell I was doing.

After four days and nights of listening to stories, I had a headful of hunches and guesses and suspicions about a tangle of lives and loves that I couldn't begin to sort out.

I didn't care.

I didn't even care about my mother. I didn't care who she'd loved, who she was. She was dead, a ghost, and she'd always been a ghost to me. All I wanted to know was if she had been a killer.

Because if she had, I could use that to excuse what had driven me into the desert in the first place: the fact that whenever I got around people I ended up wanting to kill somebody.

In the desert, the Paiutes used to say, you can be so alone that you don't even have yourself for company.

That's what I wanted. I wanted to stop feeling guilty.

I also wanted to shake the presence I sensed behind me.

I hadn't had a glimpse, a sign of him. I didn't think he could be that good; he hadn't even been good enough to escape detection by Miranda Santee. He couldn't be following me.

But I knew he was. And if I found what I thought I might, I would have led him right to it.

Then I began to sense a presence ahead of me.

Finally I saw it, first a flat gray boil of clouds, then the slash of bright snow, then the green of trees as black as the black of the reeds around Natty Stern's death pool.

Out of a flat empty desert the mountain range rose like ragged stairsteps to nowhere, ridges and rims and crests and peaks built and broken and built again by ancient upheavals and carved and cut by the tumble of water.

The desert at its foot was a muddy plain channeled by the

water that coursed onto it in scattered rivulets, water that might green the land could it be captured, water that promised life, that like the promises of life had lured and betrayed everyone who would catch it in his hands.

Abandoned ranches littered the plain, barbed-wire fences fenced in a muddy nothing.

Then a town that didn't exist.

Chokecherry sat at the base of the foothills, beside the channel of a small creek lined with dead cottonwoods.

The town had never been much: from the old barn built of rock and juniper poles and mud, a ranch or stage station; later, from the few abandoned frame buildings, a place to buy a rest or a drink or a meal before or after the trek across the mud.

Once, they'd told me at the sheriff's office, Chokecherry had been an official town. Now it wasn't even a ghost town. Now it was just a name. Nobody knew why.

But the urge that had driven people to try to make a life there still pulsed. Beside a deserted gas station was a newer one, gas and diesel pumps and a block building with plate-glass windows pasted with hand-lettered signs offering food and drink. Behind it sat a single-wide mobile home, a satellite dish, and a corral and hay shed for an old spavined bay.

I pulled in beside a gas pump, filled up, parked beside a pair of eighteen-wheelers and went inside.

The door opened into what might have been any convenience store in the country—fluorescent lights and beverage coolers and rows of junk foods and revolving racks of cheap souvenirs. Off it an arch exposed a dimmer café-cum-bar, with a handful of high stools and a row of tables along the windows and walls.

A bright-cheeked middle-aged woman in jeans and a Dodgers sweatshirt bounced through the arch. "Hi there."

"Hi." I gave her a bill. "The coffee hot?"

"Fresh, too. Go on in and grab a cup."

Two truck drivers sat at a table by the window drinking coffee. An old man in a Western-cut shirt of swirling bright colors sat at the corner of the bar before a full glass of beer.

I got a cup of coffee from the pot behind the bar and took a stool next to him. "Afternoon."

He looked at me over rimless glasses. "Forgot to duck, huh?"

"What? Oh—" I fingered the Band-Aid at my eyebrow. "Yeah, I guess so."

"Man ain't got sense enough to duck's doomed to a life of hurt. Got it comin' too." He watched me carefully, absently clacking his loose false teeth. "Where you headed?"

"Right here."

"Nobody heads for here, not on purpose. Anybody hear you say that, they're like to give you bed an' board at the Ha Ha Hotel."

The smiling woman bounced behind the bar, dropped my change beside my cup. "Leave the man to his coffee in peace, Dad."

"Hey," the old man said. "He started it."

I took out my wallet, handed him a card. "I'm trying to find a woman from around here. Mabel Margaret Madigan."

He adjusted his glasses, studied the card in a formal, teeth-clacking silence. He studied it as if it were not a message but an object, and told me in that studying that it was an object to him, that he couldn't read.

He handed the card to the woman. "Fancy that, Renata."

His daughter glanced at the card. "Now why would an attorney be looking for Peg Madigan, Mr. Ross?"

It was as easy as that. It was too easy.

"Attorney. Attorney-at-law." The old man picked up her clues, blended them into his jocular nonsense. "What's the law want with an old crazy woman, Mr. Ross? Gonna' slap her in the hoosegow? Fine her for bein' crazy without a license?"

"I'm not the law. She lives nearby?"

"Nearby as it gits in this country. Down the mountain thirty miles or so. If you could get there this time of year. Which you can't, even in that rig of yours. If she ain't dead by now."

At the thought of death, he fell silent, clacking his teeth in a ruminative rhythm.

"Quit playing with your teeth, Dad." His daughter smiled cheerfully. "Peg's a hermit, I guess you'd say, if there are lady hermits. She's had the tragedies. Lost her family, her husband and sons, all at once; it sort of sent her round the bend."

The woman smiled, her cheerfulness indefatigable. "She's up there alone, but the boys look out for her. It's better for her to be in her own home, where she's lived all her life, than to be where they'd . . . put her."

We weren't talking about the same woman.

"The Mabel Margaret Madigan I'm looking for was born here sixty years ago. She was a showgirl in Reno and Vegas." Maybe.

I took out the Harold's Club photograph and laid it on the bar. The woman looked at it, then at her father in cheerful confusion.

He picked up the photograph, clacked his teeth, smiled. This was something he could read. "That'd be Lanky Chandler. Who's the other floozy?"

I shrugged.

"Mabel. Almost forgot. Hard to believe a fella could forget a girl like that, ain't it? Course we never seen her in that kind of gitup. Close as we come was one night at a Grange dance, she's still all knees and elbows and gawky as a filly, shows up alone in this white party dress with these rainbow stripes on the sleeves, nobody could figure where she got it 'cause Peg always dressed her just like the boys. Anyhow, she's commencing to have a good time when ol' Peg comes storming in. Peg, now, she didn't think much of dancing or your basic social frivolity—a waste of good working time. So she grabs the girl and rips the dress half off her back and drags her out."

His daughter's smile seemed to inflate with good cheer. "She's Peg's daughter?"

"Yep. She's also the one who occasioned Peg getting her teeth knocked down her throat. Or so the story goes."

The old man placed the photograph beside his beer glass. He held the glass up to the dim light. Perhaps a dozen bubbles hung suspended in the beer. "There's quite a story there in that picture, Mr. Ross. Quite a story."

His clacking porcelain smile was nearly serene.

"I'd like to hear it, Mr.——?"

"Stillwell, Rafe Stillwell. But it's a long story. Attorney fella like you, got to be a busy man."

"I've got time, Mr. Stillwell."

"Well, I don't know, it's real—"

"Now you quit it, Dad. And quit playing with your teeth."

The old man picked up the photograph, read it again, handed it to his daughter. "You recognize anybody?"

She shook her head. "Just Chandler, from the billboards."

"Yeah, you wouldn't recognize Mabel. Favored Peg, but you never seen Peg when she was young. What about the other guy?"

His daughter shook her head in silent cheerful confusion.

"Why, that's ol' Single John."

The woman's smile struggled with, finally succumbed to something more powerful than her cheerfulness. Her jaw slowly dropped in astonishment.

"I—how can that be?"

"Darlin', I just tell the stories, I don't explain 'em."

"So tell me. Us."

"Oh, this one's a real long story. An attorney's a busy fella, he ain't got time—"

"Shut up and tell us!"

20

    Teeth clacking, eyes bright behind his spectacles, the old man told us a story built of guesses laid on a shaky structure of facts and shaped and molded by the logic of the land, a story that the people living in that land had told themselves.

Peg Esterhouse Madigan was the youngest of six daughters born to a scrape-and-gnaw rancher who tried to run cattle from a piece of mostly desert land that some years had a creek and some years didn't. Her mother died a year after Peg was born, worn out by childbearing and work and hopelessness.

From the start, folks said, Peg was . . . different. As a child she was largely silent and usually absent, off in the hills or the desert. Around people, even around her family, she said little. Mostly she watched.

Mostly she watched her sisters and men, watched them flirt and pose, spoon and court. She watched two marry into the life that had killed their mother and one run off with a wire salesman and one worry herself into a tight-lipped spinsterhood and one take a one-way walk out into the blinding heat of the desert.

And would have none of it—the clothes, the concerns, the work, the life. She would have none of the frills of attire and personality, the delicacies of sentiment and dream expected of women. She dressed as a boy, worked with her father, did men's work with men's tools, and at the same time expressed even more silent disdain for men than she did for women.

Exposed to the weather, set in expressions of either grim

determination or fierce disgust, her face was not one to attract more than a glance. But after puberty, under her heavy coarse pants and bulky shirts and stiff jackets, her body was such that particular gestures—the long-legged swing off a horse's back, the quick stoop after a trailing rein, the weary mopping of hay and dust from a sweat-stuck brow—drew from the more observant males a long and contemplative look.

And she would have none of it, drove off with tongue and fists even the most tentative advances, ignored the few occasions for formal socializing the country offered, spat derisively at the mention of the possibilities of marriage, romance, love.

So that everyone in the territory was stunned when sixteen-year-old Peg Esterhouse disappeared one day and reappeared three days later as Peg Madigan.

At that, no one was more stunned than Bill Madigan, her forty-year-old and, so far as anyone knew, heretofore virginal husband. A strange one himself, Bill Madigan, skittish and stumbling and silent around women, around men babbling about esoteric subjects—the movement of the planets, the history of France, the physics of electricity—a self-proclaimed expert on all matters except the matter at hand. Harmless, but useless when a man needed help or a woman needed a man.

How had this happened, this inexplicable union? Everyone had a theory that they wove into a story. Theories conflicted, stories contradicted, but gradually all blended, became one.

Bill Madigan owned a small mountain ranch he had inherited from his father twenty years before, a place he worked just enough to feed himself and pay taxes on while he hunted mustangs he could never catch and turquoise mines he could never find.

On Madigan's place a spring bubbled out of the mountain and collected in a pine-shaded pool at the edge of a small meadow.

The day Peg Esterhouse disappeared, she rode into the mountains to the spring, where she knew Bill Madigan would show up to complete work on the mustang trap he was constructing. He showed up. She was in the pool. His bachelorhood was history.

So the story went.

"Boy oh boy." Rafe Stillwell grinned. "Think of the look on ol' Bill Madigan's face when he came up on that pool and seen Peg Esterhouse there in all her splendor and glory."

"Come on, Dad," his daughter chided cheerfully. "You don't know that's what happened."

"Hey, it don't matter if it happened or not," he said serenely. "It's still true."

Once the story solidified, the women of the country seethed, the men chuckled. Peg ignored everyone.

And Bill Madigan? He seemed permanently dazed, as if he had been alone too long in the desert; from that day on, he moved through his life as if everything in it were a profound mystery.

Why this had happened was a matter of less speculation. Peg Esterhouse had looked at the land, looked at the Madigan ranch, seen what she wanted and figured out how to get it and went out and got it.

The Madigan place wasn't much, a two-room shack and a few crumbling dugouts and rickety outbuildings at the edge of a large meadow. But the ranch consisted of several pieces of patented land scattered over the mountain, land that had water spring and summer and fall, wet year and dry.

Like his father before him, Bill Madigan had never done much but run a few head of cattle on the fat grass around the water on the various parcels, bring in those he could find to winter on the desert with everybody else's, and hope like hell that he could find most of them the next spring.

The next year things changed.

The next spring Bill Madigan drove his few cattle into the mountains much as his young wife drove him. Soon they were fencing meadows, fencing the cattle out, fencing the fat grasses in. Then they began clearing pine and juniper around the ranch-house meadow, digging irrigation channels, and through the summer cutting hay in the other meadows and hauling it to the ranch.

In early fall Bill Madigan and his pregnant wife spent a month rounding up cattle. But they didn't drive them out onto the desert. They drove them to the ranch, wintered them where they could feed them hay.

The next spring, they hadn't lost a single cow. And they'd gained a daughter.

The country watched and began to understand what she was up to. The next summer Peg drove her husband into the hills to expand the nearest spring meadow, as the infant played in a basket of blankets wedged in the crook of a tree or dangled in a canvas sack from the cantle of her mother's saddle. They wintered half the herd at this meadow. Bill trailed through the snow and cold, making sure the cattle were fed and watered, while Peg handled those at the ranch.

Sure, the country said, it'll work. It'll save stock that might be lost. But there's only two of them. How they gonna do any more? Because for it to work you have to have somebody with them cows. And what happens if there's a big winter?

The next winter Peg had a son.

The next summer they hayed and built an addition onto the house. The country got the idea.

For another fifteen years the country watched Peg drive her dazed husband up and down the mountain as the Madigans improved their meadows, slowly improved and enlarged their herd, enlarged their house, enlarged their family. The four boys were working as soon as they could walk, doing a man's work as soon as they could ride. The daughter became the boys' mother, the mother the foreman, and the husband . . . the husband grew thin, gray, old.

And then one day Peg Madigan lost her front teeth and her seventeen-year-old daughter, Mabel, disappeared.

"Well, nobody in that outfit was gonna say nothin' about what happened," Rafe Stillwell said. "Wasn't till a month or so later that somebody hit upon the fact that Mabel wasn't the only one to disappear about then."

His daughter, Renata, had been refilling my coffee cup.

The old man lifted his beer, held it up to the dim light. Not a bubble stirred in it. "Dead enough," he said, and sipped slowly. "Can't stomach it till it's plumb flat. Hell of a way for a man to spend his days, waitin' for his beer to go flat."

"Quit it, Dad. Who?"

"Why, ol' Single John, naturally."

Renata held the picture up before her eyes, smiled, shook her head. "Boy, if anybody else had told me that was Single John Smith, I wouldn't've believed them in a million years."

She passed the photograph back to her father. "Never guessed a fellow that looks like him could've ever been that handsome. Boy, he's as ugly a man now as you'll see. Not that anybody sees him. He's been up in those mountains alone for thirty years. Sometimes a rancher or hunter gets a glimpse of him, which is about the only way anybody knows he's still alive. Except one morning, I come to open up and there he is, wearing a brand-new pair of jeans and packing a bedroll strung from a thirty-thirty, with this face that looks like all the pieces got put together wrong. He wants a Snickers bar, he says. He's crazier than Peg."

"No, he ain't," her father said quickly, grabbing back his audience. "Not crazy, exactly. He . . ."

I cleared my throat. "Lanky Chandler told me that Single John Smith was the only man Lanky'd ever known who didn't care about anything."

"That's more it," the old man said. "Least after he come back from the war."

Before the war Single John Smith had cared about something, the old man told us. He'd cared about women. One after another, Temporarily. Thus the moniker, which he'd picked up in his teens. And mostly other men's women, because in this country that's about all there were. That was also why he ended up in the Pacific bayoneting Japanese, on the run from a rancher with a load of rage and a horsewhip.

Three years later he drifted back. He had a different look in his eye. Six months later he was gone again.

"With Mabel Madigan?"

"That's what we finally figured. Peg must've caught him and the girl, come after him, he gives her one in the choppers."

"He hit her?" His daughter was cheerfully indignant.

The old man clacked his teeth in delight. "Hey, at least he had the gumption. Most fellas Peg Madigan come after, they'd hightailed it outta the county. Nobody messed with Peg Madigan when she was on the warpath. No-body."

He picked up the photograph again. "So he ended up a card flinger, huh?"

"He was working at a dude ranch, then left town. He showed up in Vegas around 1960. After that, I don't know."

"Shoot," Renata said. "I do. That's about when he showed up here, isn't it, Dad?"

"About." The old man clacked his teeth, stared at the

picture. "His face. He get caught with his pants down again?"

"More or less." I wondered if Hiram Vanca knew he hadn't killed Single John Smith.

"A man don't duck's in for a life of hurt. Got it coming, too. That's my phee-loss-o-phee."

"The girl, Mabel," I said, "she's never been back?"

He shook his head. "Not that anybody knows about. You'd have to ask the boys?"

"The boys?"

"The Smith boys. Single John's brothers. They got a place up by Peg's. Matter of fact, most of their place is Peg's old place. They sort of watch out for her."

"Why? What happened?"

He raised his beer glass in a raconteur's flourish. "What happened? The winter of forty-nine, that's what happened."

The winter of 1949 had buried Nevada under snow. It buried cattle and sheep. It buried the ranching business in that part of the country. It buried Bill Madigan and his four sons.

What happened to the Madigan family the country had to piece together later. After the thaw finally began, after ranchers had disposed of their dead stock and begun trying to save the living, somebody remarked that nobody had seen anything of the Madigans. The Smith boys went over to check on them.

They found a meadow full of half-frozen, half-rotting cow carcasses. They found Peg Madigan smiling, laughing, dressed in workboots and a white dress embroidered with rainbows.

Peg shocked the men who found her. She flirted with them.

Later men on horseback spread out over the mountain. They found the other fenced meadows full of dead cattle. They found two of Peg's sons frozen to death in their meadow camps. They found a third boy frozen to death along a trail to the ranch. They never found the fourth boy. They never found Bill Madigan.

What everybody knew, although they couldn't tell you exactly how they knew, was that Peg had killed them all.

She'd driven them out into the snow and ice and cold to those doomed cattle and to their own doom the way she'd driven Bill Madigan up and down that mountain for almost twenty years.

"That winter finished her. Finished lots of things. Folks knew they couldn't go on wintering cattle on the desert. Those had anything left started doing what she'd done, on a whole lot smaller scale, naturally. It was the end of the real cattle business in this country. Everybody now's just calf-farming."

"What happened to her after that?"

"Well," he said, "there was some talk about doin' something—you know, sending her away. Couple doctors looked at her, but everybody figured she was all right, woman's got a constitution like a horse, and she was crazy but not any more than she'd always been, just different. She could take care of herself an' all, so finally nobody did nothin'. Course everything she'd worked on started falling apart. Folks bought most of what stock she had left, and a couple big companies made offers on the land but she wouldn't let it go. Then finally she sold everything but the ranch house to the Smith boys."

The old man again picked up the photograph. He looked at it for a moment, then was no longer seeing it. His teeth clacked. "Now ain't that interesting."

He was creating a story.

"What, Dad?"

"Well, you know as crazy as she got after forty-nine, she wouldn't let go of them meadows for love nor money. So everybody was kind of surprised when she finally sold to the Smith boys."

"And?"

"Well, you know, it's another one of them things nobody ever put together till later. In this case, a whole lot later. In fact, it just got put together right now."

"Dad, you quit, now. What?"

The old man smiled. "Peg Madigan sold out just about the time Single John come back."

"And? What does that mean?"

"Hey, I told you. I just tell these stories. You want me to explain 'em too?"

21

mile from Chokecherry, a road graded to gravel and rutted goo left the highway to edge the foothills, twisting around sagey knolls and snow-stuffed gulleys, easing between the damp suck of the desert and the snowy ragged rockiness of the mountain.

At the turnoff to the Smith ranch, I stopped. I could see the scatter of buildings and sheds along the tree line a half mile from the open, cattle-guarded gate. A half mile straight up. A twisted series of ruts wound toward it through mud and loam and rock and snow like a braid fashioned by a spastic.

I dropped the Wagoneer into four-wheel power low and stepped on the gas. A harrowing half hour later I pulled into the ranch yard, with half of Nevada splattered over and under the Wagoneer. If anyone was going to follow me up here, he'd do it on foot.

The ranch had been worked by generations that in the desert way built and wore out houses and sheds and barns and built new ones beside them. From the crumbling mud-and-rock barn to the frame house beside a satellite dish, the buildings lay across the face of the mountain like human geological strata.

The large muddy yard was littered with rusting machinery and stripped vehicles and piles of curled and weathered lumber and small stacks of blackish bales of hay. In the meadow that spread out from a spring, black baldy cows and calves milled in the pale sunlight. In the corral beside a big barn, four horses stood like sentries staring vacantly out over the vacant desert. In the barn door a lumpish, broad-shouldered man in jeans and an orange down vest leaned on a long-handled shovel and looked at me from under a Denver Broncos cap.

I stepped out into mud up to my ankles, into the thin cold air and the rich sweet smell of cowshit and rotting hay, mountain pine and juniper, desert dust and sage.

I fought the mud over to the barn. The man hadn't moved. He looked a weather-coarsened, work-hardened sixty. He looked nothing like Single John Smith. He looked angry.

"Mr. Smith?"

"You're trespassing." Gray stubble frosted his cheeks and chin. His teeth were nearly as gray, gnarled like winter brush. Anger rasped his voice, violence seemed to drift beneath the words like virga beneath a gray storm cloud.

"Yes, sir. Seemed like the only way I could talk to you."

"Doin' the work of two men don't leave much time for it."

I didn't know what that meant. I did know, somehow, that the anger in his voice wasn't really directed at me. It was venting steam from a huge hot constant boil inside.

"I'm trying to find Peg Madigan. They told me at Chokecherry there's a road from here, that you could give me directions."

His face didn't change. "What you want with Peg?"

"I want to talk to her."

"You wanna talk to Peg? Good luck." Jerking the shovel blade from the mud, he turned and stepped inside the barn.

Then, before I could move, he stepped out again. He looked even angrier. "You wanna talk, go talk to that crazy son of a bitch in the house. You tell him he don't get out here an' help me shovel this shit he's gonna eat this shovel backwards."

He wheeled again and disappeared into the barn. If the man in the house was any stranger than this one, he was crazy indeed.

I slogged over to the house, a wooden box on which old white paint hung in strips and patches like scabs. The house had been set without a foundation on a slope; the back had sunk, so the threshold was a foot above the mud. There were no steps.

I knocked. After I knocked again, the door was opened by a slightly smaller, slightly younger man. He gave me a glance that hardly saw me. "My story's on."

He vanished, but left the door open. Grabbing the jamb, I hauled myself up and into the house.

The floor of the big room was bare, its planking gouged and slivered under a layer of dirt and mud and manure ground fine by heels and spread as if by the wind. The unpainted Sheetrock walls were adorned only by scraps and smears of mud and pencil scrawls encircling a black telephone. The room was furnished with an ancient sofa and chair covered in an ersatz pinto horsehide, a couple of rickety low tables, and a huge new television set.

Brightly colored life flickered on the big screen directly below an uncurtained window that looked out onto the drab mud and junk of the ranch yard, as if to offer an alternative reality.

The younger Smith boy was on the sofa watching a soap opera. He looked like Single John Smith might have if Hiram Vanca hadn't rearranged his face. But some inner absence marred his features. His eyes were too sharply focused on the screen, his mouth open, his jaw slack.

On the screen, between commercials for deodorants and feminine sprays and beauty soaps, attractive men and women did and said unattractive things to each other when they weren't kissing with a gaping-mouthed and sterile passion. But mostly what they did was give each other long looks apparently pregnant with a meaning underscored by organ chords.

When the music increased in volume to signal the end of the episode, he sighed, then aimed a remote control device at the screen. It went blank and silent.

He looked at me, spoke slowly, as if watching each word form in his throat. "Are Roger and Miriam gonna have a. Affair?"

"They always do."

"Not Roger. He's. Gonna be a priest. Soon as he finds out if Julie's dead. But Miriam. She has affairs with. Everybody." He giggled curiously. "She likes it. She said so. Right on TV."

He wasn't crazy.

"Makes me glad George. Wouldn't let me get married. I wanted to. A lot. One time there was this girl. She wasn't pretty like these. But she was. But George told me about them. How they. I."

His mouth remained open as he disappeared into whatever there was of his mind.

"Mr. Smith, your brother—"

"No. I'm not Mr. Smith. I'm Leo."

"Peg Madigan's place, Leo. How do I get there?"

"No." He shook his head solemnly. "You can't. Nobody can go there. Only George and—" He stopped, flinched as if he'd been struck.

"George and who, Leo?"

"Nobody." He giggled again. "George and Mr. Nobody."

"I'm Mr. Nobody, Leo."

He peered at me. "No. You're too tall. You're not. . . ." His face filled with sudden blood, grew ugly. "You. You're trying to. Trick me. You. You think I'm—dumb!"

I forced myself to smile into his rage. "I think you're smart, Leo. Smart enough to tell me how to get to Peg Madigan's."

His features set in a parody of cunning. "Ha. You're the one who's dumb. Road's right by the old barn. You can't even find it. You're the one."

"I guess so, Leo. I'm so dumb I'm going to try to find your other brother, Single John."

He looked at me the way the men and women on the television had looked at each other. "Find him. Boy. Are you dumb. He ain't even. Lost."

"Where is he?"

"Up there."

"Thanks, Leo. I guess I'll go now. And George said to tell you to come out and help him in the barn."

He gave me another TV look. "I can't." His face went as blank as the screen. "I'm too lonesome. You made me feel. Lonesome."

I thought I might know what that meant. I turned and went to the door. As I opened it, I heard organ music. As I closed it, I heard Leo Smith shout, "Boy are you dumb!"

I waded through the mud along the line of old sheds and dugouts to the ancient mud-and-stone barn. A pair of ruts led up into the trees and the snow. They hadn't been traveled in months, which suggested that they couldn't be traveled.

I went back to the new barn. Inside it was warm and dry and dusty and smelled of hay and manure. George Smith was in a horse stall, savagely shoveling manure into a wheelbarrow. He stopped as I approached, stabbed the sharp blade into the earth.

"I'd like to leave my rig in the yard for a few hours, Mr. Smith, if you don't mind."

"An' if I do mind?"

"I'll leave it down at the road."

He shook his head angrily. "Then what?"

"Then I'm going to Peg Madigan's place. There's a road out by your old barn. I'd guess it goes there."

"An' if you guessed wrong?"

"Then I'll get cold and tired and hungry and probably lost."

He nodded, as if that was the first sensible thing anybody'd said in weeks, and it was about goddamned time. "You mind tellin' me what you want from her?"

"I want to ask her about her daughter."

"You mean Mabel?" He looked past me, shook his head. "She ain't been around here for forty years. Not since she knocked her ma's teeth out."

"I thought your brother John did that?"

Anger darkened his gray face. "Who you been listening to? Probably that old gossip Rafe Stillwell. He never got anything right. Mabel did it, with the butt end of a single-blade ax. Knocked her cold. Ol' Bill found her down in the grove, thought she was dead, raised a hell of a stink. Wonder she wasn't dead."

"And Mabel ran off with your brother, Single John."

He slid his hand down the handle of the shovel, jerked, flipped the blade up just past my nose and onto his shoulder. "Why don't you get your rig and haul your ass off my property?"

I wasn't especially afraid of the shovel. I wasn't afraid of George Smith. My sense of him was that his anger, finally, could only be directed against himself.

"Mr. Smith, I'm a private investigator, and I'm investigating the whereabouts of Mabel Margaret Madigan. Thirty years ago she and my mother killed a man and stole a lot of money. My mother's dead. I want Mabel to tell me why she died."

The anger eased from his face, the shovel from his shoulder.

"Are there any fucking sane people left in the world?"

"Not many."

"Jesus Christ." His anger was back, fueled by hopelessness. "I'm surrounded by crazy people I gotta take care of.
One in the house, one up on the mountain, one over the
ridge. And now you. Thirty years ago? Your mother? Jesus
Christ."

His gray face darkened, an angry mad lost longing
brightened his eyes. Hurling the shovel to the ground, he
wheeled with a heavy suddenness and slammed his fist into
the side of the stall. Again. Again. Old damp dust rose
heavily, the thud of the blows and crack of the plank
careened off walls and corners and echoed out into the
ranch yard.

He stopped hitting the stall. For a moment he stared at the
planks. Then he shoved past me and walked out of the barn.

I hesitated for a minute. I wanted more information, but I
didn't want to push him too far.

I went outside. George Smith was at the corral, rubbing
the hard head of a gray gelding as if it were some talis-
manic object, as if it might ward off reality. Or me. It struck
me that the horses were too good for the Smith place—sleek,
handsome, the products of the careful breeding of good
blood. The gray nosed after something in George Smith's
shirt pocket.

He stepped back, fumbled in his pocket, took out something and fed it to the horse, rubbed its head. He turned and
saw me watching. He walked over.

"You tell Leo?"

I heard what he really asked. He asked if, after seeing his
brother, I understood the life he had to lead, the burdens,
the injustice, the reason for his anger.

"He said he can't help. He said I made him feel lonesome."

George Smith looked at me to see if I understood what I
had just said. Whatever he saw in my face seemed to satisfy
him. He wasn't angry now. He was exhausted.

"Peg, you know, you ain't gonna get much out of her. She's
all right sometimes, almost normal. For her, anyhow. She
don't say much then. Other times she's . . . something
else."

"Something like she was when you and Leo found her in
forty-nine?"

"Sometimes. Scared Leo half to death. Started taking that

party dress off, talking crazy talk, how pretty she was, how men looked at her. . . ."

His voice died but the memory didn't. I could see him watching it, the way his brother watched the television program.

"I'm going to have to give it a try, Mr. Smith."

He turned off the inner images, turned to look out over the distant desert. He seemed to be struggling with something. I didn't know what it was, but I did know when it ended. His broad shoulders sagged, his head bowed in acknowledgment of defeat.

"You ride?"

"Not in this country, this time of year."

"Then it's shank's mare. Over the ridge to the aspen grove, then up the draw. For Chrissakes don't get lost. I got enough to do without having to go traipsing around after you."

"Thanks." I hesitated, went ahead. "I have some questions, Mr. Smith, about your family and your business. I can understand you not wanting to answer, but it's my business to ask them."

"What difference'd it make?" He shrugged in a kind of stoic despair, reminding me of Wes James. Aging solitary males caught in the snare life had set for them, trapped in a tangle of other lives and yet isolated, unattached. I wondered if that was what life had in store for me. "What questions?"

"Why is your brother John in the mountains?"

He shook his head. "That's like askin' why the wind blows."

"Could I find him?"

"He ain't hiding. But now, in the snow, you—I doubt it."

"Why did Mabel attack her mother with an ax?"

"'Cause women are crazy." George Smith believed that. But he saw that wasn't enough. "The two of them fought night and day for years. Both of them was crazy, always at it, over anything."

"What were they at it over this time?"

Something in my voice caused the anger to flash in his face. "You been listening to Rafe Stillwell, haven't you?"

"Why didn't Peg want her daughter with John? I mean, Mabel was seventeen. . . ."

His slowly shaking head, his angry weary smile, silenced

me. "They wasn't fighting about him. They was fighting over him. The crazy son of a bitch was . . . having both of them."

I let that settle in.

"Who handles Peg Madigan's affairs?"

"I do," he said with more weary anger. "Haul her groceries, keep her plumbing running, check on her to see she ain't sick or burned her shack down. Got me running up and down that mountain the way she did ol' Bill."

"When she sold you her land, who handled the paperwork?"

"What difference does it make?"

"I don't know, Mr. Smith, but if money changed hands, then somebody has control over it, unless Peg Madigan's got it under her mattress, which I doubt the authorities would have approved."

"I paid money, yeah," he said. He looked out to the meadow, to his cattle, looked out farther, into the emptiness of the desert. "I'm still paying it off. And working it off. I'll go to my grave working it off."

But I already knew who it was.

George Smith saw that I knew. "In Tonopah, the Basco, Jim. Never could say his other name."

22

A hundred yards into the trees the ruts narrowed, in shadows disappeared under hard-crusted snow, in the sunlight became a spongy sump. I followed them up through the pine and juniper and rocks and sage, slipping on the ice, stumbling on the earth. I'd exchanged my tweed for a down-filled coat, and soon I was hot and sweating in the sun, shivering and sweating in the shade.

And so enjoying the mountain—the juniper-stained air, the crisp silence, the chill stillness, the bright white snow and black shadows—that I could almost forget why I was on it.

When I reached the rocky ridge, I looked back and down to the Smith ranch, where the Wagoneer sat in the muddy, junk-strewn yard like some alien spacecraft.

I scanned the countryside—mountain, foothills, desert. I saw nothing that didn't belong, nothing to indicate a presence. Maybe I wasn't being followed.

Ahead, the trail twisted off the ridge through more juniper and pine and rock and snow toward the entrance to a long, snow-stuffed draw that narrowed up the mountain. At the opening stood a grove of bare, skeletal aspens, white bones bruised with black like the scars of a disease that had killed their flesh.

The ruts became a trail, which, as it climbed into more and more snow, finally became just a lumpy track cut by the hard hooves of George Smith's horse.

At the aspen grove I stopped to catch my breath.

The silence on the mountain was vast. Nothing sounded

but the hush of my breathing, the squeak of the snow under my boots.

And something else, whispers, voices that weren't voices, sounds that were images flickering at the edge of my mind.

Slowly I perceived what it was, what the grove was.

I crunched closer to the aspens, read the iconographic tales carved into their skin, carved into the meat of trunk and limbs.

Some of the black on the white bark was natural, scars of growth and weather. Some was not, scars of the knives and minds of lonely men.

Initials, names, dates, obscure truncated messages in strange tongues.

Drawings. Stylized meditations on the female form—breasts, hips, thighs. Proud rigid phalluses. Stick figures or bloated beings in eternal coitus.

Sculpture. Breast and phallus, phallus and breast, carved into the limbs of the trees, carved out of chunks of trunks.

And all swollen, distended, distorted by the continued growth of the savaged trees into a nightmare of sexual yearning, as if life had transformed the crude signs of human longing into mocking monstrous symbols of the futility of all human desire.

I'd heard about these aspen groves, the living legacy of long-dead sheepherders, most of them Basque, most of them young and achingly alone in a strange land full of strange things.

This one reminded me of Las Vegas.

I turned from the grove toward the steep white expanse.

The trail edged up one side of the draw, away from the deep snow that collected in its sunken center, skirted the snowy shapes of rock and bush, climbed toward an invisible point where the draw disappeared as if the mountain had swallowed it.

The snow became icier, the air colder. I climbed crablike, sideways, carving footholds in the ice with the edge of my boots.

Halfway up, I stopped again to catch my breath. The snow was hard enough to bark my shins when I slipped and stumbled into it. The sun lay low in the sky.

Whatever I was heading for, I was going to spend some

time with it. There was no way I'd get off that mountain in the dark.

As the draw closed in, the trail eased closer to deeper snow and a lump of land that blocked out the mountain. I was halfway up when I saw the mountain again, with its cap of cloud and, closer, a wisp that looked like cloud but wasn't.

It was smoke. I could smell it, sharp, pungent. Into the silence drifted the sharp steady ring of an ax eating into wood.

The promise of warmth drove me over the crest, into a meadow that spread, then narrowed again to the base of a low escarpment that broke at its ends into rugged, pine-choked canyons.

Under the shadow of the rock, the Madigan place.

Ruins, snow-shrouded.

Rotted posts jutting from the snow at odd angles, the remains of fences and corrals. Battered buildings of rock and wood that once had sheltered stock and feed, now sagged into a distortion as severe as that of aspen carvings.

The house was a small square of mud-chinked and unpeeled logs off which ran a short succession of newer boxes of raw planking huddling under a swaybacked roof—all tenuously attached to the world by a power line that cut through the trees to a transformer and into a small circuit-breaker box.

A dozen yards from the heavy plank door, before a lean-to built of wired juniper poles, a large figure was splitting wood.

As I approached, the face I glimpsed under an old cowboy hat was just a human face, old, dark, remotely female.

She worked in a heavy wool coat of red-and-black plaid, heavy dark trousers. The ax blade flashed brightly in the setting sun. She was splitting one-foot pine logs into wrist-thick lengths and stacking them in a wooden wheelbarrow. The barrow's narrow wheel left a series of gouged ruts to the door like the ruts leading to the Smith ranch.

The ax was old, the single silvery blade sharpened and worked and resharpened to perhaps half its original size, its edge to an almost transparent thinness. Most of its weight was in the thick band of steel encircling the handle, the steel with which her daughter had knocked out Peg Madigan's front teeth.

Setting the blade in the chopping block, she stopped to collect the splits and lay them in the barrow. She hoisted another log onto the block, turned to the ax, and saw me.

Her face reminded me of the fierce masks on the wall of Marci Howe's office—weathered by wind and sun, heat and cold, deeply seamed and scarred, old and ugly, ageless and beautiful.

Her eyes were dark, bright. They turned back to her work.

She jerked the ax from the block, raised it, drove the blade into the pine log, splitting it. One half tumbled to the ground. I stepped over as she split the other, picked up the fallen half, stood it up on the block.

She looked at me, then drove the ax into it.

We slipped into a silent rhythm. I set logs and splits on the block, she split them, we stacked them in the barrow.

She worked steadily and hard, worked as if life had reduced itself to ax and log, worked with surprising strength and energy. She looked, and had to be, in her late seventies. She worked like a woman half that age.

Except that it wasn't strength and energy that powered her work. It was, I finally saw, simply will. I saw it when finally her body began to fail that will, slowly began to age.

Her dark face darkened even more, shone with sweat. Her broad back began to bend into a stoop. Her breath came out in grunting, steaming clouds, came out of, it seemed, two mouths—the mouth of flesh in her stern stiff face and the mouth of sudden darkness in her strong white clenched teeth.

The ax began to tremble in her hand. I put my hand on her coat sleeve. "We've got enough."

Twilight was dying into darkness, but there was light enough that in the look she gave me I could see what had driven her husband up and down the mountain for twenty years, had driven her husband and her sons to their deaths—a mindlessly implacable will, ominous in its purity, frightening in its force.

I took my hand off her arm.

She looked at the wheelbarrow, then reached into her pocket and withdrew a gray whetstone worn nearly as thin as the ax blade. She sat on the chopping block and began to hone the edge.

She looked up at me. "Well?"

Her voice was as raw as sand-laden wind, her tone brusquely imperative. She looked at the wheelbarrow. I got the idea.

I wheeled the barrow to the house, opened the door, saw the wheel-marks on the plank floor, and pushed it inside. The dim room was heated by an old potbellied stove near its center. I wheeled the wood over to it.

Redolent of pine smoke and dust and the sweat of old flesh, the room was lit by a kerosene lantern on a wooden table under the single window. Two wooden chairs were tucked under the table. A tight roll of blankets sat at the foot of a wooden cot bearing a thin, unsheeted mattress. On one wall, heavy clothing hung from wooden pegs. A closed door interrupted the back wall, another the wall to the right. A naked light bulb dangled from a wire cord in the center of the ceiling.

Dust lay heavily on the plank floor. Unlike the wood of the Smiths' floor, this was worn smooth by boots and feet, worn into paths around the stove, to table, cot, doors.

A scorched blue coffeepot sat on the stovetop, a heavy mug on the table.

There was nothing else in the room, nothing but the trails in the floor to indicate the contours of a past, nothing at all to indicate the shape of a future. It was a room of the eternal present.

Peg Madigan stepped into it.

Silently she took off her gloves, revealing thin, sharply boned, long-fingered hands that might once have been lovely. She took off her hat, releasing dark hair streaked with gray like veins and raggedly cropped as if with her ax. She took off her heavy coat and shrank, grew thinner, older in a flannel shirt over the long underwear that showed at her hard-corded throat.

She hung up her things, stepped to the stove, held her hands over it. "You feed it?"

The large gap in her teeth was disconcerting, like the dark entrance to a mysterious cavern around which local legends had proliferated. I tried not to look at it. "It's not my stove."

She opened the stove door, grabbed a split from the barrow, and fed it to the low flames.

"Guess you earned coffee." The gritty gruffness of her voice seemed less its natural timbre than an expression of her view of life and all human beings in it. "Cup's in back."

"Back" was a kitchen lit with a naked bulb over a long-unused wood range that stood beside an equally unused electric range, a tiny refrigerator, aluminum sink, shelves of planking holding cans and jars of food. An open door exposed a narrow bathroom with a stool and a water heater wrapped in heavy insulation and a metal rectangle of shower closed by a stiff plastic curtain.

I found a cup in a drainer beside the sink, switched off the light, opened the door to the front room.

Peg Madigan sat at the table, her hands around the coffee cup, staring out the window, talking to someone who wasn't there.

Obscure truncated messages in a strange tongue.

As I closed the door, the words stopped.

I filled my cup and sat across the table from her.

I took out the Harold's Club photograph and slid it into the center of the circle of yellow light from the lamp.

Pitch popped in the stove.

She picked up the photograph in her old, thin, scarred hand.

Her face spread into a slow, sweet, ghastly smile.

"Look at me, my heart melts and sinks to my privates. Touch me, I give milk."

I couldn't have responded to that if I'd wanted to.

Her smile vanished. "Foolishness, all of it. Twisted my sisters like wringing out wet clothes. Dumb critters got more sense. Rut. Breed."

She looked up. She saw someone, but it wasn't me. Her eyes softened. "He looked at me. He was the only one."

"Single John," I said.

She smiled her ghastly smile. "He knew me."

"Do you recognize anyone else, Mrs. Madigan?"

She didn't look at the photograph. "Ain't nobody else."

"Your daughter is there, Mrs. Madigan. Mabel."

The photograph fell from her fingers. She turned to stare out the window at a darkness gathering into gloom.

"He loves me. Comes in the night."

"The woman on the right is Mabel. Your daughter."

Peg Madigan turned from the window. "You finish that coffee and git on back with your brothers, boy. Them cows ain't gonna make it alone."

I didn't move.

"Crazy bitch-dog in heat. Frills. Pretties. Moon smiles. Like my sisters. Twisted."

"Mabel," I said. "In the photograph."

She picked it up as if for the first time. "My darlin' lover."

"Mabel."

"Mabel was ugly, she . . ."

Her hand began to tremble. Her face darkened, her breathing grew heavy, ragged, whistled through the hole in her teeth like a winter wind through a gap in a rock.

Suddenly she crushed the photograph in her hand, raised her other hand and squeezed the paper between her palms, squeezed and rolled it as if to reduce it to nothing.

She dropped the rough paper ball to the table and stared at it as if it were the essence of evil.

She ripped the ball open, pressed it flat, began scratching with dirty torn nails at the image of her daughter's face.

She snatched up the photograph and ripped it to pieces, scattering bits of paper over the table.

She leapt up, violently swept the scraps onto the floor, stomped on them, ground them under her bootheel.

Dark with rage, mad with hatred, her dark skin and distorted features a twilit, shade-strewn human desert, the gap in her teeth yawning huge, a black hole, she screamed at me.

"She done it! She done it to him! Down in the aspens, rutting like animals! She's your daughter, just like you, don't even know how to love! Mount her like a stallion! I'll kill her if she ever comes back! I'll kill her! Now git your lazy useless ass back to them cows!"

23

At my stupefied silence, she wheeled, jerked her coat from the peg, yanked open the door and disappeared into the darkness.

I fed another split to the stove against the cold and turned up the lamp against the darkness and sat and drank coffee and waited. I felt helpless. I'd get nothing from Peg Madigan but what filtered through her madness.

I felt foolish. What the hell was I doing on a mountain in the middle of the desert driving a crazy old woman out into the winter night? For what?

For what?

I sat at Peg Madigan's table and looked out the window and in the darkness saw the truth, the truth I'd had a brief glimpse of from the balcony outside Miranda Santee's apartment.

I'd told myself that Miranda Santee had told me the only story that would take me out of the desert. That wasn't true. All I was doing in the desert was waiting for someone to come and tell me a story.

Stories. They and the people who told them were all I had. They might drive me crazy, as they had the old woman wandering around in the darkness, but they were the only life I had.

It was time to get on with it.

The first order of business was to find a place to sleep, or something to sleep on. Between the expert battering of the day before and the afternoon's long icy climb, my body was weary, aching, ready for rest.

The back of the house, I knew, held nothing that would serve as bedding. The other door opened onto a small dark cold room, the air confined in it stale with the smell of dust and soiled cloth and unwashed bodies.

I felt for a light switch, found none, went back to the table and got the kerosene lamp. At the fading edges of its pale glow I could see an empty metal bunk bed against a wall, a pair of low wooden dressers with several missing drawers, a rumpled pile of discarded clothes in a corner.

The odor was faintly, unmistakably male, the subtle rankness of men and boys living in unhygienic estrangement from women.

A door opened onto a room like the first, small, cold, dark, empty. The same odor hung in its chill like a frozen memory.

The door leading out of it was locked.

The first two rooms had been the bedrooms of Peg Madigan's sons. The locked room had been her daughter's. Maybe.

There could be anything behind that locked door, whatever in the morass of her madness and memory Peg Madigan determined to be of value. There could be anything, nothing.

I could have found out for certain. The door was old, the screw in the hasp of the lock loose in the weary wood.

I didn't try it. It was none of my business. I went back to the front room, shutting the crude wooden doors behind me.

The light was on. I could hear Peg Madigan through the open kitchen door. I put the lamp on the table and went back.

She was opening a can with a clamp-handled opener. "Don't usually do much for supper. You're welcome to share the soup."

"Thank you."

"Stove could use a lookin' to."

I went back and fed the potbelly a couple of splits. She came in with a battered old saucepan, set it on the stovetop beside the coffeepot, went back to the kitchen.

She'd removed her boots, wore rabbit-skin slippers, moved with a heavy shuffle. As she brought out two chipped bowls and a mismatched pair of heavy spoons, she seemed even older, wearier.

She slowly, absently stirred the soup. "Been out to see the boys. Miss 'em sometimes. Never thought I would."

"I appreciate your hospitality, Mrs. Madigan."

"Can't have you wanderin' around the mountain in the dark. Bust a leg, never would get that power line staked out."

She glanced at me, and I got a swift brief glimpse of Miranda Santee's face lurking in the worn features and the seamed and folded skin of her great-grandmother.

"Say, boy, they all still crazy out there?"

"Yes ma'm."

"Only one I ever see is Georgie Smith. Thinks he's sane. Crazier than Leo."

"Yes ma'm." I sat at the table, the legs of my chair surrounded by the scraps of the photograph she had destroyed.

She fell silent, stayed silent until I had finished the soup she set before me. She had eaten little. "No appetite these days. You want the rest?"

"No, thank you. I'll clean up."

In the kitchen, I rinsed the bowls and saucepan and set them in the drainer.

In the front room, now lit only by the kerosene lamp, Peg Madigan was spreading blankets over the mattress of her cot. "Hard day tomorrow. Better hit the hay."

"Yes, ma'm."

"Ain't no other mattress. You make do with them coats."

From the stiff overalls and assorted jackets and heavy shirts and Peg Madigan's plaid coat I fashioned a bed on the floor on the other side of the stove from her.

She'd turned the lamp down to a feeble glow. I heard her sigh into bed, the cot creak. Slipping out of my boots, I lay on the clothing, squirmed after a padded position for my hip and shoulder, draped myself with my down jacket.

I listened to the fire, forced my mind to blankness.

I dozed, dipped in and out of those strange inconsequential dreams that you know you are dreaming, that you watch yourself dream, that you partially control, half-fashion, alter in the way you sometimes wish you could alter life. I hovered on the edge of consciousness, drifting almost beyond myself. . . .

* * *

A huge moon hung in the night out the window. Rats scratched beneath the floor.

Not the moon. The lamp had been turned up to a small yellow ball of glow.

Not rats. The silhouette of Peg Madigan's shaggily shorn head rose into the light, hovered, sank.

I raised myself onto my elbows. She was on her knees, feeling the floor for the torn scraps of the photograph, which she gathered and placed in a ragged pile beside the lamp.

Finally, stiffly, she rose from the floor and eased into a chair, slid her hands into the lamp glow and began sorting through the scraps of paper.

She began to hum, softly, tunelessly.

Rising quietly, I moved to the table, sat across from her.

I was in the vague half-darkness beyond the edge of the light. She was aware of my presence. Of a presence.

She too was in that half-darkness. Only her rough bony hands extended into the light.

Slowly she pieced the scraps of paper into images of faces.

Lanky Chandler. Celeste Ross. Single John Smith.

And finally, hesitantly, as if forming a charm the power of which was uncertain, which might vanquish evil or bring it, the face of Belle Smith.

She looked at the faces. The flesh of her own face sagged wearily. Tears shimmered in her dark eyes.

"Why did they betray me? Why couldn't they just love me?"

Her voice was thick, slow, heavy with emotion. For a moment I thought that's what made it different.

Then I realized what she had said, realized who had said it.

My own voice sounded different, strange. "I don't know, Belle. What did they do?"

She looked at me through her tears. The desert look. Everything of consequence for her was past, dead.

She brought that past, and herself, to brief life.

"Lanky said he loved me." Armies of emotion warred in her voice. "For years he kept after me to marry him. Then when I trusted him, he betrayed me."

She wasn't explaining. She was grieving—renewing, freshening her grief in the deep pool of the past.

"When was that, Belle?"

She stared down at the four faces on the table, the rips in the paper like savage scars ravaging their features.

"He knew what Hiram had done," she said slowly, quietly, to the darkness behind me. "What he'd done to John. To Echo. Especially Echo. Poor baby. At her while I was working, all those years. He made her pregnant, he thought he made me pregnant too. So did Lanky. Men are such stupid fools. . . ."

"Yes," I said. "Lanky."

"He knew I hated Hiram." Her face tightened, her eyes filled with that old hatred. "He helped me figure out how to do it, to kill him. With Natty's money, we could escape. He helped me trick Celeste. Lanky was supposed to be there afterwards, and we'd all meet in Tonopah. He said we could go away where Natty wouldn't find us. Then he wasn't there. I killed them and he didn't come."

I thought I understood that. Whether I did or not didn't matter to her. She was talking to herself.

"How did you trick Celeste, Belle?"

"She was going to Tonopah to be with you." Something happened behind her eyes. "I gave her my baby. Echo was already there, with that stupid musician. We could all go back. . . ."

She was looking straight at me. I had no idea what she was seeing. "All those years she was my friend. Then she stole my baby."

"Did you kill her, Belle?"

"She stole my baby. You—" Her face stiffened again, her voice hissed. "Where are they? Where's my babies?"

"I don't know, Belle."

She sat at the edge of the light, a mad grieving woman in her mad mother's clothes. "Where's your mother, Belle?"

Her eyes flickered, dried. Her face swelled with rage. "Belle she called herself. Mabel wasn't good enough for a whore. Comes running back here wanting John. My John!"

She slammed her thin fist onto the table. The paper faces jumped, fractured, fell apart.

"What did you do?"

"I used the right end of the ax."

I didn't doubt it for a minute. I sat in the shadow, looked

across the circle of pale light, into the shadow that held her. "What did you do with her?"

Belle Smith smiled a bright showgirl's smile made grostesque by the dark absence at its center.

"She made love to him in my old room. She knew he didn't want her, he wanted me. She thought she could be me, that he'd want her then. She wore my clothes, that ratty old dress I sent away for on the sly, that she ripped off me the night of the dance. She . . ."

Her gaze flickered again. She looked at me. "Who are you?"

I didn't know who she was then. I did know who I was. "I'm Celeste Ross's son."

"Who's Celeste Ross? What you doin' on my land?"

"I got lost, Mrs. Madigan," I said. "I appreciate your hospitality. I'll be gone in the morning."

24

I left at first light, closing the door quietly on the old woman's snores and sleeping dreams.

The trek down the draw was treacherous, the trail icy, gray in the morning shadows. It dumped me hard a half-dozen times.

Halfway down, out of the shadow of the mountain, I stopped to rest.

Out beyond the foothills, the desert slowly brightened, as if soaking up the light. Closer, on the distant rocky ridge, George Smith sat astride the big gray gelding, watching me.

He waited for me at the aspen grove, handed me a steaming cup of coffee from his thermos. The gesture belied the anger that seemed to swirl through the frosty steam of his breath.

"Break your fool neck."

"I'm all right."

"Is she?"

"I guess."

The gelding snorted, defecated. The mound steamed in the cold air. I noticed the thick, humanly carved and naturally deformed branch around which he'd wrapped the reins.

George followed my glance, stared angrily. "Goddamn place. Like to cut it for firewood. Leo used to sneak up here all the time, sit and gawk."

I sipped the coffee. "Who knows, George?"

For a moment he didn't answer. He looked over at the horse, as if for help. He rubbed his hand hard over his stubbled cheeks, as he had the day before over the gelding's head.

"Me and the Basco." He sagged, as if he'd shrugged off a long-borne burden, scowled angrily as if he'd lost something important. "Now you."

"No one else?"

He shook his head. "I—another fella, a while after . . . it happened, he showed up. I tried to stop him. Older than me, but he whipped me pretty good." For a moment he drifted into memory.

"You don't happen to know the man's name?"

He shrugged. "Don't matter. Jim, the Basco, told me he's dead. He—if you was to shave, I'd say he looked like you."

My grandfather got this far. And left no file, no record.

"Why did you do it, George?"

"I been askin' myself that all these years," he said slowly, angrily; but his violence had turned inward. "Every time I haul myself up this goddamn mountain I ask myself."

He looked again at the horse. "I shouldn't've gone after her. She wasn't calling me, she was calling John. She was in a motel in Indian Springs with a guy that'd picked her up. We figured it took her four days to get to the highway. God knows how she did it, middle of summer, on foot, alone."

"You brought her back here?"

He shook his head. "First to Tonopah to meet this other woman there, get this baby. I really didn't follow the whole deal. But the woman wasn't there, that really sent her round the bend. I didn't know what to do. But her daughter was there, told me about them Mafia guys and all, told me to bring her here."

"So the daughter knows too?"

He shrugged. "I guess. Never seen her since."

"What happened—" I nodded at the mountain—"up there?"

He shook his head. "We never really figured it out, exactly. She went up the mountain and never came down. Then the Basco shows up, goes up-there and then comes and tells me. . . . Well, they'd always been at each other, Peg's crazy after that winter and now Mabel's as bad and . . . well, you seen it."

I hadn't seen all of it. I hadn't seen what was behind the locked door. But I'd seen enough.

"Jim, he figured out how to handle it. I'd buy the place, so's nobody'd be after her about taxes and stuff, let her live in the house, nobody'd know. She'd already . . . Jesus, can you imagine what it'd take to knock your own teeth out like that?"

A shudder ran through his body. "Anyway, used to be all kinds of crazies in these mountains. Folks just let 'em be."

The last statement came as both a hope and a challenge.

"Makes sense to me," I said.

For a moment he seemed relieved. The moment passed. He straightened his back, shoulders, as if resuming his burden.

"How did you buy Peg's place? Where'd you get the money?"

He flushed with renewed anger. "At the bank. Signed my goddamn life away."

That could be checked, wasn't a lie. George Smith knew nothing about Natty Stern's money.

"Any strangers around after I left?"

"The only stranger around is you."

I finished the coffee, handed him the cup. "Tell me about your brother, about Single John."

He flushed angrily. "Tell you? I wish to hell somebody could tell me. Crazy son of a bitch, he was always like he is. All that about the war or getting his face smashed doing something to his brain, it ain't true. You know who give him that nickname? My mother, when he was a kid. She said he was born alone."

He looked at me, at the gelding, at the mountain.

"Son of a bitch, even when we was kids, you'd talk to him, he'd just smile that little smile of his, like you was nothin', like just looking at you gave him an ache but he was too polite to complain."

He looked at me again, this time as if I might be able to tell him what that meant. I couldn't.

"You bought twenty-five years of trouble, George. Why?"

"Didn't matter," he said. "I had Leo. One more wasn't gonna make much difference. And there was this other. . . ."

For a long time he was silent, somewhere else.

"Went to a Grange dance one night, first one I'd been to as a . . . sort of man. Spruced all up and scared to death.

Mabel was there, she'd snuck out and walked down the mountain. Wearing a white dress with these little colored stripes on the sleeves. God knows where she got it. She walked in and everybody loses their teeth, just like that she's the belle of the ball. Every hand in the place was after her to dance. Then Peg storms in, rips that dress halfway off her and drives her out."

George Smith looked at his horse, at the limb the horse was tied to, at the aspen grove.

"She was dancing with me at the time."

George went up the mountain. I went down.

I drove to Chokecherry, stopped and had breakfast with cheerful Renata and her teeth-clacking, story-telling father.

I told them I had no story to tell them. Rafe Stillwell had a story to tell me.

After I'd left, a thin young man in denim had come in and asked questions about me and someone named Belle Smith. Snotty little shit, asked a man questions, then didn't listen to the answers. Told the guy he didn't know no Belle Smith but that the guy in the Wagoneer had said he was headed for Ely.

I laughed. Renata smiled cheerfully. Rafe Stillwell clacked his teeth in delight.

I drove across Nevada. Still, silent, empty.

A few miles before Tonopah, I turned off into the Big Smokey Valley.

The southern end of the Big Smokey was filling up. Dirt roads diced the sageland between the Toquima and Toiyabe ranges into bite-sized pieces. Cheap new houses spread over the sage—ten, twenty, forty fenced acres cut out of abandoned old ranches.

I stopped for gas and directions at a new station beside an old bar draped with rainbow swirls of neon.

A few miles up the road, James Bacigaluplaga's place sat near the center of the valley, exuding prosperity—irrigation ditches bearing water to neatly fenced hayfields in which fat cattle nosed through the stubble; pipe corrals and chutes for handling stock; metal sheds for machines and equipment; a huge wooden barn beside a pasture in which a dozen horses ambled.

Beautiful horses. Sleekly groomed, hard-muscled bays and sorrels; a pair of perfectly matched buckskins, hides the color of summer sand with manes and tails of startling black. A gorgeous big blue-black stallion.

The brick ranch house was wedged at the V of a Lombardy-poplar windbreak. I pulled up before it, parked beside James Bacigalupilaga's pickup and a new Thunderbird thick with winter grime.

His wife answered my knock. She gave me her strange savage silent smile.

"Good afternoon, Mrs. Bacigalupilaga, I'd like to talk—"

She shut the door. I knocked again. The door didn't open.

I took a slow walk around the ranch yard, checked the barn, the sheds. I let my gaze swing over the pastures, hayfields, out to the irregular salt flat that patched the valley floor.

Against the distant drab darkness of the mountains, a large darker shape that might have been an illusion seemed to move at the edge of the flat. A smaller shape did move.

I walked out toward it.

The sandy earth turned easily under my heels, the scattered gray sage seem to quiver at its tips, threatening green. The sun was pale yellow in the pale blue of the sky, the afternoon air was crisp, tinged with the scent of the sage like a promise of spring.

The large shape was a horse, a young bay mare with fine hard lines and a blazed face, tethered to a clump of sage.

The smaller shape was a man, digging.

James Bacigalupilaga stood chest-deep in a hole the shape of a grave. Under his hat his face was damp, furrowed by anger or exertion. His shovel sliced into the earth, flashed as he scattered dirt over the sage. He saw me, stopped.

"You taking somebody out or putting somebody in?"

"In," he said, crawling out of the hole. "Me."

"People talk about digging their own graves. Normally it's a figure of speech."

He stabbed the shovel into the sandy earth. "I'll be in it just long enough to get a mustang stud in my sights." He nodded at a splash of dark green a hundred yards away. "He and his mares come in about dark. I'll be waiting. Then he goes in the hole."

He went over to his horse, removed a thermos from a saddle-sack, poured coffee.

"I had to put down one of my studs. He tried to go over the fence at the mustang and didn't make it."

"So you're going to shoot him."

He shrugged. "I can't catch him."

"It's against the law, isn't it?"

"There's town law and desert law. There's killing a horse and killing a human being. They're not the same, Mr. Ross."

"Probably not." I turned, looked out at the pale empty playa slicked with scattered puddles silvered by the sun.

"Belle Smith told me that my mother was on her way to Tonopah to be with a man. That man was you, wasn't it?"

How else to explain what happened to his voice when he looked at her picture?"

In the silence I heard him reopen the thermos, pour coffee. "You got to Chokecherry faster than your grandfather did."

"I got lucky." I turned back to him. He held out the coffee cup. "Why didn't you tell me where Belle was the other day?"

He looked down into the hole he'd dug, both ambush and grave. "I considered it," he said slowly, "but I thought it was better if you found her yourself. If you could. I thought it might help you to . . . understand what you found."

I wasn't sure I understood yet.

"What happened when my mother left Vegas?"

"I waited all day." He looked out over the salt flat, up over the Toquimas, into the empty sky. "The longest day of my life. In a sense, it isn't over yet."

I remained silent, sipped his coffee as he told me a story about my mother.

They met in a Las Vegas grocery store. He was picking up a six-pack for the drive back to Tonopah. She was in jeans and a sweatshirt, no makeup, hair in curlers. She was three inches taller and five years older than he was. She was what he wanted.

"I fell in love with her the moment I saw her, the way it happens in silly movies." He smiled in irony. "It took her a while longer, but she . . . We were going to live out here. It wasn't much then, but she liked the idea of what we could make it. She—thought she could get you, that you'd like it too."

The smile that had lingered on his lips like a memory

disappeared. "I went ahead and did it, but it wasn't the same."

He had his memories, his stories, and maybe they were true, maybe it had been as he said. Or maybe it had been as Lanky Chandler had suggested and he was just Joe Tourist from Altoona.

It didn't matter. I had my questions.

"She left Vegas with Belle's infant daughter?"

He nodded. "The highway patrol found her car the next day near Indian Wells. We looked, did everything we could think of. Three weeks later she called. She was with Jude Bascomb. She—"

He stopped, as if his mind had suddenly gone blank.

"What did you do?"

"What I was told." His voice had grown thick, scratchy. He cleared his throat. "Nothing. And it killed her."

He looked again into the hole he'd dug. "I've lived with it ever since. Or not lived."

She'd told him what happened. Her car had broken down, and Jude Bascomb had come along and offered her a ride. Instead of taking her to Beatty as he promised, he took her into the desert. She'd had opportunities to escape Jude and his sexual fantasies, but she was in the desert, and she had Belle Smith's infant daughter. She couldn't take a chance with the baby's life.

I tried to envision it, tried to see incarnate the ghost that to me had always been my mother, out in the Nevada desert enduring Jude Bascomb's pathetic advances so that she could protect another woman's child. I couldn't. She remained a ghost, a shadow, as insubstantial as the steam drifting over Natty Stern's death pool.

"So Bascomb had his fill of her in the desert and then brought her into Tonopah."

His broad fingers tightened around the shovel handle. "She told me what had happened but not where she was. I wanted to come after her, but she wouldn't let me."

His story was starting not to make sense. "Why would she call you and then not . . . and anyhow, Tonopah's a small town, how could you not know where she was?"

He shook his head. "It was Jim Butler Days, the town was a mess. I—I could have found her, but she asked me not to. She asked me to trust her. I did trust her. I loved her."

"What was she doing? Why all the secrecy?"

"I know it doesn't make sense," he said. "We determined that she'd been to see Belle's other daughter, Echo, at the Mizpah with Cletus James. We know she was in the Waterhole twice, once to talk to Cletus, and then . . . when she was killed. Your grandfather and I debated it a hundred times. I've been trying to make sense of it for over twenty-five years."

He looked at me as if I might be able to explain it.

I shook my head, trying to clear it. "Why did my grandfather stop trying to find out who killed her? He must have found out the truth. He wouldn't have stopped otherwise."

He looked down into the hole. I didn't know what he was seeing in it.

"He found the truth, Jack. The truth about Celeste. Not about how she died but about how she lived, what she was."

The truth. I didn't know if I believed in the truth anymore. Maybe it was a mare's nest, a fantasy. Maybe there was no truth but only stories. "What truth?"

"She was a good woman."

"He said that?"

"Finally," he said. "When he understood about the baby. She died for that baby of Belle's. That's what killed her."

This story wasn't any more preposterous than most of the others I'd heard recently, but I didn't believe it. Or, more precisely, I didn't believe James Bacigalupilaga. I still had the sense that he was jacking me around.

"What happened to the baby?"

"Belle's other daughter, Echo, took her."

"The baby have a name?"

He gave me a small smile. "She must have. All I remember it being called was the baby."

I hurled the cold dregs of the coffee into the brush. "So who killed my mother, Mr. Bacigalupilaga?"

He left his hole, his shovel, and took the cup. "Bascomb."

I didn't believe that.

He saw that I didn't believe it. "I can't prove it. We couldn't even put him there that night. But I know it, in my bones, and your granddad knew it."

"Of course," I said. "Which is why you've been keeping him alive out there at Sand Creek, bringing him groceries and dirty videotapes he can masturbate to."

He flushed. "I like to go out and look at him. I like to see what he's become. It's a kind of justice. I take from it the vengeance that the law has denied me but life has provided."

That last rang, in its measured formality, like an oft-repeated pronouncement. It was so bizarre it was probably true.

"You keep Jude Bascomb alive in the desert because he killed your lover and George Smith keeps Belle alive on the mountain because she danced with him once."

He shrugged. "Life is . . ." He looked at me. He didn't know what life is either.

But I knew what it frequently was. "George Smith's got a herd of fat cows and some horses that look as good as those expensive beauties in your pasture, Mr. Bacigalupilaga. You've got a showplace surrounded by ranches going under or already carved up into lots. And Belle got out of Natty Stern's limo with a suitcase full of Natty Stern's cash."

He started to speak, stopped.

I heard it too. The sand-muffled drumming of a hard-running horse.

The big blue-black stallion raced toward us through the sage, flinging showers of sand from its heels. Low on its back, Lois Bacigalupilaga clung like a succubus.

She reined the horse to a hard stop before us. His big chest heaved, steamed. He shook his head, pranced for the mare.

The woman sat stiffly straight, smiling at me.

"Lois," her husband said, "you're going to break his leg if you keep running him that way."

She smiled at me, silently, savagely. Then she spoke, quietly, calmly, reasonably.

"It isn't fair, you know. It really isn't."

She smiled savagely at me until I nodded agreement.

She gave the reins a hard jerk, turning the stallion's head cruelly. He half-reared and raced out across the salt flat.

She ran him straight toward the mountains. For some reason I thought of the girl with the blowing hair riding in an eternal circle on Miranda Santee's childish bedspread.

James Bacigalupilaga watched her.

"Will she be all right?"

He nodded. "Sometimes I have to go find her. Not often."

He stepped over to the mare, put the thermos back in the

saddlebag; as George Smith had with the gelding, he began to rub the hard bones of the mare's head.

"George had nothing to do with it, Mr. Ross," he said finally. "He has what he has because he's been lucky, and because he's worked himself half to death for forty years."

It took me a moment to connect. "How much was there?"

"Enough to make improvements on her house, feed her, keep her alive. The rest is in the bank, drawing interest."

"George says he borrowed money from the bank to buy the place."

"That's right."

"Then what—" I looked at him and understood. "So you did a little Nevada-style deal with your friendly banker and set up a blind and George borrowed Natty Stern's money."

"In effect."

"But not all of it."

"There was a hundred thousand dollars, Mr. Ross. I can show you receipts for about forty thousand. I can show you a bankbook accounting for the rest."

"And I can go to court and get into the bank records and show the world and Natty Stern what you did with his money."

"You could, Mr. Ross. But you won't."

25

We walked back to the house. James Bacigalupilaga led the bay mare through the sage. I led him through a list of questions.

He didn't know where the baby he said my mother had died for was. He didn't know where Echo was. He had never met either Miranda Santee or Dalton James.

I asked him if he'd known Single John Smith.

He shook his head. "I never met him. All I know is what Celeste told me. She said he was pure loneliness."

"George said something like that."

"You used to see a lot of it out here. I've heard old herders talk about what the loneliness could do. They'd go months without human contact, grow desperate for it, but only to a point. They'd reach that point and they weren't desperate anymore, they didn't care, nothing mattered. They wouldn't walk ten feet to talk to somebody."

"I've seen it," I said.

He nodded again. "We've all come to that point, one time or another. Most of us stop there. Some don't."

James Bacigalupilaga had thought a lot about that point. I asked him three more questions.

"How did you know where Belle was?"

"I knew who Belle was the first time I met her. My father herded in the Chokecherry country, I'd spent summers with him. I'd seen Mabel and Peg. Celeste told me how at first Belle was hiding because she thought she'd killed Peg, then because she was afraid Peg would find her and kill her. When it happened, I had a hunch. I wanted to ask her . . . if Celeste had been in on the killing, the robbery.

It didn't make any difference, but I wanted to know. The woman I found couldn't tell me."

"That's a pretty big coincidence, and a pretty lucky hunch."

He didn't deny it, couldn't explain it.

I asked the second question. "Why would Jude Bascomb kill my mother?"

He shook his head. "We came up with a dozen motives, from jealousy to insanity. Finally, I don't know. Normal people do strange things for strange reasons. Strange people . . . ?"

He couldn't explain that either. "Why did the mention of my mother's name upset your wife?"

He could explain that. "Lois knows that I don't love her, at least not the way . . . she knows I never got over Celeste."

He looked at me, couldn't look at me, looked out where the small darkness that was his wife had vanished against the huge darkness of mountains.

"She was in trouble once, and I got her out of it. She'd had a brutal life and I was about the first man who ever did anything for her and not to her. Then a few years later, we met again. She fell in love, and I was lonely. I thought it might . . . then she lost the baby and somehow she connected it with Celeste and Belle's baby. Ever since then she's been . . ."

We were standing in the middle of the ranch yard, in the middle of the Big Smokey, in the middle of Nevada. This man my mother had loved was telling me strange stories.

I didn't know if they were true stories.

I didn't know if it mattered.

I had dinner at the Mizpah, had a beer in the bar, lost my change in the same poker machine as I watched what seemed to be the same news.

Two things were different. The grief-ridden face of Cleo James didn't appear on the screen, and the end of the inversion over northern Nevada appeared imminent.

The weatherperson showed us the satellite photo of the storm series stretched across the dark Pacific like a fraying rope full of kinks. The first storm cell was pelting the coast with rain.

I walked out and across the street and into the Waterhole.

No bandstand, no old bloodstain in a corner, no answers.

Just a large open room with a cracked linoleum floor, brief rows and clumps of slot and poker machines to which a few old men and women fed coins, a bar at one end of which sat a buxom middle-aged woman in black slacks and a crisp white blouse.

I slid onto a stool, she slid off hers. "What'll it be?"

I ordered a beer, asked about the weather.

Two beers later I knew that for Carlene Stiles life was an endless sequence of events whose primary purpose was to illustrate profound but obscure principles.

Her husband had been crippled in a mine accident and was on NIC, which wasn't hardly enough to keep him in smokes let alone support a family, which just went to show you.

Her son in the Navy was doing real good but the government didn't pay its fighting men enough that he could help out, which just went to show you.

Her high school daughter was starting to give her trouble, which just went to show you. "Girls get sixteen, hormones make them crazy. Did to me. Came out of it, though. I guess she will."

I nodded. "I met a woman up in the Big Smoky today, seemed to be permanent with her. Bacigalupilaga was her name."

"Lois." Her plump features set in the automatic sororal sympathy of one woman for another. "Poor thing. Just goes to show you, though. They can make good wives, I hear. Never known a case of it myself."

"They?"

"He married her out of Bobbie's."

Bobbie's was the local whorehouse.

I had another beer, left my change on the bar, and walked out into the disappearing day.

26

Nevada by starlight: shades of darkness, shadows, solitary distant specks of light, confused clusters of lights in silent little towns; along the highway brief flashes of lights in predatory eyes, on the highway lumps of bloody furry death.

I got to Reno at midnight, with the rain.

As I drove out of the Truckee River Canyon, the lights of Reno and Sparks glittered as they did on the postcards mass-produced by the Nevada Tourism Commission, bright, colorful, enticing, promising whatever you wanted them to promise. Above them black clouds spat rain through tattered gray scud.

I checked into a Sparks motel and went to bed.

The next day my daughter and I house-hunted in the steady rain, finally renting an old small frame two-bedroom place on Ralston Street, well within siren distance of St. Mary's Hospital and neon distance of Circus Circus.

We spent the next rainy day moving in.

As my daughter was unpacking the box of photographs she had packed the previous fall, I showed her the one from Natty Stern's casino, showed her her grandmother, told her the story that James Bacigalupilaga had told me, told it as if it were the truth.

The story brought tears to her eyes.

She looked at the photograph for so long, with such intense absorption, that I finally asked her if she wanted it. She gave me a curiously shy smile and slipped it into her pocket.

At her request, as she watched, I shaved off my beard.

The next day I got a phone installed, hooked it to the answering machine, and began recording Frank Calvetti's ironic, carping insults. I didn't call him back.

I called to make arrangements to reinstate my license. I called to reestablish my information network. I called to let those people who often availed themselves of my services—lawyers, mostly—know that those services were again available.

I didn't call Sage or Lanky Chandler. I started to call Miranda Santee a dozen times, but finally I couldn't.

I didn't know what story to tell her.

Frank Calvetti sent me a package and a note.

The package held copies of official documents, information on the list of names I'd asked him to check.

The note said: "Miranda Santee's in the clear. The slug that killed Dalton James was not fired from her popgun.

"James *père* was done with double-ought shot. The setup is suicide, *sans* note. Vegas likes notes with their suicides.

"Pardun wasn't following Ms. Santee that night. He was following you.

"All we've got gives us zip. Vegas has less.

"You don't write, you don't call. . . ."

The rain ended, and February, and winter.

I did a small job, found a wayward wife who had not, as her realtor husband insisted, run off with the bass player in a third-rate country band but instead was working at Wendy's and living in a studio apartment on Grove Street's welfare row and being alone. I told her that if she'd call her husband, I wouldn't tell him where she was.

I did a few other jobs—some background checks, witness interviews.

I ran, worked out, read a little, listened to old records.

I got on with my life, such as it was.

And came home one balmy budding late-March late afternoon and punched my answering machine, listened to several dial tones, then to the stiff tones of an impervious old hooker.

"This is Linda Goshgarian. I'm at the Silver Sage. I'd like to talk to you tonight, about you doing a job for me."

I'd been waiting for some kind of contact.

I hadn't seen the ghost, but I knew he was around. Natty Stern knew that I was making no apparent attempt to find Belle Smith. He would be wondering if maybe I hadn't already found her.

I'd expected goons. What I'd got wasn't much different.

27

I called the Silver Sage Steak House and made a reservation for two at eight o'clock. I called the front desk, asked the clerk to see that Linda Goshgarian got the message that I was taking her to dinner and would pick her up at seven forty-five.

I got out the package that Frank Calvetti had sent me and went over what he had on her. Not much. The few documents told essentially the same story Marci Howe had given me.

Born Linda Rolfner forty-two years ago in Fresno. Divorced waitress at the Starlight twenty-three years later. Four years later suspected hooker, mob connections. A couple of years later a solicitation rap, dismissed. Another, fine and time served. Then for years nothing. Then Tawny's Fillie Ranch.

I called Frank Calvetti. He wasn't in his office, wasn't home. I asked his wife to tell him I'd meet him for breakfast the next morning.

I listened to Bessie Smith for a while, to Hank Williams, to Mozart. Then I showered and dressed in a gray pinstripe, soft white shirt and gray-and-red tie, glossy black boots. When I finished I looked like an attorney, which was one of the things I was.

The Silver Sage was only six blocks away, but I drove, parked in the garage, walked from the gray oily silence of the garage into the bright stale clamor of the casino.

The place was full, tourists in from the Bay and Sacramento by bus, priming themselves with free booze, convincing themselves that they could beat Lanky Chandler at his own game.

At the desk I asked for Linda Goshgarian's room number. The clerk, a fiftyish bottle redhead and ex-tray carrier I'd known for years, didn't give it to me. She gave me a silent look.

I knew that look. It was a specialty of casino workers, reserved for tourists whose play was being watched, gamblers whose credit had run out, hookers who were about to be escorted out, drunks and crazies who were about to be tossed out. It said that I didn't exist, was a nonperson.

Tom Pardun appeared at my elbow. He nodded grimly at a door beside the desk. We went into a small office. He sat behind the desk. "Prostitution is a crime in this county, Ross."

I didn't bother to respond. It was his show.

"You running her or renting her?"

Again I tried to read him, his smooth face and empty cop eyes. I couldn't. All I knew was that he wanted something. I didn't know what it was.

"Whichever it is, it isn't going on in the Silver Sage."

"Excuse me," I said. "I have a dinner engagement."

"You move and you'll have a dozen men whaling on you."

"Let's cut through this, shall we, Tom? What do you want?"

"I want you out of the Silver Sage, out of its business."

"Afraid I'll find something?"

His face smoothed even more. "I hate bastards like you, Ross. You scam a cop like Calvetti and get him to do your work, you play fast and loose with the law, you bleed the poor bastards who come to you with problems, and you end up with your name in the paper and everybody thinking you're a dashing, romantic hero when you're just one more slime-ball hustler."

"That's me." I about let it go at that. But my mouth kept going, tugged my brain behind it.

"But the real question is, What are you? An ex-cop with a taste for razor cuts and fancy suits? Lanky's hand-picked successor? How come, Tom? Why would Lanky make you his heir apparent? Because you're so smart and tough? Or is it something else? I think it is. I think that's why you're worried about me; you think I'll find out what it is."

His eyes went emptier, empty all the way down. "You've got everybody around here fooled, Ross, but not for long."

He was more ambitious than I'd thought. "I assume that Sage Chandler knows I'm having dinner with a hooker."

He smiled again. "An old hooker."

"You think you can play in that league?"

He stopped smiling. "You want me to tell you what she keeps in the drawer beside her bed up in her suite?"

I thought I understood the purpose of his little game.

"Good luck," I said, and left him sitting there.

I went back to the front desk. The clerk gave me a piece of paper and a different look. The paper held a room number. The look held an apology.

"Thanks," I said, accepting both.

Lanky wasn't dealing. He wasn't drinking. When I got into the elevator, I hadn't seen Sage. But I knew I would.

Linda Goshgarian answered my knock wearing a warm smile and softly waving hair and heavy makeup that shadowed and softened her features, but she couldn't do anything about the agate-shine of her eyes.

Her black dress displayed all of her smooth back and ribs, all of her smooth front except what half-hid under flaps of pleated cloth that rose from her waist, narrowed over her breasts and became a thin strip tied at the back of her neck.

"Stunning outfit, Ms. Goshgarian."

"I—" She had been staring at me. She recovered, turned to give me a better view of her breasts, smiled to give a promise of carnal delight.

"You—would you like a drink? I ordered champagne."

I smiled. "Maybe later. Our reservation is for eight."

She smiled harder. "We could have a better time here, Jack. We could relax. . . ."

I smiled harder.

Her smile weakened. "Yeah, okay, I guess I could eat. . . ."

We made our way to the dining room, leaving a trail of silent stares. The maître'd knew enough to smother his smirk the way his palm smothered the bill I handed him, worked to keep his eyes off Linda Goshgarian's chest, led us to a table near the center of the room.

Our entrance created a momentary sudden stilling of

voices that was like a gasp. Linda Goshgarian's face darkened. "I'm not dressed right. You should have—"

I smiled. "You're perfect."

She looked at me with perfect hatred. "You're a perfect asshole."

With the help of a couple of bottles of wine and a glum accusing scowl, she got through the meal. I chatted, about the food mostly, and watched her. Over the last of the wine, I asked, "And how may I be of service, Ms. Goshgarian?"

"You're really enjoying this, aren't you, you bastard?"

"What's not to enjoy? An excellent meal, fine service, a delightful companion. But you did say you wanted to discuss the possibility of retaining my services? Or was I mistaken?"

I smiled innocently into her glare. Slowly it faded. She made her mouth soft-looking even as her eyes stayed hard.

"I'd rather not discuss it here, Mr. Ross. It's a private matter." Her gaze flickered past me, back to me.

"I really don't think I want to be private with you, Ms. Goshgarian. It might be dangerous."

Her smile brightened, her glaze flickered. "Not half as dangerous as it'd be with somebody else. If looks could kill, you'd be one dead dude about now."

I followed her gaze.

Sage stood in the doorway. The look she gave me didn't seem mortal. If anything, it seemed sad. Then she was gone.

"This complicating your private life?"

I shook my head. "There's nothing to complicate."

Her eyes got harder. "I think you forgot to tell her that."

We finished the wine, went back to her room, in silence.

At the door she put a bright hooker's smile on her face, a hand on my arm, a breast on my elbow. "Let's have that drink."

The sudden shift didn't confuse me. She hadn't gotten what she wanted from me yet. I stepped back. "How about we just talk about that job you wanted me to do?"

She tried to work her smile. Then she gave up, opened the door.

But for the two cheap prints of bucking broncos on one wall, the room was as functionally furnished as a barracks—TV on a cheap bureau, small round table before the window, double bed beside a lampstand. The drawer in the stand wasn't quite closed.

She slipped out of her shoes, uncorked the champagne bottle, poured herself a glass. "Might as well drink it. It's paid for."

"No, thanks."

She shrugged, sat on the bed, not quite absently nudged the drawer shut with her knee.

I took a chair at the tiny table by the window. Outside Reno sparkled, the stars sparkled, the Sierra between them seemed not a dark presence but a darker absence, reminded me for some reason of the darkness in Belle Smith's smile.

"You were saying, Ms. Goshgarian?"

"Knock it off, goddammit. You had your little joke."

"All right," I said. "I know what you want. But why you?"

She looked past me, into the night. "Marci Howe thought I could do it with less fuss. She said you looked at me. I told her you were just looking at tits. She said try it."

"Fair enough," I said. "Tell her and Natty Stern that I don't know where Belle Smith is, that I don't care anymore."

"That's not enough."

"That's all there is."

"They won't buy it."

I shrugged.

"Where did you go from Tonopah?"

"Ely. It was a hunch that didn't pan—"

"You didn't go to Ely. And there's an old geezer at a truck stop who found a dead horse in his corral."

I looked into the night."

As James Bacigalupilaga had said, there was killing horses and killing people. It could have been worse. But it was bad enough. And it was my fault.

To see into the darkness I had to look through Linda Goshgarian's faintly reflected image. I saw her mouth move.

"He'll be receiving another visit soon."

They had me. "What are they waiting for?"

"They tried him once. They didn't get anything. They're letting him think about the horse."

I tried to imagine Rafe Stillwell silent. "Who's got the job?"

"The one who lost you."

The denim ghost. Better him than Goon. Small consolation.

"Let me tell you a story, Ms. Goshgarian."

I told her everything that had happened since the stormy afternoon Miranda Santee wandered into my camp in the desert. I told her all the stories, the stories within stories. The only thing I changed was the sequence, set the telling of the tale I heard in the Big Smoky instead in Bacigalupilaga's Tonopah office. I took her right up to Chokecherry.

She listened in silence. "They don't care about that."

I didn't want them to care. I wanted her to care. She didn't seem to. I told her another story.

"That's important only because it explains what happened, Ms. Goshgarian. I stopped at Chokecherry, talked to Rafe Stillwell, showed him a picture I had of my mother and Belle and Lanky Chandler and another man. He knew the other man. Single John Smith, the one Hiram Vanca thinks he killed. Smith is a recluse, lives alone in the mountains. I went up in them and tried to find him. I got lost, and I found myself."

"Shit."

"I know," I said. "But there it is. I was on that goddamn mountain, freezing, lost, stuck in the snow and trying to shovel my way out, not knowing which way out was, and I finally sat down in a snowbank and tried to figure out what the hell I thought I was doing up there. What drove me into the desert wasn't the past, it was the present. What difference did it make how my mother died? I was alive now. So I said the hell with it."

"Shit."

I shrugged.

She sat on the edge of the bed and looked at me. There had been just enough truth in my tale that I could tell it as if it were all true. In a sense it was.

"Did you find him?"

"Single John? I quit looking for him."

"And you expect me to tell Natty Stern all that?"

"Yes," I said quietly. "I'd also like you to ask him for me to leave Rafe Stillwell alone. I'd like you to tell Stern that if any harm comes to that old man, I'll kill him."

She smiled. "I know you think you mean that, Ross, but you know you don't."

I smiled. She smiled. Something was going on behind her eyes. "Even if all that's true, I can't take it back to them."

"Why not?"

"It isn't what they want."

I thought I understood what she was really saying. She wanted me to understand. I also thought I understood what she was doing. She didn't want me to understand that.

Our delicate little dance had just begun.

"So what?"

"So if I don't give them what they want, they do things to me I don't want them to." This time she even managed to dull the bright hardness of her eyes.

"I'm sorry," I said. "There's nothing I can do. I can't give them Belle Smith because I don't know where she is."

She smiled, a brief small smile that would bravely and foolishly ward off visions of inevitable suffering. I was impressed. I was almost moved.

"You don't want me to tell Natty Stern that if Hiram breaks any of my bones you'll kill him?"

"I'm responsible for Rafe Stillwell's fix, not for yours."

She rose, moved beside me, stared out the window at the lights and the stars and the darkness between them.

"There might be a way," she said finally. "It probably won't work, but we could try it. If you'll . . . do me a favor."

28

She wanted me to spend the evening with her in the casino, gambling and drinking. The people who were watching her would tell Marci Howe and Natty Stern that she had worked hard. That might ease their dissatisfaction with what she had to tell them.

I didn't believe her, but it didn't matter. It would give me a chance to do a little watching of my own. "Why not?"

"Let me change and—"

"You don't want to fit in, you want to stand out, right?"

Something that might have been genuine feeling flickered in her eyes. She looked past me into the darkness. "Right."

We took the elevator down. Just before it reached the casino floor, I slipped my arm around her. "Let's make it look good."

I kissed her hard startled mouth. I felt her body relax, her mouth soften, open. The elevator door opened.

I broke the kiss, leaned back, grinned. "It's show time."

Despite herself, she laughed.

We stepped into the dazzle and the din.

I caught a glimpse of Lanky Chandler's gray Stetson bobbing behind the bodies collected around the Hold 'Em table.

I led her on a long twisting half-circle around the floor. We came up on the poker pit from behind. Lanky's voice rose into the cacophony—disembodied, mythopoeic in his tale-telling.

Slipping my arm around her shoulders, I pulled her

closer, ignored the grind of her pelvis on my hip, saw a break in the barricade of bodies around the table, stepped with her into it.

Lanky was in the middle of a deal. His gaze flicked over me, stopped. He continued the deal, but he looked at me.

He grinned. "Jack, good to see you." His gaze expanded, took in Linda Goshgarian, didn't flicker. His grin expanded. "Good to see you enjoying yourself."

I'd expected more.

I could think of a number of reasons why I hadn't got more, and all of them made sense, but finally what I had to believe was that Lanky Chandler had never seen Linda Goshgarian before.

"My credit still good?"

He grinned again. "Whatever's fair, Jack. Gonna beat me with my own money, are you?"

"I'm going to try."

"Good luck."

Three hours later I was broke. I'd lost a thousand dollars. I'd gotten a run going with the dice, then crapped out, marked time at a Twenty-One table, gone back to the crap table and brought my hex with me and gotten killed.

Linda Goshgarian, on the other hand, walked through rain drops.

Three silver dollars after she started she hit a jackpot that rang bells. As I slaved over the dice, she played silly bets, carelessly dropping chips, changing bets, littering the table with so many chips that she often bet against herself, yet somehow always won. She got such a run going at twenty-one—hitting sixteen against the dealer's deuce showing, splitting face-card pairs—that the pit boss came up to watch the play and watch the dealer and watch her and watch me and scowl.

By the time I was tap city she had a change carton filled with black twenty-five dollar chips.

All of which rendered her performance believable, motivated the working of her red mouth and pale hands, the grasp and grope and caress, squeal and whisper.

Through it all she managed to display most of her body to most of the people in the big room, managed to get my hands on most of her body, managed to cling to me as Lois Bacigalupilaga had clung to the big blue-black stallion.

Through it all, too, I managed to watch her, watch others watch her, watch her watch me.

I didn't detect the audience she was playing to, if there was one. There might have been an audience watching us from the screens in the security office, from the catwalk above us. Lanky Chandler might have been watching, or Sage. Or Tom Pardun.

For all the other revelers in the room, we were just one more boozing bozo and bimbo, Joe Tourist from Altoona about to get lucky with a lucky hustler.

I lost my last chip and decided to call it a wrap.

It was after two. The crowd had thinned and quieted, then swelled in one last dying surge of noise and jostle before its inevitable disintegration into solitary men and women, drunk or desperate, begging Chance to do what Life couldn't and make them winners, into lonely couples wandering off with aching heads and stinging eyes and burning lungs and tired surly souls.

I was one of them, and looked it. In the various images that flashed back at me as we drifted toward the elevator, I saw my twisted tie, the grin of lipstick on my shirt collar, the glaze of alcohol in my eyes.

Linda Goshgarian looked better, and worse. Her eyes glowed with the excitement of her success, and alcohol had softened the set of her mouth. But her makeup had thinned, slicked, left her face stiff and somehow artificial.

Among the naturally flowing lines time had left on her face I noticed others, straight as a knife's edge, creeping from under an eyebrow, slanting off the bridge of her nose, slicing across her cheekbone.

She hadn't wanted to cash in her chips, seemed to think the black chips were more real than money. As the elevator came, I again suggested she cash in.

She shook her head. "I've got plans for them."

The elevator door shut. "What plans?"

She took my arm, surrounded it with breasts. "I'm going to spread them on your body and scrape them off with my tongue."

"Forget it." I moved my arm. "The show's over."

She pressed the length of her body against the length of

my body, put her mouth to my ear, flicked her tongue. "I know."

Stepping away from her body, I looked at her. I didn't know how drunk she was. I didn't know how drunk I was. Not so drunk as she and anybody who'd watched us might think. Not so drunk that I was about to believe a word she said.

I still didn't know what she really wanted.

She smiled, kept her motor revving at cuddle and purr.

Inside her room, she switched on the light, handed me her carton of chips. "Get comfortable. I won't be a minute."

"Don't bother," I said, but to the closing bathroom door.

I set the chips beside the television set. She'd won nearly a thousand dollars of Lanky Chandler's money. I'd lost a thousand. Lanky'd broken even.

At the window I gazed out into the darkness between the lights and the stars. Something was battling the alcohol in my body, glands opened by emotion were secreting their potions into my bloodstream. I didn't know which emotions were doing it.

Fear, maybe. Maybe anger. Maybe even lust.

I heard the bathroom door open, turned into darkness as the lights went out. In the darkness a fainter, shadowed darkness moved silently toward me.

"I told you I wasn't interested, Ms. Goshgarian."

"You're interested," she said, moving closer. "Otherwise you wouldn't still be here."

There was a bit of truth in that.

Her breasts swung softly, brushing shadow across her belly. Her body in the shadowing darkness seemed pale and smooth and perfect, her features harsher, as if hacked from hard wood. At the same time her face seemed human, the face of a real woman atop a plastic body.

My voice seemed to have harshened. "What do you want?"

She put her hands on my chest, lifted her face close to mine. "It's not what I want, it's what you want."

I took her hands and pressed them together and pushed them away. "I don't want you, that's for sure."

"I know." She smiled, and the shadows moved on her face, and her shadowed smile seemed full of old pain and dead hope and the ghosts of youthful promises.

"I know what you want, Ross. You don't want me, you don't

want a woman, a person, a human being. You just want a body, a female body, a body you can lose yourself in. Here it is."

I found myself suddenly, deeply angry. Not because she was wrong. Because she was right.

I pushed past her, found the light switch.

Linda Goshgarian stood before the window, her body unreal and beautiful and her face real and ugly. "You asshole."

I tried to control my anger, couldn't quite do it.

"Right. How about if I beat on you, break some bones, give you a few more scars you can try to hide with makeup? Will that make me more like your true love Vanca, less an asshole?"

"All men are assholes," she said savagely. "The only difference is that Hiram Vanca is pure asshole, and he doesn't try to hide it. He doesn't pretend to be what he isn't. He doesn't pretend to want you when he just wants to use you."

"Blessed be the pure at heart," I said.

She was as angry as I was. Angrier. Her gaze blazed, shot suddenly toward the lampstand drawer, shot back toward me.

"At least you could turn off the goddamm light."

I understood why she wanted darkness. Not to mask her body, which was smooth, unmarred, nearly pristine, as if it had never been touched, but to mask her face. And to get at the drawer.

I turned off the light, watched her move like a pale shadow to the bed, turn back the covers and slip beneath them.

"I don't suppose you'd consider hanging around for a couple of hours, so they'll think . . ." The bitterness in her voice shriveled the words to nothing.

I went back to the table, sat, watched her pale shadowed face, listened to the silence. Then I broke it.

"What's in the drawer, Linda?"

"I—what drawer?"

"The drawer four inches from your hand. The Gideon Bible? Or a condom? The last woman I was with in this hotel had a condom in the drawer. A gun? But what would you be doing with a gun? Be a little hard to explain, wouldn't it?

You'd have to come up with a whiz-bang story to talk your way out—"

"You stupid bastard! I saw you operate, remember? You think I was going to let you work on me that way?"

"Did you really think I would?"

"Why not? You're no different than any other asshole. You'd do anything you figured you could get away with."

I let that go. "What's going on, Linda? I've been expecting the goon squad for a month. What's Natty waiting for?"

"He's waiting for you," she said. "He's waiting for you to do something. He says you will."

I sat and watched the darkness and realized that Natty Stern was right. So I did something. I told her the truth.

"I found Belle Smith. Tell Natty if he wants to know where she is, he'll have to ask me himself."

She made a strange sound, a sound that seemed to issue not from but through her.

I heard another sound, but she hadn't made it.

"She's alive? After all this time?"

I identified, located the other sound, and as I did I realized that it was too late.

I leapt up and threw myself toward the door just as it opened and a thin dark shape framed itself in the rectangle of light.

I threw myself against the wall just before the soft damp pop and tiny spark of flame and I was about to throw myself at the shadow because I couldn't do anything else.

A loud hard pop and small sharp pain in my arm.

The shadow grew very still and a larger shadow appeared behind it. The room exploded in a huge expanding blast and the small shadow hurled toward me and I saw it was the denim ghost.

He was dead before he crashed into me and we both went down.

I struggled out from under his wet and insubstantial weight.

The light switched on. Tom Pardun stood over me, his eyes empty, a dark 9 mm. steady in his fist and pointed at my eye.

The room suddenly was quiet, thick with the smell of cordite and blood and fear. Tom Pardun and I stared at each other.

Then I slowly climbed to my feet.

"It's too late. The moment was there, and now it's gone."

He knew I was right. The pistol dipped in his hand. "I don't need to kill you, Ross. Natty Stern will do it for me."

An inch of barrel of the little silver gun extended from under the denim ghost's leg. His chest was an ugly ragged gory hole. Blood spattered the wall, soaked the carpet, smeared my shirt, ran warm and thick down my arm, soaked my jacket sleeve.

Sage Chandler appeared in the doorway. Or I imagined it. My mind seemed not to be working right.

Tom Pardun smiled. "Maybe he won't have to. I'd guess you've got a blown artery."

"What?"

My knees didn't work anymore. I leaned against the wall, felt myself slide slickly down it.

Then Linda Goshgarian was kneeling beside me, wrapped in a blanket.

She shouted at somebody. "Call an ambulance, you asshole!"

She leaned over me, ripped open my shirt, slid her hand into my armpit, smiled.

"It's show time."

She smiled strangely, and the light began to dim, and this smile was the same as the smile she'd given me in her office in the whorehouse and the light grew dimmer and I'd seen that smile before and the light grew even dimmer and I remembered where I'd seen it and then I forgot again. . . .

29

When I came out of it, I discovered that I was a sleaze ball.

I'd drifted up once, like a drowning man toward the hazy light, and the sun that cast that light was my daughter. Later Frank Calvetti's grumble drifted as faintly as distant thunder. On a warm breeze I caught the scent of the desert after rain.

I awoke and found myself taped and tubed and weak and found my daughter sitting on a folding chair beside my hospital bed.

I assured her I was all right and she cried and sat with me and told me that she knew what the paper said wasn't true.

Frank Calvetti came the next day, scowling. "Tell me a story. It won't be the truth, but try to make it interesting."

I told him the truth.

"Terrific, Jack. Stern thinks you have information he wants, so he sends a hooker to get it and a kid to kill you before she can. It's so logical, I don't know why I didn't think of it."

I borrowed Rafe Stillwell's line. "I just tell these stories, Frank. I don't explain them."

"Right," he said. "So you don't explain why both Tom Pardun, who despises you, and Linda Goshgarian, who despises damn near everybody, would go to such lengths to save your life."

"You'll have to ask them."

He smiled. "We did. Tom says his men saw the kid come in, got the old just-doesn't-look-right feel, watched the elevator to see where he got off, called Tom. He figured it

192

had to be the hooker's room, figured there might be trouble. Tom did what a good cop does. You ought to be thankful he was a good cop."

"And Ms. Goshgarian?"

"She said she wouldn't let a dog die like that, although she expressed some regrets when she found out you hadn't croaked."

"And Sage Chandler?"

Frank frowned. "What about her?"

"What did she say?"

"Why should she say anything, Jack? She wasn't there."

Maybe I had hallucinated. Suddenly I remembered remembering where I'd seen Linda Goshgarian's smile. But I couldn't remember what I'd remembered.

I changed the subject. "From my daughter's distress, I'd guess the media had lots of fun with it."

"What do you expect? A dead goon and a naked hooker and a shot-up private eye in a hotel room littered with champagne bottles and twenty-five-dollar chips—especially when it turns out the dead goon killed Dalton James."

"How do you figure that?"

"Ballistics figures it. Same gun."

"Why?"

"Natty Stern had the kid—Billy Landrum, his name was— follow Miranda Santee on the chance that she'd lead them to Belle Smith. Dalton James got in the act, shot her once, so Landrum made sure he didn't kill her before she found Belle."

"Neat," I said.

He nodded wearily. "I don't much like it either, but there it is. Case closed."

"Who did Cletus James?"

He shrugged again. "Not my case, Jack."

"Did Dalton James and this Landrum know each other?"

Frank knew where I was going. "We can't connect them, but the odds are good that they might have. How else could Landrum get that close to him? James had to know he was there."

That was true. "What kind of gun was it, Frank?"

"It was right in front of your nose, Jack. But then with the hooker in nothing but a bloody blanket, you may have been looking elsewhere. A little bitty .32 revolver, pearl handle, the kind stage-door johnnies and sugar daddies used to give to their bimbos. Probably a present from his mother."

"Neat," I said.

I got out of the hospital a week later.

My car was at the Silver Sage, so I walked the few blocks to my house. It was April, and warm, and budding and flowering and greening. The air was soft and smelled of growing things.

Before my door a man and a woman stood in a strange isolated togetherness.

Cleo James was in black—trim black skirt and sweater under a short black jacket. A small black hat trailed a net of black mesh over to her pitted cheekbones. The clothes looked expensive, the hat as ridiculous as her melodramatic pose that at once presented and parodied real suffering.

Wes James was in gray, a shiny suit he was twenty years too old and as many pounds too heavy for. He looked doggedly unhappy.

I expressed my sympathies, they expressed theirs. I parked them in the living room while I made coffee and tried to decide what I was going to do about what I knew was coming.

Cleo James sat primly on the edge of the couch. "I want to . . . retain your services."

I parked myself across from the couch. The room held my furniture, my books and records and pieces of desert. Nothing looked quite as if it belonged yet.

"The police say the man who killed your son is the one who shot me. He's dead. It's over."

"No." Cleo bowed her head, peered through the veil that hung like virga over a desert range. "I don't care who. I want to know why. Why would Dalton want to harm that girl? Why would that man kill Cletus? I—I want what you wanted when you came to talk to me."

"I don't think I can help you, Mrs. James."

Her hands wrestled in her lap. "If it's a question of . . . remuneration, I can pay you. I've come into a . . . legacy."

"It's not that," I said. "I just don't think I could find out what you want to know."

"I—did you find out what you wanted to know?"

What had I found out, really? I didn't know. "Sort of."

"Was it . . ." She stopped, fumbled for a pin in her hat, removed the hat and veil and held them in her lap. "Is it that you think the truth will be painful, Mr. Ross? Wesley thinks so. He was against my coming here."

I looked at Wes James. He stared at me with a sort of defiant melancholy.

"I really don't know what you want, Mrs. James. Do you want to know why your husband and son died? Do you want to know if they were evil men? Or if somehow you're responsible for what they were, or responsible for what happened to them?"

The face of her flesh trembled. She was made up expertly if not heavily, as if someone had recently shown her how to soften the ridges and pits of scar tissue, smooth the old torn flesh.

"Yes."

"Yes what?"

"Yes to all of it. Yes."

When I didn't answer, she took a deep breath. "My son and husband were murdered. I have . . . benefited from their deaths. All these years I kept up the insurance on all of us. . . ."

She hesitated, her gaze fixed and blank. Wes James reached his thick hand toward her, stopped it an inch from her arm. He looked at me. An inch. An unbridgeable gap.

"I'm not rich, Mr. Ross, but I have enough money to make a different life for myself. I'm going to have plastic surgery. I'm going to enroll in college. I'm going to make something of myself. But first I need to understand. I'll grieve for my husband for a while. I'll grieve for my son forever. But I can't go forward, I can't bury them, until I know."

I was moved, not by the words or the dreams they exposed, but by the pain that quietly drove them. I was also moved, in a different way, by the expression on Wesley James's odd ugly face as he listened. Something else would be buried—his hope.

He looked at me, understood that I understood, and did something I doubted I'd ever be able to do.

"Here's the deal, Ross," he said with forced gruffness. "You help Cleo and I'll tell you all I know about Tonopah."

I didn't answer for a while. I wasn't deciding. I was

waiting to see what decision would come out of my mouth.

I knew that if I agreed, somebody else would probably die.

I knew it might be me.

"All right."

Cleo James sat back, tugged her skirt down over her slender knees. Wes James leaned toward her, touched her arm gently with his thick fingers. "I need to talk to Ross . . . in private."

She shook her head. "This is part of it. I need to know."

"It's not that," he said. "It's just . . . man talk."

She smiled brightly, Nevada-style. "I've been a cocktail waitress for twenty years, Wesley. I've heard man talk."

He looked at her, at his hand. He slipped it from her arm.

"I didn't say nothing about it in Vegas . . . I mean she was your mother an' all. I—she was there with this guy."

He stopped, looked at Cleo James. She smiled brightly.

"I seen them three times. When she came to the hotel, he was in the hall. Then in the bar, he was with her too. He . . . while they was talking, he started telling me . . ."

He shook his head, as if in renewed disbelief. "He was just this ordinary-looking guy, but when he opened his mouth this . . . stuff came out. Stuff about him and your mom, what they—"

"Jude Bascomb," I said. "I've talked to him."

"Yeah," he said, "But the thing is, he was always there, watching her, like she was sort of a prisoner. I know that sounds crazy, but—and he had the baby, like it was his prisoner too."

"They were his prisoners, Wes, sort of."

He nodded. "He was there that night, too."

"You saw him?"

He nodded again. "She come in during a set, was waiting for Cletus. I—I wondered where he was, kept looking and I seen him come in back an' slink over in the corner, the one they found your mom in. He was there while her and Cletus was talking."

I thought I understood what he was telling me. "You didn't tell this to the sheriff?"

"They asked me about your mom, not about the guy. I didn't want to go volunteering, you never know what it's gonna mean, what's gonna happen, we still had a couple weeks on the gig—"

He stopped, looked away, into his past and his shame. "Wasn't no better than Cletus."

"You think Jude Bascomb killed her?"

He nodded. "She was fixing to dump him, you could see that. He was crazy. So he . . . you know."

"Who had the baby that night?"

"I—neither one of them."

"Do you know James Bacigalupilaga?"

He furrowed his brief forehead. "I don't think so."

"Was the band doing a set when the fight started?"

"No, we'd just finished one."

"So Cletus was talking with her."

"I—" He looked at Cleo James, panic in his eyes.

"No," she said. "Tell him. Tell me. The truth, Wesley."

His face filled with suffering, his own, and hers. "They'd been talking, yeah. But when it started, Cletus, he come up to try to cover his guitar, he didn't . . . I mean, for crying out loud, he's the one called Natty Stern and told where she was! He wasn't about to kill her. Nobody's that dumb."

"Why did he call Natty?"

He looked down, into the depths of his brother's shame. "A favor. You do him one, he does you one, you know? It was gonna be our big break, playing in his lounge."

"What were my mother and Cletus talking about, Wes?"

When he didn't answer, Cleo James did.

"That baby. She wanted him to take a baby to its father. He told me that once, when I found out I was pregnant with . . . Dalton. Cletus wanted me to have an abortion. He said babies cursed his life." Sudden tears sprang to her eyes. "Maybe he was right."

Wes James sat frozen between his impulses to touch her and his knowledge that she wouldn't recognize the nature of that touch.

"Who was the baby's father, Wes?"

"All's I heard was a name. Vanca."

"Did you hear a name for the baby?"

He shook his head.

"Why would she want Cletus to take the baby? Why not Belle's daughter, Echo?"

He shook his head again. "I don't—all I know's that Echo

wanted to take the baby one place and your mom said
another. That's . . . I don't even know that for certain."

"What happened to Echo, Wes? Where is she?"

He continued to shake his head. "I don't know. We went
back to Vegas and she had her baby and they . . . gave it
up, and she started . . . runnin' around, got into some
trouble, dope or something, and then she was just gone."

"No," Cleo James said quietly.

Neither Wes nor I spoke.

"She's . . . not far. Cletus—sometimes he'd be gone a
day or two and come back with money he shouldn't have. It
was her." Again tears sprang to her eyes. "It was always
her. Echo."

"Why would she give him money, Mrs. James?"

"I don't know. I—maybe she still loved him," she said.
What she didn't say, but what Wes and I both heard, was *He
still loved her.*

"Could it have been blackmail money?"

From one eye tears carved a narrow channel down her
cheek. "It wasn't much money. It was just a few dollars,
when he'd come to the end of . . . everything. I don't
know."

"Wes, was Echo in the Waterhole that night?"

"For a while. She left early, right when your mom come
in."

Wes and Cleo James had given me all they had. I couldn't
give back less. I told Cleo James that I'd find out what I
could about the deaths of her son and her husband.

I tried to convince her that I didn't want her money. She
insisted that I take a check. I finally did, only to assure her
that I'd help her. When they left, I tore it up.

I spent an hour with the package Frank Calvetti had sent
me.

When I put it away, I knew more about some of the people
but nothing more about what had happened nearly thirty
years before or what had happened less than a week before.

I knew nothing more about Belle Smith or Natty Stern or
Hiram Vanca or Marci Howe.

Cletus James's rap sheet repeated the story his wife had
told me in Las Vegas. Dalton James's rap sheet repeated the
story his uncle had told me in Las Vegas.

Echo Smith's rap sheet told me what Wes James hadn't been able to tell me. For three years after the adoption of her baby, she had been hauled in on various drug and prostitution beefs. Probation, suspended sentence, time served and counseling.

Then nothing.

I called Frank Calvetti, listened to his insults, then told him about my client and what she had hired me to do.

"You don't like the official story?"

"Not much. Did you get anything more from Miss Santee?"

"Nada. She professes to find both of Master Dalton James's appearances in her life inexplicable. Did he rape her?"

"No. That little job was taken care of by Hiram Vanca."

Finally Frank spoke. "Somebody ought to shoot that bastard."

"It's against the law. But speaking of shooting, why did you put my S and W with my things? It could have stayed in the property room forever. I wondered if it was a message."

"I wondered too."

"On a slightly less cryptic note," I said, "when you talked to Tom Pardun, did he tell you who else was following Miranda?"

He phrased his answer. "He didn't mention anyone else."

"Tom was a good cop, you said?"

"You're alive because of how good he is."

"So you say."

He paused again. "I don't like your implication, Jack."

"No implication, Frank. Just questions."

"Then I don't like your questions."

"Sorry," I said. "But don't worry. Tom Pardun didn't kill Dalton James."

This silence was longer. "You're not implying anything, I know. But I'm inferring. I'm inferring that you think you know who did kill him."

"Sort of."

"What the hell does that mean?"

"I'll tell you when I find out."

He didn't say anything for a while. When he finally did speak, what he said surprised me.

"Welcome back, Jack."

30

Miranda Santee didn't answer her phone.

I locked up and walked downtown. In the soft afternoon light, tourists lazed about the streets as if resting up for the bright excitement of the night. At the Silver Sage I retrieved the Wagoneer, then drove to Miranda's apartment.

Her lock had been fixed, but the flimsy door echoed hollowly under my knock. None of the basting bodies around the concrete pool knew anything about Miranda Santee. All the manager knew was that the rent was paid.

At the television station, the receptionist informed me that Ms. Santee was on vacation. The receptionist had a number at which Ms. Santee could be reached, but she wouldn't give it to me. Instead she gave me a promo: when Ms. Santee returned, she was to begin a weekly "feature format" called *Real Nevada,* for which she would serve as host and chief reporter, and about which station management was "extremely excited."

I found a phone and called the Silver Sage and asked to speak to Sage Chandler, listened to a scratchy tape of the Beatles crying for help and then to Tammy Wynette counseling the unhappy women of the world to stand by their men.

Sage came on with a comic drawl: "Howdy, stranger."

I told her what I wanted. "I need to talk to Miranda Santee, but she doesn't seem to be around. I thought maybe the attorney you hired for her—"

"You don't need a lawyer. All you need is me."

The last remark was a bouquet of significance. Something in her voice told me that it was a bouquet I'd never smell.

"You know where she is?"

"I'll be in the street in fifteen minutes, stranger," she drawled. "Be there with your guns on."

I drove back downtown, eased around the walkways and the cranes of the construction that had resprouted with the spring, and pulled up to the entrance as Sage stepped through it.

Her dress was thin and summery, patterned in subtle streaks of pale yellows and subdued lavenders that reminded me of cheat grass. The cloth fluttered with her movement and her smile.

She slid in beside me. "You look better than you did the last time I saw you. Still too pale, though."

I remembered the last time I'd seen her. Or thought I'd seen her. I didn't mention it. "'Alone and palely loitering.'"

"I hope not. That would make me a woman without mercy."

"A *beautiful* woman without mercy," I said. "Where to?"

I followed her directions and we continued the banter. Better banter than talk about real things. Dead things.

I drove across the river, to Plumb Lane, west through an older, elm- and cottonwood-shaded residential section and out to a new development of large houses on large raw hillside lots carved from an old ranch and overlooking the river and the city.

The road twisted up the hillside. Near the top, Sage pointed at a huge house and a concrete driveway and Miranda's rainbow-striped Bronco. I pulled in beside it.

The house was mostly stained redwood and glass. At the corners the stonework foundation seemed to climb the wood like a parasitic growth. A tiny creek curled across the corner of the lot, which Sage or someone had had sense enough to leave in its natural state—sage, sand, a lone juniper.

Sage smiled. "Miranda's been staying with me. We've become friends."

"She could use one."

"Me too." Her smile brightened a bit. "We discovered, as we became friends, that we didn't have any friends. We've been trying to understand why that was."

I nodded, but didn't respond.

"I won't ask you what you want to talk to her about, Jack. I just hope it won't—she's had a hard time."

"I know," I said.

"Harder than you know, Jack. A lot harder."

Sage smiled. She waited for me to smile. I tried, but I couldn't quite manage it.

She got out, and I followed her to the door.

It opened onto a sunken foyer that looked into a vast room with cathedral ceilings and redwood beams that took up both stories of half the house. The walls were broken by glass and a few paintings and a massive river-rock fireplace, the space broken by careful arrangements of rugs and furniture; the principle was the same as that organizing Sage's office, but the effect was like that of Marci Howe's restaurant: it was a room in which you couldn't hide but where no one could sneak up on you.

At that, we nearly sneaked up on Miranda Santee. Before the fireplace, she and a blond boy sat cross-legged on the floor, seemingly mesmerized by the chessboard on the table between them.

Miranda glanced up, saw us. Her face held more color, her gaze didn't scatter. She still seemed a bit pale to me, a little weak, but not so fragile, vulnerable.

As we approached, her mouth tightened. I had a sudden vision of her grandmother.

"Come on, Miranda," the boy said impatiently. "Move."

She glanced absently at the board. "There isn't much I can do, is there? You're about to kill me. You already took my horses, and yours are right—"

"Knights," the boy said sharply. "They're knights, not horses. And I'm not going to kill you, I'm going to put you in check. And then mate. But you have to move."

As I came into his line of sight, the boy had directed his last remark, and a glare, at me.

Sage put her hands on his shoulders. "Miranda and Mr. Ross have to talk, honey. Why don't you try to get me in mate?"

The body squirmed from under her touch. "You're too easy."

But he wasn't talking to his mother. He was talking to me again, not so much with the words as with his baleful glare.

He was ten years old, and he was already in big trouble.

Miranda rose. "Let your mother try. We can play tonight."

Sage stood beside her son, looking for something to do

with the hands he had rejected. "Why don't you go out on the patio? I'll bring you something. A drink, Jack?"

"No, thanks."

"Maybe later," Miranda said. "But this won't take long."

Sage smiled at her, at me, at her son, looked around as if she would smile at someone else. No one else was there.

Miranda wore what might have been the same designer jeans, and a crisp salmon-colored blouse that cast faint color onto her face. Her bare feet were very white and beautiful.

I followed her across the room, through a glass door, out onto a patio of flat river-rock bordered by desert flowers in carefully tended beds. Near the house a huge hot tub steamed.

Miranda took a chair at a heavy table shaded by a tilted canopy of brightly colored canvas. I sat across from her, where I could look past her and over the city to the rumpled brown mass of the Virginia Range.

She folded her thin hands, put on a mask of journalistic sympathy. "I'm sorry you were shot. I guess we're even."

"You're still one up on me, Miranda."

If she knew what I meant, she ignored it.

"Congratulations on the new job."

"Thank you. I—it isn't what I really wanted, but it's better than what I had. And it could lead to big things."

"How did it happen that you got it?"

She gave me a small ironic smile. "All I had to do was get shot and fall under suspicion for murder. When I made the news instead of reporting it, the station management decided that the taint of notoriety might be just the thing to boost ratings. They resurrected an idea that I'd thrown at them and here I am."

She seemed to believe that. I didn't, but it didn't matter.

"So now you don't need the story of Belle Smith."

"There never was a story, was there?" She smiled again, faintly, ironically. "Not one I could tell, anyway. I was just . . . fantasizing."

"What about the story of what Nevada, and men, do to women?"

She looked at me with a quiet ferocity. "I'll tell that story. In a sense that's the only story I will tell, and I'll tell it over and over."

"How?"

"I'm under the usual editorial restraints, but I can do it the way women in Nevada have always done it, surreptitiously—a shot here, a remark there. I'll get the story told."

I didn't doubt it.

"Belle Smith," she said stiffly. "Did you find her?"

The brightly colored canvas stretched over the table cast a sharp shadow diagonally across the upper half of her face. I thought of Cleo James and her pathetic black veil.

I looked past her. The sun was slanting yellow rays over the city and onto the desert hills; shadows deepened, the land lay in fleshlike folds.

I had no reason not to tell her. In fact, I had to tell her in order to get her to tell me what I wanted to know.

"There's only one way this will work, Miranda. We can sit here and tell each other stories, and neither of us will get what we want. Or we can tell each other the truth."

"You think I'd lie to you?"

I didn't answer.

"All right," she said rigidly.

But Miranda wasn't really all right. I had the sudden sense that she was again holding herself together by an act of will.

"Did you find Belle Smith?"

"Yes."

Behind the slash of shadow, her eyes brightened with a passion I couldn't read. "Where is she?"

"Your turn. What did Dalton James say to you?"

"What? I don't—what difference does it make?"

I didn't understand her sudden panic, confusion. Her gaze started to scatter. She gathered it quickly, firmly, but the act took something out of her.

"I want to know what he said to you and why he shot you and why he came back the night he died."

"But—why?"

"His mother wants to know why he died."

I saw her pain. I saw her will herself past it. She looked at me as her grandmother had.

"He said he was my brother, or half-brother, that our father was a drunk and a criminal and an ex-convict. He told me that my mother was a prostitute. He called me names, filthy . . . names. He told me that I thought I was better than he was but that I was just a bitch-whore like my mother. He told me he hated me."

The words had come stiffly, to a strange invariable rhythm.

"Why would he—"

She shook her head hard. "That wasn't part of the question." Then she answered it. "He was stupid, crazy. He looked crazy and he acted crazy."

"What did he want from you?"

"He wanted me to tell him where Belle Smith was. He said she was going to make him rich. He was too stupid to realize I was telling him the truth, that I didn't know where she was."

She spoke with the same artificial rhythm, like a child reciting a poem she had memorized but didn't understand. I was feeling uneasy. Something was wrong. But I kept going.

"Why did he shoot you?"

"Because he was stupid and crazy. He stood there screaming at me and got crazier and crazier and he shot me and he ran."

She sat, nearly slumped back in her chair, as if exhausted. Her fierce face was now all in shadow.

"Where is Belle Smith?"

I told her. All of it.

It shook her, but finally her will held. "She . . . killed her own mother?"

"Yes."

Her face didn't change. "Who is she?"

What she meant was who was Belle Smith to her. "I think you know, Miranda. You checked the records, you talked to Cletus James. He told you, didn't he? She's your grandmother."

Her face lost its fleshy texture, stiffened even more. In the shadow, it stared at me as if frozen in a block of ice.

"My mother was Echo Smith?"

"Probably. You can find out for certain if you—"

"The . . . one with you when you got shot—is she . . . ?"

I'd thought so for a while. I could tell a dozen stories about how it worked. But I could tell another dozen and have Lois Bacigalupilaga as heroine. It was also possible— probable—that neither was Echo Smith, that Echo Smith

was a Keno runner in Laughlin or a Henderson housewife
and not involved in what was going on.

I didn't tell Miranda any of that. "I don't know."

She had constructed her barricade of will to ward off
certainty. But it was uncertainty that cracked it. "The
records, they don't prove—I mean, I don't have to
be . . . hers."

I looked at her, listened to her, saw and heard what had
made Dalton James crazy: revulsion twisted her mouth,
loathing ground in her voice.

"There isn't much doubt that Echo is your mother, Miranda. You could find out for sure if you wanted to. But
finally you were right, out in the desert. The Santees were
your parents in the only way that matters."

I'd been trying to console her. I didn't. Her gaze seemed
not so much to scatter as to splinter, like shatterless glass
under a brick.

"It doesn't really matter, Miranda."

She didn't answer.

"It's not what your parents were that matters, Miranda, it's
what you are."

She didn't answer. She didn't move.

"Miranda?"

She didn't answer. She didn't move. She wasn't there.

Shaken, I got up.

Miranda didn't move.

I started toward the glass door, saw Sage standing behind
it watching us. She opened it as I neared.

"Something's happened, Sage. I don't—"

Color roared through her face. "You stupid bastard!" she
hissed, "I told you—"

I grabbed her arm, gripped it tightly until she was silent.
"You can scream at me all you want later, Sage. Right now
she needs help. And you need to calm down."

"I'm calm," she said, and seemed to be. "I can help her."

"What do we do?"

"*We* don't do anything. *You* get the fuck out of my way."

I let go of her arm, turned to step out of her way, and saw
her son watching us from across the room.

He was smiling with delight.

Sage hurried to the table, bent and got her arms around

Miranda and somehow got her to her feet and held her like a child. She seemed to be talking to her, softly.

As I came near, I realized that Sage was singing to her. I recognized the song, a nursery rhyme my grandmother had sometimes put me to bed with:

> *Ride on your pony, child*
> *Ride all the way*
> *Ride through the mountain to the end of the day*
> *Ride through the desert to the end of the night*
> *Ride on your pony, child*
> *And all will be right.*

Fiercely refusing my help, Sage got Miranda into the house, into a bedroom. She shut the door.

I found the bar and stepped behind it and found the Scotch.

Sage's son sprawled on a couch watching an ill-made cartoon in which massively muscled warrior types jerkily slaughtered first nightmarish monsters and then one another.

At the end of the show, the boy sat up, turned, propped his head on the back of the couch. "You ever kill anybody?"

"Yes."

"Was it fun?"

"No."

He didn't believe that. "Are you a cop?"

"No."

"My mom's boyfriend used to be a cop. He killed some guys."

"Did he think it was fun?"

"He says he never killed a guy who didn't need it."

The boy seemed to think that summed up everything. I thought of weary Carlene Stiles and her reading of the lessons of life.

"Just goes to show you."

While he was thinking that over, his mother came out of the bedroom, saw me, shut the door, strode over, saw my drink, slipped onto a stool in front of me. "I could use one of those."

I fixed her a drink. She took it, swallowed deeply. "I thought you'd be gone. "

"I thought you might want to yell at me some more."

She looked at me, then into her glass. "I always seem to end up doing that, don't I."

"How is she?"

She tried to smile. "She's . . . all right."

"It's happened before?"

She nodded. "It isn't . . . serious, Jack. It's just certain things make her remember . . . certain other things."

"What things?"

She looked away. "Horrible things."

"What things, Sage?"

"What does it matter? What business is it of yours?" But she wasn't angry. She was just looking for a reason to tell me.

"I don't know. I can't know unless I know what they are."

She shook her head. "They happened a long time ago, Jack. They have nothing to do with what you're doing."

"That isn't true, Sage. It never is."

Especially in this case. It was the reason Miranda hated men and the desert and Nevada and herself. It was the reason she got shot and Dalton James got killed.

She drained her glass, pushed it toward me. I looked at it, at her, left it there.

She turned and called to her son. "Honey, why don't you go to your room to watch that?"

His face rose slowly up from behind the back of the couch. He stared at her. Then he turned and slowly sank out of sight. The volume of the television increased.

"He . . . needs a father." She looked at me, looked away.

The boy needed more than that, but I didn't say so. I didn't say anything.

"Did Miranda tell you about . . . her father?"

"Which one?" Charley Santee, the man she'd thought was her father when she was a child? Cletus James, the man she thought was her father now?

"Her adoptive father."

"She said he died in the desert, alone. That he fell off a ledge and broke his legs."

"He wasn't alone," she said quietly.

I waited.

"They were rock-hunting, they were out on a ledge. She says she looked down and thought that all she had to do was step off and she would kill herself and it would be over. She says . . . she says she decided to. She was going to just step off and kill herself. Then, somehow, it was him that was falling. She didn't even know she'd pushed him until she heard him scream."

I didn't ask why. I didn't want to know. I already knew.

"He had been . . . abusing her. For years, since she was just a . . . she was five when it started."

It was, as Sage had said, horrible. But it was only one of the horrors visited upon Miranda Santee.

She wouldn't know one of the other horrors, at least not from me. I wasn't going to be the one who told her that the man who raped her in Las Vegas was her biological father.

Sage looked at me, telling me why she had told me the story. Like Wes James, she wanted to know if it could be true. She wanted me to tell her it couldn't.

I couldn't tell her that. Instead I asked her a question. "Do you think you're up to it, Sage?"

"Helping her, you mean?" She started to shake her head, stopped. She started to nod, stopped.

"I don't know. I—we've talked about her seeing a doctor. She doesn't want to, and I don't know that it would do any good. She just needs somebody to listen. I can do that."

"Does she know that you got her her new job?"

"I—what makes you think that? She . . ."

"What was it, advertising? You giving the station a bigger slice of your budget?"

She nodded, slowly. "Is that bad, Jack? Is there something wrong with helping someone who needs it, helping a friend?"

"No," I said. "I'm just wondering why."

"Stop wondering. It's because of you."

I didn't respond.

"You don't know what you did to me the other morning, do you? When you left?"

"What did I do?"

"You left me alone."

I didn't say anything.

"I mean *alone*, Jack. Completely alone. I—I don't know how to describe it without sounding . . . It was the worst feeling I've ever had, feeling that alone. I finally realized that it wasn't your fault, it was mine. And I decided that I'd do whatever I had to to make sure I was never that alone again."

I didn't know what to say. At my silence, she said something else. "I'm sorry it didn't work out, Jack."

"So am I."

"You—I thought it might. You were one of only two men I ever met who wasn't afraid of me."

I nodded. "Tom Pardun is the other."

She smiled, faintly, fondly. "It's funny, Jack, the way you two dislike each other. Do you know why?"

I knew what she was going to say. I also knew she was wrong, as wrong as she'd been in saying that I wasn't afraid of her.

"You're the same kind of men. You're alike."

"How did it happen, Sage, that Tom got picked to take over the gaming end of the business? With so little experience."

She nodded. "That's what I asked Dad. He told me that what the job needed wasn't so much a man with experience or knowledge as with character. Somebody who wouldn't blink. Somebody who would make the hard decisions, the hard choices."

"Like Tom."

She smiled. "Or you. But you weren't available."

I finished my drink and came around the bar. "I've got to go. Tell Miranda I'm sorry."

She walked me to the door. "Good-bye, Jack."

"Good-bye. I—will you promise me something, Sage?"

She frowned. "I—if I can."

"Never enter into a business deal with Marci Howe."

For a moment she seemed stunned. Then she smiled. "That surprises me, Jack, coming from you. I know about Marci and Natty Stern. But that's past. He's an anachronism, a tourist attraction. I—I didn't think you could be that naive."

I could tell her a story and it would be true and she wouldn't believe it. "One of us is naive, Sage," I said instead.

"You think I am, but I'm not. I'm a businesswoman. I can't make decisions based on gossip and rumor and fairy tale. I have to live in the real world."

And I was a private investigator, and the world I lived in was nothing but gossip and rumor and fairy tale.

"Good-bye, Sage," I said.
She smiled, gave the Nevada benediction. "Good luck."

I drove back to my house, loaded up the Wagoneer, and
drove out of Reno, into the gathering night, into the interior
of Nevada.

31

In the darkness I could sense the softening that spring had brought briefly to the land. The shadows were deeper, fuller, textured in the starlight. The scent of sage sweetened the night.

I couldn't sense anyone following me, but it didn't really matter. If I was being followed, that meant I could end things. If I wasn't, that meant things were already over.

I stopped at Tonopah, spent the night, had breakfast and gassed up and drove out of town.

What I had sensed in the darkness I could see in the daylight. The desert pastels were fresher, cleaner. Tiny flowers scattered spots of color through the deeper desert tan. The sage tips shimmered gray-green in the sunlight, playa and salt flat puddled, bunch grass greened, cheat grass waved soft yellow and pale lavender and brought Sage Chandler into my mind.

The mountains still glittered with snow at their crests, rose so hugely in the silence that they seemed to speak.

The mud flat at Chokecherry was a suck of gumbo and goo.

Everything at Chokeberry looked the same. Everything but the corral beside the mobile home. The corral was empty.

As I stepped inside, Renata again bounced cheerfully in from the bar. When she saw me, her smile skipped a beat. "Mr. Ross?"

"I came to apologize. Is he all right?"

Her cheer picked up where it had left off. "He's fine."

"I'm sorry about the horse."

"That hurt him most. But he's too old to be gallivanting around the country on a horse anyhow. Almost like doing him a favor."

"Almost," I said. "But not quite."

She nodded. "It seems you took care of that little matter, if what we see on the TV is true."

"As true as anything else on TV."

"Yep." Her cheer radiated like the warmth of the sun. "He's in there, be real insulted if you don't say hello."

The old man was standing watch over his glass of beer. As I came in he began to grin. "Forgot to duck again, I hear. A man don't duck's in for a life of hurt. Got it comin', too."

"How are you, Mr. Stillwell?"

"Just dandy." His teeth clacked. "Can understand why you didn't duck, what with the feminine distractions. Sounds like you got what ailed ol' Single John."

"Maybe," I said. "They weren't too hard on you?"

He grinned again. "Hey, what was he gonna do? I told him us old guys break awful easy. We're like horses, bust something and you have to shoot us."

"Speaking of horses, I owe you one."

"Speaking of shooting, I figger we're even."

"I didn't kill him, Mr. Stillwell."

He clacked his teeth, checked his beer. "He's still dead, son. That's all that matters."

I told him where I was going, told him that if anybody asked he should tell them where I was.

"Big doin's on the mountain, is there?"

"Big enough."

"You gonna tell me what it's about?"

"Better you don't know, Mr. Stillwell."

"Somebody gonna get killed?"

"What makes you think that?"

He clacked his teeth, looked at me. "You're coming from Reno, I know. But you got the look of the desert on you."

"That means somebody's going to get killed?"

He grinned. "Usually does, yeah."

An hour later I pulled into the muddy yard at the Smith ranch. The horses were still in the corral, but the meadow was empty. George Smith was draped over the radiator of a huge stock truck, vanished to the waist in the motor. His brother stood below and behind him, shifting from foot to foot in the mud.

I walked over, catching on the soft breeze the smell of sage and juniper and the incantatory chant of George's obscenities.

Leo watched me with uncertainty, tugged silently at his brother's pant leg.

With a fresh fierce spew of obscene rage, George drew himself out of the motor. Grease smeared the bright orange of his down vest, the pale flesh of his thick forearms.

He saw me and bit off his anger. His face became a rough stubbled ball of gray. "Had a feeling we wasn't shuck of you."

He rubbed at a spot of grease on his cheek. Then he shoved his hands deep into his back pockets, as if to remove them from temptation. "What do you want?"

"I want to end it, George."

He looked past me, up the dark mountain. His brother looked too, seemed surprised to see nothing but what was there.

"Yeah," George said finally. He turned to his brother. "Leo, we ain't gonna get this thing going today. Might as well go watch one of your stories."

Leo smiled in delight. Something in the smile reminded me of the photograph of his brother, Single John.

"Yeah." He hurried off across the muddy yard.

George watched until Leo had pulled himself up over the threshold and into the house. Then he turned to me. "How?"

I told him what I planned to do, and what I expected other people would do, and what I expected would happen.

I told him why I expected it. I told him everything I knew.

He listened attentively, his rage freshening, swelling.

"Goddamn sons a bitches. You want help?"

"I'd like to leave my rig here, if we can get it out of sight. Can a car make it up there this time of year?"

"In a rig like yours. The road ain't much, muddy in spots, but if you're careful . . . yeah."

"When they come, tell them how to get up there."

He looked down the muddy road to the house, to the dirt road, along it toward the highway and Chokecherry thirty miles away.

"When you figure?"

"Tomorrow. Maybe the next day."

"Goddamn sons a bitches. You sure you don't want help?"

I did want help. But I didn't want anyone killed who didn't have to be. I shook my head. "Don't try to stop them, George."

He nodded, seemed to be waiting for me to tell him something else. When I didn't, he looked past me to his empty meadow, to the horses in the corral, to his house, back to the horses.

"You talk to the Basco, Jim?"

I nodded.

"All that gonna come out?"

"Not if it doesn't have to. But a lot of what's going to happen I'll have no control over."

He nodded. "Don't matter much anymore, I guess. Not to Mabel, for sure. What do you suppose the sheriff'll do to me?"

"Nothing."

"I—it's just about Leo. I'm all he's got. This place's all he knows."

"I wouldn't worry about it, George."

But he would. That's what his life was about.

We hid the Wagoneer in the old barn. As I was unloading, I heard the roaring of an engine and the harsh hard clashing of gears in the yard. I came out to find George tearing up the muddy yard with the hard-knobbed tires of a pickup, wiping out the tracks of the Wagoneer.

He got out and looked me over—knapsack stuffed with dried food, two canteens of water, sleeping bag. The weight of the Smith & Wesson tugged down my jacket pocket. The weight of the .30.30 tugged, faintly, comfortingly, at my arm.

"You want a horse?"

"No, thanks."

"Make the climb a little easier, wouldn't be—"

"I wouldn't want to be responsible for what might happen to it."

"They're good horses. But that's all they are. Horses."

I shook my head, then held out my hand. For a moment he stared down at it, uncertain of what to do.

Then he took it. "Kill them sons a bitches once for me, will you?"

32 _____

The mountain was alive.

Buds spread, leaves shimmered. Pine and juniper scented the air with new growth. Mountain flowers whose names I didn't know—white, blue, orange, red—seemed to glow in the sunlight.

The mountain was silent.

In that silence songbirds sang their challenge, a squirrel scurried, a distant woodpecker drummed, an even more distant cow lowed for her missing calf.

Above it all a hawk swooped in its deadly circle.

From the ridge, I looked back. Nothing in the ranch yard but what should be there. Nothing on the road. No wisp of dust for as far as I could see.

Down in the aspen grove, leaves shuddered green to silver, blurred the lines and shapes of the tree limbs. It looked like any other aspen grove.

I stayed on the ridge, followed it up the mountain.

The juniper thinned, twisted into strange shapes as it sought water, sunlight, purchase on the earth. The ground grew rougher, the climbing more difficult. Soon I was sweating under my pack, breathing hard.

After half an hour, I stopped to rest. I looked back, and out, and could see, it seemed, forever.

Desert and mountains, ranges rising in a bluish haze like dark waves from a drab sea of earth. The Chokecherry mud flat glistened in the light. The foothills buckled up smoothly, took on a fur of grasses and brush, a stubble of pine and juniper.

I had a sudden sense that I was the only living human being on the mountain. In the universe. It was the same sense Sage Chandler had had when I left her in her dark bed. Unlike Sage, I took comfort from it.

I resumed my climb. After another half hour the ridge crested, the land dipped, broke into a series of narrow rocky washes choked with brush and sage and juniper.

I was a quarter mile away and a hundred yards above the Madigan place. In the bright sunlight and still silence, the ranch looked abandoned, a ghost ranch.

Without its cover of snow, the meadow looked in worse shape—posts down, rusted wire curling here and there toward the sky, old irrigation ditches silted up and thick with weeds, grasses struggling to grow in scattered patches, sage and juniper seedlings advancing toward the small willow-choked spring.

Directly below me, near a clump of old junipers, barbed wire on steel posts blocked a space for a few small marble headstones.

There was no sign of life at the house. It looked, in its weather-worn darkness, as if no one had lived in it for years.

Perhaps Belle Smith wasn't there. That would be good. One less person who might get killed.

I sat and listened to the silence of the mountain and heard everything in it. I didn't hear what I was listening for.

I'd planned to climb around and up onto the low escarpment behind the house. But I was as well off where I was. I could see the meadow, and hear well beyond it. I was too far away for the .30.30, but a deer trail wandered down to the clump of juniper near the graves. I could reach it quickly, fire from it unseen.

I shucked off my pack, spread my bag over a bed of needles beneath a stunted pine, found a rock and sat and watched and listened and waited.

Sunlight, starlight.

No light shone at the windows of the house to ward off the darkness, no smoke rose from the chimney.

I spent the night in the sweet cold air, watching the whirl of the stars and listening to the song of the mountain.

* * *

At mid-morning the mountain silence sang complex harmonies. In the still air sounds carried, mingled, shaped
themselves into patterns of nuance, suggestion, promise.

And then a sound not of the pattern, faint at first, then
slowly swelling—the high growling whine, rising and falling like the contours of the land, of a laboring engine.

Grabbing the .30.30, I half-ran, half-slid down the needle-
slick hillside, slipped behind the junipers, propped the rifle
barrel in the crook of a limb and led the sound and aimed
the rifle at the emptiness where the vehicle would appear.

And stood stunned and angry and confused as the
rainbow-striped nose of Miranda Santee's Bronco eased
over the hump.

I didn't know what her being there meant. I didn't know
what to do about it. So I did nothing.

Miranda stopped the Bronco, climbed out, for a long time
looked at the house, as if waiting for something to happen.

Finally she opened the back of the Bronco and tugged out
a video camera, hauled it up onto her shoulder, and panned
across the meadow, lingering at the spring, the house, the
graveyard.

Slowly she moved toward the house, adjusting the focus,
panning back and forth over the land and the buildings of
the Madigan place. At the door she stopped, lowered the
camera, stared at the ground, the chopping block. She
straightened suddenly, as if straining after a sound. She set
the camera beside the door and opened it and stepped
inside and closed it.

I waited, watched the door, listened to the mountain.

After a while a thin wisp of smoke twisted up out of the
chimney. Then nothing. Finally I stepped into the meadow
and walked toward the house.

The marble stones in the graveyard were old, chipped,
wind- and water-worn, their lettering indecipherable.

Before the door the ruts cut by the barrow had been
smoothed by wind and feet to small rolling ridges. Over
them lay another trail, pools of darkness soaked into the
earth, smeared, as if by a wounded animal crawling to a
private death.

The trail began at the chopping block. On it stood a length
of pine as thick as my waist. An ax had driven into it, sliced

through the wood and struck a railroad spike buried in its pulpy flesh, sliced out on an angle, sliced into human flesh.

The ax lay beside the block, specks of rust eating at its bright edge, spatters of blood stiff on its thin blade.

I leaned the .30.30 against the wall beside Miranda's camera, opened the door, and stepped inside.

The room was cold, dim, foul with the rank of rotting flesh.

Belle Smith lay on the cot under a blanket. Her face was as blanched, her skin as stiff and rough as aspen bark. Her eyes were open, glazed with shock, saw nothing.

Miranda sat beside her on one of the wooden chairs, her own face slick with tears, her own eyes dark with grief. Her smooth pale hands held one of her grandmother's rough dark hands.

"Miranda, are you all right?"

"I'm all right," she said, and the slow low steadiness of her voice seemed to confirm it.

"I've tried to get her to eat, but . . . I was going to go back down and call for a doctor, but she . . ." She looked at the three hands in her lap. "She won't let me."

Belle was clinging, with what little strength was left in her body, to Miranda's hand.

Belle didn't want to die alone.

"Please, Jack, go for help. The keys are in the Bronco."

"It's too late." I stepped closer. "Where did it get her?"

"In the leg. It's . . . please, go call."

I lifted the edge of the blanket, waited till the wave of stench and my sudden nausea passed.

Miranda had cut away the pant leg, exposed the deep slash in the lower thigh, the jagged jut of the broken bone, the gray ugly distorted gangrenous flesh.

There was little fresh blood, mostly because there couldn't be much left. The cot was soaked with it.

"Please, Jack?"

I looked at Belle Smith. She looked vacantly at the window. I'd seen that look before, too many times.

"I'll go if you want me to, Miranda. But it won't matter."

She nodded. "I know. But we've got to try."

"Are you sure you'll be all right?"

"I'll be okay," she said quietly. "I've done this before."

*   *   *

I went outside, sucked up sweet mountain air, thought about Miranda's calm, about the curves and spirals of fate.

I went to the Bronco, fired it up and turned it around, nudged it toward the hump in the land at the top of the draw.

The Bronco had churned deep ragged ruts in the damp earth in the center of the draw, dodged mudslicks and small patches of shaded snow. That she'd made it to the meadow spoke to Miranda's skill, but it was going to make the trip down a little tricky.

As I was about to ease the tires into the ruts, movement tugged my eyes to the low rocky ridge above the aspen grove.

A horse in hard flight clambered over the crest, jumped and scrambled and crashed down the hillside.

It was George Smith's gray gelding.

At the aspen grove he swerved and started up the draw, saw the Bronco at the top and stopped, turned, reared, his front legs flailing at air. A back leg slipped. With a squeal of pain that cut through the mountain silence like a blade, he went down.

He started to get up, couldn't.

He struggled violently, frantically. Finally he managed to pull himself up onto three legs. The other leg dangled, angled abnormally below the knee.

Then he just stood there, his head drooping as if in despair, as if he knew what it meant.

There was more movement on the ridge. A man appeared at the crest. As the gelding had, he threw himself down the hillside, arms flailing at brush and limb, stumbling, running.

He ran into the aspen grove and didn't come out.

Leo Smith wasn't running after the horse. He and the horse were running from the same thing.

33

I put the Bronco back where Miranda had left it, got out and jogged to the house, grabbed the .30.30, went inside.

Belle Smith's eyes were open and empty, Miranda's wide and full. "Why are you—"

"We're about to have company. You didn't happen to bring your little pistol, did you?"

She glanced at her coat pocket. "I always do, when I come out . . . here. Alone."

"You may need it. You'll hear shots. Don't panic. Stay away from the window. If the door opens, shoot whoever comes in."

"I—who is it?"

"Our pals from Vegas."

"Why are they here?"

"To finish what that ax blade started."

"But—how did they know?"

"They followed one of us. It doesn't much matter which one of us, does it?"

"But—"

"No buts, Miranda. Stay inside. If anyone comes in, shoot him. If you don't, you'll die."

I left her with her questions and her dying grandmother.

As I stepped outside I heard the sound of a large laboring engine, faint but clear in the thin air, softened by distance into a tuneless hum.

I hurried across the meadow to the juniper blind, ducked in behind it, waited, listened. The sound of the engine swelled, ebbed, swelled. Tires whined in a muddy spin. Sage cracked. Metal scraped bark.

The engine slowed, steadied, then revved in rhythm to an apprehensive foot on the accelerator. The sounds took on an added resonance, a richness that told me they'd started up the draw.

The engine raced, slowed. A horn blasted a long steady blast like a scream of rage. The engine wound itself into a shriek that was soon drowned out by the scream of tires.

Then suddenly, as if the machine had died, the mountain again was silent.

I heard a reedy angry voice, the thunk of a slamming car door, a string of human sounds that could only have been curses.

Then silence. Then the boom of a large-caliber gun. I found myself out of the juniper blind, scuttling fast and low toward the crest of the draw.

The gun fired again. Dropping to my knees I crawled until I could see.

Two hundred yards up the draw from the aspen grove, the long gold Mercedes leaned with the slope, a rear wheel axle-deep in the soft hillside. The driver had tried to swerve around the gray gelding and hadn't made it.

The horse lay on his side a few feet from the car. It didn't move. Even at that distance I could see that half its head was missing.

Hiram Vanca stood over it, in a jumpsuit as white as the bark of the aspen trees. As I watched, he fired again. And again. Shooting a dead horse.

Apprentice leaned against the driver's open door, his hands in the pockets of his jacket, watching. A shape I assumed to be Goon sat in the front seat. Another shape I couldn't identify sat behind him.

I backed away, crawled, walked back to the blind. There was no hurry. They'd be walking up. That would make it easier.

Another door slammed shut. Faint voices, then silence.

I picked out a sturdy limb, set the barrel of the .30.30 across it, sighted toward the low knoll at the head of the draw.

I had a nice window to shoot through, large enough to cover the meadow from the draw to Miranda's Bronco, small enough that I couldn't be detected. I waited, listened.

Silence. Voices. A high reedy cry like a curse.

The top of a blond head appeared. Apprentice's head slowly swiveled to scan the meadow, the large dark gun in his hand moving as if tied with invisible thread to his eyes. His eyes and the pistol fixed on Miranda's Bronco.

Goon appeared, with a large dark gun in his hand. At the sight of the Bronco, he dropped to a squat, called, "Wait."

He signaled with his pistol. Apprentice slowly moved toward the Bronco. Then he stopped, pointed his pistol at various spots on the rainbow-striped mass of metal as if performing some ancient rite of exorcism.

Goon stood up. "Okay."

I laid my cheek against the rifle stock, nudged the front sight to a spot between where the two men had appeared, waited.

Two heads appeared. One seemed a skull. Only the buckskin-colored hair, and a certain familiar hooker's holding of her body even as it stumbled forward under the force of Vanca's hand, told me it was Linda Goshgarian.

She wore white sneakers and jeans and a light-blue jacket, like a housewife off to fetch kids. Between jacket and hair, her face was a wide swath of white tape across the bridge of her nose, dark eyes enlarged by dark and brutally bruised flesh so that they seemed skull-like holes.

Vanca shoved her again, stopped, bent to catch his breath.

His white jumpsuit, gold zipper pull, gold chain at his throat, all gleamed in the sunlight. His patch gave him one eye like Linda Goshgarian's two. His face was dark from the climb, but still white enough.

He straightened up, started toward the Bronco. He too had a large dark gun in his hand.

I put the bead of the front sight on his forehead, adjusted until the bead settled into the crook of the back sight.

The world reduced to a dark metal bead on white flesh.

He was thirty yards away. He was a dead man. I wrapped my finger around the trigger and got ready to squeeze.

I couldn't.

For a moment I couldn't do anything.

Then, because I had to do something, I did something totally insane.

I lifted the rifle from the limb, stepped out from behind the junipers, stepped into the meadow, and shouted. "Vanca!"

The still, silent mountain meadow exploded in thunderous movement.

Apprentice wheeled in a crouch and he fired and I fired and he wheeled up out of the crouch, his arm soaring up over his head as if in a ballet pirouette, and his large dark gun spun flatly down and hit the ground just before he did.

Vanca had a handful of Linda Goshgarian's hair and was dragging her toward the Bronco as he fired over her shoulder.

Goon was in a shooter's squat, his elbow steadied on his knee, forearm steadied by his left hand, the .45 like a third eye focused on the center of my chest.

I was a dead man. I knew it. He knew it. He knew I knew it.

His face exploded, disappeared, became a bloody maw with dead eyes, and the sharp distinctive crack of a rifle cut through the booming echoes of Hiram Vanca's fire.

I dived, rolled, scuttled behind a scruffy sage, tried to find Vanca with the end of my rifle.

The echoes dissipated, yet the sound of gunfire seemed still to mingle with the silence as the scent of it stained the air.

The door to the ranch house hadn't opened.

Vanca was behind the Bronco. He had Linda. I could see her ankles, her white-sneakered feet. Then I heard him, his high reedy jaylike screech. "You wanna play, asshole?"

Linda's feet jerked suddenly. Her body jerked stiffly from behind the Bronco. Vanca's gun rested on her shoulder, an inch from her ear. He huddled behind her.

For a moment nothing in the meadow moved. Then her head jerked. Slowly he backed her toward the ranch house.

He didn't fire. At that distance, hitting me would be pure luck.

He didn't seem to know that there was another rifle on the mountain. I was alive only because George Smith had refused to do what I'd told him to.

I tried to figure out where he was. I couldn't remember the exact angle of Goon's head, didn't know the angle the slug took.

It didn't matter. He couldn't get a clean shot at Vanca

either. Whatever the size of his rage, he wasn't going to take a chance on killing a woman. Men like George Smith didn't.

When Vanca was fifty yards from the ranch house, I leapt up and ran to the Bronco. He didn't stop, didn't bother to fire. I tried to put the bead back on him. I couldn't get past Linda Goshgarian. I put the bead on her forehead, bone-white with pain or fear. Her eyes and mouth were black holes.

Slowly they backed toward the house, the door.

There were only two chances that Miranda would come out of this alive. If Vanca was going in firing, he'd have to toss Linda out of the way. If he did, I'd have a shot. If he tried to back in with Linda, Miranda would have a shot. If she was able to do what I'd told her to.

I didn't think much of either chance.

They reached the door. The dark gun in his hand wavered. His free hand felt for the handle of the door.

Suddenly Linda threw herself toward the chopping block. I fired. Vanca spun toward the door and the door opened and he lurched through it and a shot fired and he slowed and another shot fired and his gun fell from his hand and he stopped.

I fired and knew I'd missed and then knew it didn't matter.

Slowly Vanca backed out the door, a spreading stain at the top of his shoulder, his hands holding his middle.

He stumbled, turning as he fell, hit the side of the house and slid down it, his hands still at his middle, clawing at the splotches of red that stained the white jumpsuit.

For a moment, again nothing moved in the mountain meadow.

Then I got up and started toward the house. Slowly Linda Goshgarian struggled to her feet. From her jacket pocket she took a small silver pistol.

She turned toward me. I stopped, tensed. I was still twenty yards away. She'd have to be very good or very lucky to get me with one shot. She wouldn't have time for another.

"Drop the rifle." Her voice was hard, harsh. Yet something in it told me she wasn't preparing to shoot me.

I let the .30.30 fall to the ground.

With the toylike gun, she directed me toward the chopping block. Then she backed away from me, over to Hiram Vanca.

Blood seeped slowly from under his stained hands, ad-

vanced down his white abdomen like the stain of fall down
a mountain. His face was flushed and damp, his single eye
wild. "Shoot the mother-fucker!" His reedy voice was dry
with pain and rage.

She looked at him.

His eye went wilder, moved in its socket like an enraged
animal trying to escape a cage. "You fucking bitch! Shoot
him!"

She looked at him.

Miranda appeared in the door, her own small gun hanging at her side. I slipped my hand into my jacket pocket and
found the Smith & Wesson, fit my hand around the butt, my
finger around the trigger.

"Shoot him, you fucking whore! Shoot!"

She shot.

He screamed as the gelding had. His eyes closed, opened
in agony and rage. A small splash of blood appeared at the
crotch of his white jumpsuit.

She shot again. Now his scream was weaker, scratchy,
half moan. Another small splash of blood stained his white
crotch.

She fired again. One of his hands jerked bloodily. The
other clawed across his stomach toward it.

She fired again. The clawing hand jerked, flopped bloodily. He made a sound that was low, soft, not quite human.

I knew I should probably stop her. I didn't.

Miranda stood in the doorway, watching.

Linda took a step forward, knelt in the dirt beside Hiram
Vanca, raised the little silver pistol up to his eye.

"Can you see it, Hiram?"

His eye had stopped its erratic movement. Its brightness
dimmed, swelled, dimmed, like sunlight in a sky of storm-
driven clouds.

"Can you see it? I want you to see it. I want you to know."

His lips moved. He might have been trying to speak.

Miranda Santee spoke. "Let me."

Linda Goshgarian didn't look up. "No."

"Please."

"No. I know what he did to you. But you don't know what
he did to my mother, my father, what he's been doing to me
for thirty years."

Miranda looked at her. "All right," she said, giving her mother permission to kill her father.

Echo Smith brought the end of the barrel of the silver gun up an inch away from Hiram Vanca's quivering eyes.

"Look, Hiram. Look."

She pulled the trigger.

34

From the wild beyond the meadow, a mountain bluebird burst into song.

Echo Smith rose, Vanca's blood spotting her cheek, chin. She turned to her daughter, who stood in the doorway staring at her. "Is she all right?"

"She's dead," Miranda said quietly.

The mountain silence swelled. Miranda stepped out the door, past her mother and the body of her father, walked slowly into the meadow. Echo Smith and her little silver pistol turned on me.

Up close, her face looked worse, not dead and skull-like but alive and battered and ugly, a vessel of pain. "Let's see if I can do it right this time."

"You don't want to do that, Echo."

"Yes, I do. And my name's Linda."

"The one you use now. I've never known a woman in the life who didn't have a few. But you were born Echo Smith."

"You don't know that. You're guessing."

But I did know it. What she'd said about her mother and father and Hiram Vanca had told me. And something else. I'd remembered what I'd remembered. "You've got your father's smile."

"And you're full of shit. But not for long."

"You can't kill us all, Echo."

"I can kill you," she said evenly.

"Maybe," I said. "But if you try, probably I get you too. And even if you do kill me, you can't kill everybody. Your daughter. And George Smith, your uncle. And your uncle Leo."

"Daughter," she said slowly, as if trying out a new word in a new language. Her eyes, voice got strange. "I can kill anybody I want to. It doesn't matter now. She's dead. I'm dead too."

"Not necessarily."

She almost smiled. "You and that gun in your pocket, Marci Howe and a contract, the little needle up in Carson City, one way or the other I'm dead."

The bluebird sang again.

"One way or another, we're all dead," I said. "But not now."

She looked at the dark open doorway to the house. Her body seemed to lean toward it, as if in yearning, but her feet didn't move. "How did my mother die?"

I told her, and watched for some sign of feeling in her eyes, her battered masklike face. I didn't see any.

"What about . . . my grandmother?"

She didn't know how her grandmother had died. I wasn't going to tell her. "She's been dead for years."

A fly droned, settled on Vanca's black eye patch, wandered over his nose, found the gory hole that had been his eye.

"Everybody's dead," she said strangely.

Echo Smith was sinking into the muddy suck of a despair the depths of which I couldn't imagine. I could hear the sinking in her voice, see the power of the downward pull on the swollen flesh of her face. "What do you want, Ross?"

Still, she was talking. Not so much talking as thrashing after hope.

"Tell me why you killed Dalton James."

She looked again at the dark doorway. She turned and looked out to the meadow, where Miranda wandered among the bodies.

A bit of bright orange flashed through the trees by the graveyard. George Smith stepped into the meadow, a rifle in his hand. Something was wrong with his face. He looked at us, at the Bronco, at Miranda, then walked toward her.

"Why, Echo?" I asked again.

"Dalton was going to kill Miranda if she didn't tell him where my mother was. He—he was crazy. Besides, he might have gotten lucky and found out where . . ."

"Why was he looking for Belle in the first place?"

"He had this deal with Natty—"

"No."

Her hand tightened on the toy pistol. "All right. So what? He was going to muck around in it anyhow, and turn her over to Natty if he found her. I made a deal with him, let him think we . . . It was the only way I could keep tabs—"

A rifle exploded, sending sound reverberating through the silence of the mountain.

In the meadow, George Smith and Miranda Santee stood over the body of Apprentice. George lowered the rifle from his shoulder. Miranda gently touched his face, took his arm, led him toward the Bronco.

"I still don't understand why Dalton tried to kill Miranda," I said.

Echo continued to look at her daughter. "Dalton was nothing, a loser, a nobody, and he knew it. He was like his father, he tried to blame the world and everybody in it for his stupidity and bad luck. He thought Miranda was his sister, that Cletus was her father. It drove him crazy that she was pretty and smart, everything he wasn't. She was—everything he might have been but never would be."

Then she smiled, that same hard proud hooker's smile she'd given me in the brothel. "He was what I made sure my daughter wouldn't be when I gave her away."

She didn't know what she had given her daughter away to. I wasn't going to be the one to tell her. "So you killed him."

Her smile disappeared. "Better him than her."

"And you killed Cletus."

Her laugh was brief, bitter. "Cletus killed himself."

"Why?"

"How should I know? He probably thought Natty'd killed Dalton and was coming after him. I don't know. Who cares?"

"You don't?"

She laughed again. "Why should I? Who do you suppose it was that turned me out, Ross? When he couldn't play anymore. Who made me turn a trick when I was eight months pregnant. Who put me on the streets and then couldn't take care of me."

"You didn't have to do it."

She looked at me with that perfect hooker's hatred. "Easy for you to say. You don't know anything about it. You don't know anything about anything. You're too stupid to be alive."

"Probably," I said. "I'm so stupid I might even understand why you've stuck with Hiram for thirty years, in spite of the beatings and God knows what else. He keeps you close, in case Belle gets in touch. You keep him close, in case he happens to find out where she is."

"Real symbiotic, isn't it?"

"Symbiotic" was a word she'd picked up somewhere. It didn't explain anything. She knew it, used it bitterly, mocking herself.

She looked again at the dark doorway. "I've been thinking about this for thirty years. Now I don't even want to go in."

"You must have loved her very much."

"She . . ." Echo's voice broke. She tried to fix it, but she couldn't. "She did it for me. All of it, for me and . . . When she found out what he'd been doing to me, she kept putting herself in his way. She took the beatings, the . . . she finally tried to kill him, to get him to leave me alone."

I didn't know if that last was true. Or at least all the truth. But it didn't matter.

"Why didn't you kill him before, Echo? You must have had chances, over thirty years."

She looked down at the body. Her hand, and the little pistol, dropped. "I almost did, a couple of times. But if I killed Hiram, Natty would kill me. Then who'd . . ."

"Protect Belle. The way she tried to protect you."

It made a twisted sense. But not enough. "Why else?"

When she spoke, it was in a voice I hadn't heard from her before, soft, quiet. "You wouldn't understand."

"Maybe not," I said.

But maybe, although I doubted I'd ever be able to explain it, maybe I did. Maybe "symbiotic" was the right word after all.

Miranda and George were at the Bronco. The back was open, and he sat on the tailgate while she dabbed at his face with something white.

"Come on, Ross. Let's get it over with."

She had the toy pistol pointed at my middle.

"Why did you shoot me in Reno? And then save me?"

"Show time." She laughed again, her hard bitter grating hooker's laugh. "You knew where my mother was. If I could get it out of you, so could they. Then those bozos show up. What a farce! I wasn't trying to save you. I just needed a reason to be next to you, to switch the guns."

"Why was the ghost after me?"

Her laugh grew more bitter. "Not you, me. Me. Marci Howe didn't send me, I was on my own. I had to find out what you knew. They thought . . . I was trying to queer the deal."

I followed it, sort of. "Why didn't they kill you later?"

"Too soon. The Silver Sage had enough sleaze publicity. They didn't want any more, especially a hooker's hit. I could be connected with Vanca, and to Natty. They don't want that."

I thought about it. "They're moving in?"

"They're trying. It's not a done deal, but it's close."

"Does Sage Chandler know?"

She gave me a hooker's hard appraisal. "What difference does it make?"

"She's a friend of mine."

She continued to look at me. "She knows what she wants to know, Ross. Just like anybody else. It's all right in front of her. If she doesn't see it, it's because she doesn't want to."

The back of the Bronco slammed shut, the distant disturbance sending a small cloud of flies into brief flutter above Vanca's eye. Quickly they resettled.

Miranda and George Smith started toward the house.

Echo Smith waved her little gun at me. "Show time, Ross."

I took my hand out of my pocket. Empty.

"You want to shoot me in cold blood, Echo, in front of your daughter and your father's brother?"

She looked at me. Then, slowly, her eyes, her look changed, spoke of a desolation as bleak and barren as the most desolate of deserts, where all hope was gone, all promises betrayed.

She lifted the toy gun to her temple.

"You can do that too," I said, "and give your daughter one more wonderful memory. Or we can make a deal."

She looked at me, at Miranda and George. They'd stopped twenty yards away, stood quiet and still. Everything on the mountain seemed to have stopped, gone quiet and still.

Her gaze fixed on Miranda Santee. "What deal?" What hope?

"Go to Vegas and explain to Cleo James why her son died."

The pistol flashed in the sunlight, wavered, lowered. "That's all? And then what?"

"Then it's up to her."

"And what do you do?"

"I don't do anything."

"That's stupid, Ross. I could kill her too."

"That's right," I said.

She didn't, couldn't quite believe it. "But . . . why?"

I shrugged. "I don't know. Why not?"

Her voice was barely a whisper. "You're crazy, Ross."

"I know."

The whisper softened. "You're as crazy as your grandfather."

"How crazy was that, Echo?"

But I already knew.

35

Echo Smith put the little silver pistol into her jacket pocket. She looked at the dark doorway. She turned to me and almost smiled. Then she stepped inside.

Miranda and George came over. Miranda looked at the dark doorway. "Is she all right?"

"Hard to say."

"Is she . . . my mother?"

"Why don't you ask her?"

Miranda tried to smile, couldn't. She stepped inside.

George didn't try to smile. The left side of his face was swollen and bruising up. He'd lost a grayish twisted tooth. "What the hell was all that?"

"Hard to say," I repeated. "What was that back there?"

"Son of a bitch wasn't dead. Is now."

"You all right?"

"Yeah. You seen Leo?"

"He's down in the aspen grove, hiding. He's scared, but he's okay."

George shook his head, his anger more memory than emotion. "I tell that maniac he won't get up here in that fancy rig, he says they'll take the horses. I said no way, and the son of a bitch whacked me with his pistol, then was gonna shoot them."

He shook his head again, in angry mystification. "Leo run and let them loose. Saved them. Never thought Leo gave a damn about horses."

"He didn't save the gelding, George." I told him what had happened in the draw. I could see him seeing it. His gray

234

face went grayer, darkened the swelling bruises. "But you sure saved me. Saved all of us."

He gave me a blank look. He seemed still to be seeing in his mind the dead horse. "I—who are they, the women? The young one said she was Belle's—Mabel's—granddaughter?"

"And your brother's. Single John's."

"John and . . . ? Who's the whore?"

"She's your niece, George. She's John and Mabel's daughter."

He turned to stare into the dark doorway. The silence from inside the house seemed to overwhelm the silence of the mountain.

"The whole goddamn world is crazy, you know that?" He shook himself, as if to throw off a nightmare. "Now what?"

"Now we work like hell, concoct a little story, and maybe we'll get out of this mess."

Walking down the draw, I told him what we were going to do.

When we reached the dead horse, he looked at it for a long time. I expected him to explode, but he didn't. He just looked.

At the grove, he called for Leo, enticed him from the trees, silenced his frightened babble and heaped praise on him for saving three of the horses, and sent him up to the ranch house.

An hour later the sun stood high in the sky as we pulled his pickup and my Wagoneer up to stop beside Miranda's Bronco.

Miranda and Echo stood beside it, in a strange strained silence, together but not together, as Wes and Cleo James had stood before my door. They looked at the ranch house, tried to look at each other, looked at the mountains, the sky.

Leo Smith sat on the ground staring at them.

I climbed out. "Here's the plan, ladies. We clean up this mess. . . ."

They were listening. "What's the matter?"

Miranda turned to me. Her smooth face was bone-pale, her eyes huge. I looked at Echo. In her battered, masklike face her eyes looked out with a misery close to madness.

"What's the matter?"

Miranda tried to speak. "Jack, did you see . . . ?"

George came up beside me. Miranda turned from my confusion to him. "In the back room, did you see what's there?"

A softness, a strange gentle sadness settled into George's face. He looked at Miranda, at Echo. Then his lumpy old body moved toward them, his arms rose and bent in an ancient ageless gesture of humanity and hope.

"I seen it a long time ago," he said.

Miranda's eyes blurred with tears and she stepped into his arms. He looked at Echo. She looked at his swollen face, and whatever it was she saw in his eyes took some of the mad misery from hers and she also stepped forward into his embrace.

In the still silence of the mountain meadow, they did what humans, when all else failed, always did. They came together.

Leo stared at them. Then he got to his feet, brushed off the back of his pants, moved toward them tentatively, like a child uncertain of protocol. He put his hand hesitantly on Echo Smith's arm. "I seen it too."

Her face was buried in the bright orange of George's down vest. Without looking up, she lifted her arm and Leo Smith stepped into it and the four of them huddled together in silence, holding one another.

I hadn't seen it. I didn't want to see it.

Long shadows splashed George Smith's muddy ranch yard by the time we were finished.

The Mercedes was hidden in George's old barn. In a week or so, after things quieted down, he'd take it down to Chokecherry at night and run it into the mud flat and leave it.

The gray was in a deep grave deep inside the aspen grove. The other three horses were back in the corral.

The road up the mountain was a muddy rutted mess. George had a story to explain it, and a story to explain his face.

The gore splattering the meadow was scuffed under sand, scratched away with brush.

I had a rig filled with a sackful of guns and three bodies piled on and under layers of black plastic garbage bags.

"You know what to do, George?"

He nodded, "Wait till dark, then call the sheriff and report finding the body. Tell them stories."

"Miranda?"

"I don't see how it will work. Anybody who looks around at all will see—"

"They won't look," I said. "They'll come in darkness, see the body, look in that back room and have more than enough to occupy their imaginations. George will tell his stories. They know George, they trust him. You'll tell your story. They'll have you interview them so they can get on TV. They'll see what they want to see, Miranda."

She nodded. "And if they don't?"

I shrugged. "That's the chance we take."

"Why? Why take a chance, break the law? Why don't we just forget the stories and tell them the truth?"

She knew why.

She looked at her mother, looked down at the mud.

The embrace in the meadow, the reuniting of the Smith family, hadn't held. The four of them stood in the ranch yard, alone, the space between them as vast as the spaces between the stars. Between us.

Much of the afternoon Miranda and Echo had worked together, perhaps grieved together, but they spoke, as far as I could tell, little.

They had removed or hidden all traces of death from the meadow, all traces of Vanca's death from the house.

Miranda had followed Leo Smith up the ridge to get my stuff. Leo had followed her back down, as if in awe or love. To get him into the grove to dig the gelding's grave, we had to send Miranda with him. An hour later, when George and I came back from hiding the Mercedes, all three of them were in the grove. Miranda had her mini-cam.

I didn't know what had happened, or been said, in the house, the meadow, the grove. It didn't seem to have made much difference.

Through her daughter's questioning, Echo had been silent. Finally, she spoke. "Yes, Ross. Why?"

I looked at her, then looked directly at Miranda Santee.

"Because that's the way we do it in Nevada."

36

I drove down the mountain to the county road, over to the highway, down to Chokecherry, into the desert.

The night fell from the sky and onto the land in waves, until the desert was one broad black shadow and the mountains were another massive ragged black shadow outlined against the silky black shadow of the sky.

Echo Smith sat silently beside me, thinking her thoughts. I thought mine. Then I spoke one of them.

"What happened to the real Linda Goshgarian?"

"Real?" she said after a while, "There never was a real Linda Goshgarian, at least not—it was the phony name of one of Hiram's girls. She did something he didn't like and she ended up in the desert sucking sand. He had her papers, he had a collection of them, the one's he . . . took to the desert." Her hard hooker's laugh battered the darkness. "When they brought me in to run Tawny's, I had a choice of a dozen different names."

After a long dark silent time, as we eased over a low ridge, a spot of the sky ahead of us began to soften with a faint light, cast a pale shadowy nimbus into the night.

Tonopah.

I heard a strange sound, realized that Echo Smith had made it, realized that it was a laugh. "I was just thinking. If we got stopped for a burned-out taillight or something, you'd probably try to make up a story about those guns and the three bodies in back." She laughed again. "I'd sure like to hear that story."

"So would I."

I'd been thinking about those bodies. About the curious

and curiously fortuitous fact that three men had been shot to death on the big mountain behind us and I hadn't killed any of them.

Echo had killed one of them, and George Smith the other two.

Except that I'd been thinking about George, about the blank look he'd given me when I thanked him.

"Tell me about your father, Echo."

"What's to tell," she said finally. "He was just a man, just like every other man. He came and he went."

"Your mother loved him."

"My mother was crazy."

"You loved him."

I looked over at her. In the faint light from the dash her face was all rough flesh and dark shadow, like the masks on Marci Howe's office wall.

She felt my look, turned away, to the desert and the night.

"She loved him. He didn't love her, or me, or anybody. He was just a bum, a drifter. All he wanted was to be alone. My mother wouldn't leave him alone."

She turned from the darkness, into the glow from the dash, stared into the distant growing glow of Tonopah.

"I've met others like him. Every girl in the life has her true love. Some of them are like Single John Smith. Empty all the way down. The girls think they can fill them up, but all they do is get lost in the emptiness. And call it love."

"Like your mother."

"My stupid, crazy mother."

"Like your grandmother."

"Shut up, Ross."

"Like you."

She turned to look at me. "Just shut up, will you? Please?"

I shut up.

Like Single John Smith, Tonopah came and went.

I drove through the darkness, down, toward Las Vegas.

My mind began to wander, drift. Echo Smith dozed. I realized that she was exhausted. I realized that I was too.

At Beatty, I stopped for gas and coffee. Echo awoke, got out and went looking for a restroom. Before she got back in, she stood for a while and stared up into the sparsely starred sky.

"I always liked this little town," she said as I handed her a cup of coffee. "It's pretty, in a rough ugly sort of way."

I pulled the Wagoneer back onto the highway.

"What I saw of it, anyhow, from Fran's. I was young then. The men liked me. Miners mostly, rough and dirty, but they always got real quiet with me. I scared most of them, especially the young ones. Some were real sweet."

Even old hookers had pleasant memories.

As if she'd guessed what I was thinking, she gave a short hard bitter mocking laugh. "Fucked a fortune out of those hills."

Down onto the Amargosa, the highway like a black blade cut across its edge.

"Your mother talked about you sometimes, Jack."

I didn't say anything.

"That's one of the reasons she was going to marry the Basco. To get you back."

"One of the reasons?"

"She was in love with him," she said. "She wouldn't have done it, agreed to marry him, otherwise. She . . . she was a nice woman. She was nice to me. I liked her a lot."

"That's probably not why you killed her."

I let it hang in the dark silent space between us.

After a while, Echo said something similar to what Natty Stern had. "Celeste liked to laugh. She kept me and Mom in stitches. But her humor could be strange. Sometimes you couldn't tell if she was joking or not."

Soon, despite the coffee, my mind started drifting again. I knew how tired I was when, at the spot in the night where the headlight disappeared in the darkness, I began seeing faces. My mother's face. My daughter's. My grandfather's.

Faces from photographs, faces from life. Different faces but the same faces. Belle. Single John. Sage. Lanky Chandler. George, Leo, Miranda. Lois and James Bacigalupilaga. Wes James and Cleo James. Marci Howe and . . .

I shook the faces out of my mind and as I did, two of them came together.

What had Echo said to me about Sage, what had I said to Miranda about the sheriff and his troops?

They'll see what they want to see.

I knew that Echo Smith had killed my mother. What I'd just seen was why.

"Sage Chandler," I said.

"What?"

"She's your sister. She's the one all the fuss was about in Tonopah. The one everybody's been protecting and lying about."

She didn't answer.

"You took her to Lanky, from Tonopah. To get her away from Vanca. My mother didn't want to let you have her. She wanted to keep her. So you killed her."

When she spoke it was with the soft quiet voice she had used, that one time, on the mountain. "I wish Celeste had wanted to keep her."

"What did she want?"

"She said . . . she said a child's place was with its parents. She wanted to give Sage back to my mother and father."

I didn't understand. "What was wrong with that?"

"Everything, Ross. For one thing, my mother, out in the desert, she'd gone . . . round the bend. For another, Natty and Hiram were after her. For another, my grandmother was there. For another, my father was there. I—she wanted to put Sage into all of that, when Lanky had a chance to give her a real life, a good life, to get her away from . . ."

I thought about Sage, about her life. About what she'd gotten away from and what she'd gotten into.

Echo seemed to know what I was thinking. "That was her in the restaurant that night, wasn't it?"

"Yes."

"Are you and she . . . ?"

"No."

"Is she . . . ?"

I knew what she wanted to know, what she couldn't quite ask. She wanted to know if the life she had given Sage Chandler was worth the life of Celeste Ross.

"I don't know, Echo."

In fact, I didn't want to know. I didn't want to think about it. I asked something else.

"Does Lanky know he's not Sage's father? He's not, is he?"

"Sage and I aren't half-sisters, we're just . . . sisters." Her voice was ribbed with a curious pride. "Mom told Lanky

he was the father to get him to help, and Hiram that he was
the father to keep him from killing Lanky. Single John Smith
is her father, and mine."

"How does Sybil Chandler, Lanky's wife, fit into it?"

"You'd have to ask Lanky."

I didn't know if I would or not.

"That night at the Silver Sage, Lanky looked right at you
and didn't blink. He didn't know you."

She laughed her hard hooker's laugh. "He saw what he
wanted to see." That didn't do it, and she knew it. "I've been
hooking for almost thirty years, Ross. You figure it out."

The life, the scars. I figured it out.

The lights of Vegas threw up a pale-pinkish glow into the
night like the flames from a distant plague-ridden city put to
the torch. Or so it seemed. I was very tired.

"I know it doesn't matter," Echo said, "but I didn't mean to
kill her."

"What happened?"

"She came to the bar, and I left. Then I saw that creep she
was with, Bascomb, sneaking in the back. That meant that
the baby was alone. I went to their motel, but she wasn't
there. I—I panicked, maybe I went a little crazy, I don't
know. I went back to the bar and there was a riot going on.
Celeste—she was hiding in a corner. She . . . wouldn't tell
me where the baby was. I—I hit her. I didn't even know I had
a bottle in my hand. I wasn't trying to kill her. I didn't even
want to hurt her. I liked Celeste. She was my friend. But she
wouldn't tell me where my sister was."

Finally, the truth. Or at least a final story.

"Is that what you told my grandfather?"

"He knew most of it by the time he showed up. He . . . he
just sort of looked at me when I told him. Then he went
away."

But how did he already know most of it? There was only
one answer.

"Where was the baby?"

"What?"

"Sage, where was she that night? Where'd you find her?"

"Celeste's boyfriend had her. The Basco."

"He was baby-sitting Sage when my mother was killed?"

"Sort of. He was working, too. He was there with this kid,

she wasn't much more than my age. She was working at Bobbie's and somebody figured out she was underage and he was trying to help her, I guess. I—I remember looking at her, knowing she was a hooker, and feeling so sorry for her. . . ."

For a long time she was silent. Then she laughed. It died into the night.

"No one else knew you killed her, besides my granddad and Bacigalupilaga?"

"Only your granddad," she said. "The Basco doesn't know."

"He does know who Sage really is, doesn't he?"

"Yes." And was still lying to protect her.

"But he doesn't know that Sage isn't Lanky's daughter."

"No."

The lights of Tawny's Fillie Ranch flickered and jerked in sad obscene comedy.

"Those trees back there, where we buried the horse. My mother told me about them, but . . . it was different, seeing them. She told me I was conceived under those trees. They . . . the carvings, they aren't really about sex at all, are they?"

I almost said something. But, as tired as I was, I knew how fatuous it would sound. Even if it was true. So I didn't.

I pulled into the parking lot. Only two cars. It was three in the morning, the time for drunks and crazies and lost souls. Rocks and islands. I drove around the building, pulled up in back, parked beside Echo's gray Pinto.

"What are you going to do, Ross?"

"Right now I'm going to go in and borrow one of your beds. In a few hours I'm going to deliver a present to Natty Stern."

"Not that. I mean about me, about my killing your mother?"

"I'm going to do what my grandfather did," I said, and opened the door.

The night air was warm, desert-sweet. The scent of it made me aware of how foul the Wagoneer had become, gore, rotting flesh.

We went in the back. Music drifted down the long hallway. I didn't recognize it. Echo Smith stopped at one of the doors, opened it, turned on a light. "Will this do?"

"If it's got a bed."

I stepped past her. The small room contained other things, but all I saw was the bed. I eased myself onto it, tugged off my boots.

Echo stood in the doorway. "You want a girl to go with it?"

"No."

She smiled her proud hooker's smile. "Yes, you do."

She was right. "Shut up and turn off the light and go away."

Her smile got prouder, and ironic, and bitter, and something else.

"You want me, Ross? You wouldn't have to kiss me, or even look at me. I'd be just a body."

"Shut up," I said. "Please. Go away."

She reached out and turned off the light. I sagged back against the pillow.

She remained in the doorway, silhouetted against the light from the hall. The light flashed briefly on the tiny silver pistol that appeared in her hand.

"You could go to sleep and never wake up, Ross."

"I'll trust you to see that that doesn't happen."

She laughed, bitterly. "You'd trust me? Why?"

"Because my grandfather did."

She stood there for a moment, still, a shadow. Then she was gone and the door was closed and there was only darkness.

As I drifted off, I discovered that I, and she, had been wrong. It wasn't a girl I wanted. It wasn't a body.

I wanted what she and her daughter and her uncles had had, if briefly, as they held one another in the middle of the meadow on the top of the mountain.

The last thing I thought before I stopped thinking was that that was what Echo had wanted, too, as she stood in the doorway.

37

Sunlight. From the next room came the sounds of what might have been music, the sounds of what might have been love.

I sat up, stuffed my feet into my boots, rose, washed my face in a small low sink that was designed for washing something else, and stepped out into the hall.

The office door was open. Echo Smith sat at the desk. In her hand was the picture of Hiram Vanca. She looked at it strangely, with an emptiness at once passionate and hopeless.

On the desk lay a photograph that had been torn to pieces and then carefully taped back together into a coherent image.

She saw me, laid the photograph face-down on the desk. "I don't know what to do now."

Now, she meant, that she no longer had anyone to hate. Or love. Or protect. "Find something. After you talk to Cleo James."

Her hair was brushed smooth and hard, her mangled face shone cleanly, she wore a fresh-looking yellow robe. The room was filled with the scent of some musky flower. Still, for some reason, I didn't think she'd slept.

"That's really all you want?"

"The easiest thing you've ever done, Echo. Or the hardest."

"Linda. I'm Linda here. Now." Again. Forever.

"That's up to you, isn't it?"

She gave me a small hopeless smile. "Cletus's wife—all I'll do is tell her a story, Ross. You know that."

I knew that. "Tell her the right one."

She reached out toward the photograph she'd pieced together, stopped, dropped her hands into her lap. "Then what?"

"Whatever."

"Miranda . . . despises me."

"That's her problem."

She almost smiled. "Yes. I—is she all right?"

"I don't know, Echo. I'd guess we'll find out in about a week, when she does her first television show."

"Why? What's she—" Her mouth continued to move, but no sound came out of it.

"I don't know. We'll see. In the meantime, I'm off to deliver a present to Natty Stern. And tell him a story. I killed all of them, Echo, remember that."

"Why?"

"Just remember it. What did you tell him about the money?"

I was going too fast for her. "What money?"

"The money your mother brought out of the desert."

"I—there wasn't any money. She lost it in the desert."

"Is that what you told Stern?"

"Of course it is, it's the truth. Isn't it?"

"Of course it is. And that's what I'll tell him too."

It was an early April mid-morning, but already hot. The bare desert earth sent waves of heat back toward the sun.

I opened the Wagoneer's door, then opened all the windows before I got in. The smell wasn't too bad. But it was bad enough.

I drove to Natty Stern's place as fast as I could. The rush of dusty desert air cooled me, but couldn't blow away the smell of death.

The gate in the fence was locked. As I had before, I climbed out and up onto the fender and waited.

The sun still gleamed on the lacquered wood of the house, the steam still drifted over the hot spring's pond, the pump still groaned into the silence. But in the morning heat the land seemed not quite dead. Scattered tufts of brush stood stiffer, seemed healthier, stronger. Here and there over the rocky, sandy earth, bits of color showed—maybe new desert growth, maybe broken bottles from a drunken goons' gala.

I was growing angry. I tried to control it. Anger wouldn't help in what I was about to do.

But then, I didn't really know what I was about to do. Or why. All I knew was that I had to.

I had to end it.

Someone stepped from the goon shack, stared, disappeared. A minute later, two someones stepped out of the house. From the large body and dark suit, a goon. From the slim body and bright head, Marci Howe.

The goon strolled down toward the fence.

The goon's suit was beautiful, brown with a faint pale-blue pinstriping as subtle as the promise in a lover's eyes. The goon's gun was a 9 mm. The goon's eyes were empty. Empty all the way down.

Through the gate, he gave me a grim empty look and a message. "You're dead, Ross."

I grinned at him. "Hey, Tom, how's tricks?"

He unlocked the gate. "There are a dozen guys in there who'd love a piece of you. Natty gave you to me. As a present."

"For services rendered, no doubt. Maybe for the service I'm about to render him, he'll give you to me."

He didn't know what that meant. I didn't either.

I slid off the fender as he swung open the gate. As I got in behind the wheel, he followed the gun over to the window, stuck it in my ear, looked in the back.

"What's tha——" Then he smelled it and knew.

"Hop in," I grinned. "No point in getting that suit dusty."

He shoved the barrel deeper into my ear. "I'll walk. You drive. If this comes out of your ear it goes off."

I started the Wagoneer, dropped it into power low, eased out the clutch, took my foot off the gas, idled through the gate and inched down the dusty road. Tom Pardun walked alongside.

Three men came out of the goon shack. Another came out of the main house. Then came a wheelchair and a bundle of blankets that was Natty Stern, pushed by muscles in a white T-shirt.

"The Silver Sage a done deal yet, Tom?"

"Shut-up, Ross."

"Gotta hand it to you. You get Sage, take over the casino end from Lanky, he kicks off, you work it right and she doesn't even know what's going on. Impressive. A fella that ambitious and slick might even end up running this whole shooting match. If Marci Howe doesn't kill you, that is."

He looked down at me, smiled. "I went to an execution a few years ago, Ross. Tough guy, like you. Phony tough, like you. At the end, when he knew he wasn't going to get out of it, he got to babbling. Like you."

"By golly, you got me there, Tom."

The dirt road arced up toward the house. A pair of ruts broke from it, led toward the steaming pond and groaning pump. I aimed the Wagoneer at them.

"Where you going?" The barrel of his gun dug into my ear. I winced at the pain, felt the ooze of blood. "To the house."

"Somebody'd just have to haul me back down," I said. "Think of all the work I'm saving you."

The gun jabbed again. "Do it, Ross, or—"

"You do it! Shoot or shut up!"

He couldn't shoot. Not yet. He shut up.

I put the Wagoneer in the ruts and eased along the thick barrier of black-green reeds. The steam dampened my nostrils, the sulfurous scent drove off the smell of death.

A rickety-looking wooden walkway led through a gap in the reeds along the edge of the water to a wider gap in front of the pump house. I nosed the Wagoneer just past the opening.

Tom Pardun took the pistol out of my ear and stepped back. I carefully opened the door and got out.

"You know what to do," he said.

I assumed the position. "You think I'd insult Mr. Stern's hospitality by bringing a weapon in here?"

"Shut up."

Metal creaked. I turned to see Natty Stern in his chair moving toward us. And Marci Howe. And four men.

I watched them approach. Mostly I watched Marci Howe. I'd almost forgotten how beautiful she was.

"Mr. Ross," the old man said, "you have something for me?" Swaddled in blankets, he was much like he'd been in his pool, a talking head.

"I do, Mr. Stern."

"Belle Smith?"

"She's dead."

"My property?"

"I'll get to that. First, I have a present for you."

I stepped to the back of the Wagoneer and opened it. "I'll need some help. We don't want to show disrespect for the dead."

Marci Howe smiled at me. Tom Pardun kept his gun on me. Natty Stern nodded, and two of the goons came over. One of them peeled back the corner of the top black garbage bag, exposing what was left of Goon's face. He dropped the black plastic as if it were death itself.

"They won't bite," I said, and pulled the plastic off.

The goons lifted out the body and carefully set it on the ground. They lifted out the body of Apprentice. Natty Stern wheeled closer. He looked briefly at the bodies on the ground, longer at the body still in the Wagoneer.

"A strange present, Mr. Ross. What do you imagine that I will do with it?"

"Whatever you want with those two, Mr. Stern. But Oedipus here goes where he's put so many himself."

"Oedipus? Oh, yes. He now has no eyes." He laughed his cackling laugh. "Like your mother, Mr. Ross."

"Tom will have to help me, if that's all right, Mr. Stern. Everything's pretty much drained and dried. It shouldn't hurt his pretty suit."

The old man laughed again. Marci Howe smiled. Tom Pardun flushed with anger.

"Certainly, Mr. Ross. Do what you will. Then we talk."

I reached in and grabbed a pair of ankles, stiff under the socks, clammy cold through them. Tom Pardun stuffed his pistol into his holster, reached in and picked up the body under the arms. "I'm going to enjoy doing you, Ross."

"Yeah," I said, "you can tell Sage's son all about it."

The body wasn't heavy. Tom Pardun had most of the weight. I had the easy end. I had something else. For the first time since I'd left the mountain, I had something resembling an idea.

We hauled the body over toward the planking. Marci Howe walked beside us, looking into the gory dead ugly face.

The planking was narrow, old, smooth, slicked with dampness. That was good.

I grinned at Marci. "You want a moment of silence, a last

farewell to dear old dad? How about that devilishly dashing patch as a keepsake?"

She smiled her smile. "He was my father, of course. But he hasn't been of use for a long time. He couldn't even handle you."

"Past his prime," I said,"if he'd been a horse, you'd have put him out to pasture."

She smiled again. "Get him as far out as you can. That way he might not clog the pump."

"Right. You ready, Tommy-boy?"

"Shut up," Tom Pardun said. He was sweating in the heat.

I carefully backed onto the boards. They sagged, squeaked with the weight. I began to sweat.

I didn't have to try it. It might kill me. But I thought about Sage Chandler, how I'd made her feel so alone the morning I'd left her. I wanted to make her feel alone again. It was the only chance she had.

The water lapped at the supports of the walkway, the pump groaned, the wood squeaked, our shoes scuffed, Tom Pardun grunted. The sun was bright, the sky blue and empty, the desert silent.

I started to laugh. My mother had died for Sage Chandler. Now I was probably going to do the same thing.

"You're crazy, Ross," Tom Pardun grunted.

We reached the pump and the opening. I could feel the heat of the water. The pump groaned louder, like a tired old whore.

"Remember," I called above the sound of the pump. "Way out. You got a grip?"

His scowl darkened on his damp face, his fingers dug into the stiff cloth and dead flesh.

"On three. Ready?"

He glared at me.

"Uhh . . . one!"

We dragged the dead weight back a foot or so, swung it forward, fought physics, won.

We pulled the body back even farther.

"Uhh . . ." We swung it forward farther.

"Two!"

I let go.

The lower half of the body flew out over the water, caught

against Tom Pardun's weight, swung, tugged, jerked him forward. He let go of the body. Too late.

The body thunked against the walkway and slid into the dark water. Tom Pardun fought for balance and lost. He cried out in rage and fear, his arms flailing for balance, his hands clawing for purchase in the nothing of the air.

He toppled, hit the water. His cry became a scream and his scream became silence.

He went under, came up. His mouth was still open, but no sound issued from it. His eyes stared as Belle Smith's had. He went under again, almost came back up.

Set in his death scream, his face swam for a moment near the surface of the dark steaming water. His mouth was open and dark, his eyes open and dead. Slowly the darkness of the water grew, the whiteness of his face dimmed, and he disappeared.

Vanca's body floated for a few seconds more. Then, as if in the grip of a firm, steady hand, it sank into the darkness.

I looked back at the figures standing on solid desert ground. I was a little surprised I was able to.

No one had moved. The goons were stunned. Natty Stern looked as if he might be dead. Marci Howe's smile floated a foot in front of her face.

I walked back along the wooden planks.

A goon moved, a gun appeared in his hand. He stepped forward and Natty Stern put out a crablike hand and stopped him. Marci Howe gathered her smile back, met me at the foot of the walkway. "I may have underestimated you, Ross?"

"You can thank me later."

She smiled again. "I think maybe Sage is the one who should thank you."

"Yeah," I said. "But she probably won't."

Natty Stern stared at me. I walked up to him. "Oops."

His sagging face split into a sudden smile. "Ah, Mr. Ross," he laughed. "So like your mother."

"I guess so."

"And what entertainment have you planned for us now?"

"I thought I'd tell you a story, Mr. Stern. Then I thought I'd tell you where your property is. Then I thought I'd leave."

"One thought too many, Mr. Ross. But tell me your story."

I told him Belle Smith's story. I told him what happened to Belle at Chokecherry thirty years before, and what happened to her at Chokercherry the day before. I told him that I'd killed the goons and Vanca.

He listened attentively. "Very interesting, Mr. Ross. About your mother, I'm happy to learn that she had no part in that business. She was a good girl. I enjoyed her very much."

"So you said."

"And my property?"

I waved my hand toward the gate and what lay beyond it—rock and dirt, greasewood and yucca, snakes and scorpions, hot springs and salt flats and sand pits and a dozen ways to die and a hundred hungry desert creatures to pick the bones.

"It's out there, somewhere. It's never been more than twenty miles from this place. Unless the suitcase came open and the wind got to it. Then it could be anywhere. Some of it may even be in the trash collecting along your fence."

He wasn't happy. "You expect me to believe that, Mr. Ross?"

"I don't care if you believe it or not, Mr. Stern. You wanted to know where your property was. You do."

"I know what you told me. Another story." He nodded. Each of the four goons suddenly had a gun in his hand.

Marci Howe stepped over to the chair, leaned, whispered. Natty Stern listened, but his eyes didn't leave my face. Marci Howe stood straight, smiled at me, shrugged.

Natty Stern looked at me. Then he laughed his cackling laugh. "In memory of your mother, Mr. Ross. You may go."

His head jerked and the guns disappeared. The muscle man in white turned the chair and pushed it slowly up the slope toward the house. The goons followed.

Marci Howe didn't.

"What did you tell him?"

She smiled. "That you would be of use to us someday."

"Not a chance."

"I also told him that you were hopelessly romantic and sentimental and guilt-ridden. That because I was saving your life you would come when I called you. That you did have a code, you just didn't know it."

"No way."

She smiled her smile.

"Why did you do it?"

"I have a code too. You've just done me an immense favor."

"Pardun," I said. "What did he want?"

"He wanted it all."

"How did you get to him?"

She smiled, shook her head. "So naive, Mr. Ross. We didn't. He came to us."

"How did you get to Lanky?"

She smiled again. "Mr. Stern has always known who Sage was, Mr. Ross. He's also known that Lanky would do anything he had to to keep that knowledge from Vanca. And from Sage herself."

There was only one way for that to make sense. "The Silver Sage has always been a done deal."

She smiled.

So much for the myth of Lanky Chandler.

Marci Howe again smiled her wonderful smile.

"Good-bye, Mr. Ross. Give my love to Sage."

38

The gray Pinto wasn't parked at Tawny's Fillie Ranch. It didn't matter. I wasn't planning to stop anyway.

I wasn't planning to stop in Tonopah either.

James Bacigalupilaga's dirty pickup was parked in front of his office, and for a moment I slowed. Then I said the hell with it and drove through town and into the desert.

After a mile, I turned around and went back.

He sat at the desk of his denlike office. I stood in the open door. "Peg Madigan is dead."

He looked at me from his cavelike eyes. "I heard."

"You probably have her power of attorney, and will execute her will, if there is one. Her heirs are her granddaughter, Linda Goshgarian, neé Echo Smith, care of Tawny's Fillie Ranch, and her great-granddaughter, Miranda Santee, of Reno."

"I'll see that the estate is handled properly."

"There's another daughter. No one knows where she is."

He sat, looked at me, said nothing.

"Tell me again that you don't know Lanky Chandler."

The animal that lived in the caves of his eyes went wary, shifted furtively.

I could feel the anger burning in my belly.

"Lanky told me that about all my mother wanted was a man who wasn't a total asshole. Too bad she never found one."

"You know . . . ?"

I had to get out of there.

"Yeah, I know. I know who you've been bleeding for thirty years, I know whose money paid for that pretty ranch of yours. And I know something else. Jude Bascomb didn't kill my mother. I know who did. And you never will."

I was in the desert for an hour before the burning stopped.

I got to Reno late, showered until I stopped smelling death, went to bed and slept till the next morning.

I called my daughter, listened to her, talked to her, and began to feel faintly human.

Then I waited.

The call came at sunset.

Cleo James didn't seem to know what to say. "She . . . was here. She came yesterday. She just left."

"Did she tell you what you wanted to know?"

"She . . ." Emotion or a fault in the line scratched out what she said next. All I heard was ". . . more than I wanted."

"Are you all right?"

"Yes. I—did you tell the police?"

"No."

"Am I supposed to?"

"That's up to you?"

There was a long silence. Then she spoke. "I . . . hope you don't take this wrong, Mr. Ross. It's just—I hope I never see or hear of you again."

"Good-bye, Mrs. James."

I had another wait to get through.

In the middle of it, a couple of days later, I had breakfast with Frank Calvetti. I told him I knew who had killed Dalton James, and that I wasn't going to tell him.

He didn't say anything.

He finished his breakfast, stirred his coffee. "Several people have disappeared. Hiram Vanca and a couple of Stern's goons, Vegas says. And Tom Pardun."

"Imagine that," I said.

"Lanky reported him missing. He didn't seem especially distraught by the disappearance. Then we checked Tom's house. We found some things that shouldn't have been there. Little things, odd. Some people say they don't mean anything. Others say that if you put them together, they tell an ugly story."

"Imagine that."

He sat and stirred his coffee. Then he shook his head in genuine sorrow. "Yeah, imagine."

Outside, we stood for a moment in the cool morning air.

"You going back to the desert?"

"No."

"Good. You going to resign from the bar? I only ask because it's important. Not to a lot of people, maybe, but to you. To you, violating an oath matters." He looked at me. "Or it used to."

"It still does," I said.

"Did you find out who killed your mother?"

"Yes."

"That wasn't what you really wanted to know, was it?" When I didn't answer, he went on. "You really wanted to know who and what she was, and who and what you were. Did you find that out?"

I hadn't learned very much about my mother. But maybe I'd learned enough.

"Everybody has always told me that I was just like my grandfather, Frank. That's true, I think. But since I've been out of the desert, everybody's been telling me I was just like my mother. I think that's true too."

"Does it bother you?"

"Nope."

"Yeah," he said. "Thanks for breakfast."

The Silver Sage was busy, filled with middle-aged men and women with plastic smiles pasted on their faces and paper name tags on their chests.

Lanky Chandler was dealing Hold 'Em. He looked better. He saw me, grinned his billboard grin, dealt, raked, talked.

I watched and listened, tried to merge the image of Lanky Chandler in the stories I'd heard with the image of Lanky Chandler the Legend. All I could see was the old man in the silly cowboy costume who sat before me pretending to be himself.

Finally he grinned, held my eye, nodded toward the bar.

The bar was crowded. I squeezed onto a stool, ordered a beer, checked my watch, asked the bartender to turn on the TV, told him the station I wanted, told him he didn't need to turn on the sound yet.

The news was on. I didn't watch the soundless images. I

sipped my beer, then decided I didn't really want it. Like Rafe Stillwell, I sat and watched it go flat.

I looked up as Lanky's image appeared in the back mirror. A sort of seismic shudder ran along the bar, and an empty stool appeared beside me.

Then Lanky Chandler did something he'd never done to me before. He held out his hand. "Jack, how are you?"

I shook his big dry soft hand, ignored the sudden memory of Belle Smith's thin scarred hand. "Fine, Lanky. You look good."

He took the stool. "Amazing what a month off the booze and a couple nights' sleep will do."

The bartender positioned himself directly before Lanky. I saw fear in his face. Lanky washed it away. "Gimme a Coke.

"I'm glad you came in, Jack," Lanky said. "I wanted to apologize for what happened, for me . . . slapping you."

"I brought it on myself."

"No," he said. "But it wouldn't matter if you did. Booze or no booze, a man ought not to act that way to his friends."

"Apology accepted," I said, knowing he might soon act that way again. "Belle died a few days ago."

Along the bar the drinkers kept drinking, the talkers kept talking, the machine feeders kept feeding machines.

Only Lanky Chandler changed.

His face set in a mask of hope and despair, like the masks of Comedy and Tragedy somehow imposed on one another.

His voice, when it came, was a whisper. "Where?"

I told him where. When. How. I told him everything.

Tears formed in his eyes. He wasn't Lanky Chandler anymore. He was just an unhappy old man. "I thought she was dead."

"You thought you'd killed her. You thought that when you didn't pick her up after she shot Vanca, she tried to walk out of the desert and didn't make it."

Tears smearing his eyes, he stared at his reflection in the back mirror, as if trying to determine who and what he was. "You talked to her before . . . ? What did she say about . . . ?"

"She said you told her you loved her and then betrayed her."

Tears trembled in his pink-rimmed, red-veined eyes. He seemed unaware of them. "I chickened out."

It was a strange expression, strangely expressed, a bit of childish slang spoken as if from a remembered childhood.

"As long as I was with her, it seemed real, like it could work. But as soon as I was away from her, it turned into a dream. Where could we go that Natty couldn't find us? How could we hide? And leave everything I'd managed to . . ."

He stared into the mirror. I watched him watch himself.

After a while, he said, "I know it doesn't matter, but I suffered for it. I've had to live with it all these years, the idea that I'd killed her. It . . . takes something out of you."

"I'm overwhelmed with sympathy, Lanky. Especially since it also killed my mother."

He rasped at me. "Jack, I didn't kill Celeste. I swear—"

"You left Belle to die in the desert. That started the process that ended up killing my mother."

That wasn't completely true, but it was true enough.

"Your granddad didn't think so. He didn't hold me—"

"What were you afraid was in his file? The file he didn't have? The file you were afraid Miranda Santee might get."

He seemed in pain. "People would have been hurt."

"What people? You thought Belle was dead, so it couldn't be her. I can see how knowledge of your abandoning Belle to the desert might shoot the Legend of Lanky Chandler to hell, but—"

"No," he said, "I don't care about that. I—didn't want Sage to know . . . what I'd done."

"Or to know that she's Belle's daughter?"

His voice went hard. "If I thought you'd tell anybody I'd kill you, right here, with my bare hands."

"Why? What possible difference could it make that she's your daughter by Belle rather than by Sybil?"

"It would . . . all these years a lie, all she went through with Sybil, thinking . . ."

I thought I understood what he was trying to say. It wasn't enough. "The whole charade, Lanky, what was the point?"

He looked at his hands, looked at them as George Smith had looked at his, as if they'd failed him. Lanky suddenly called to the bartender. "Wild Turkey. The bottle."

"Chickening out again, Lanky?"

He turned his hands into fists. "You son of a bitch, Ross."

"Maybe, Lanky," I said. "But that isn't what everybody's been telling me. Everybody, including you, has been telling me what a nice person my mother was, how like her I am."

Although there was no reason it should have, that remark took everything out of him. His fists slowly fell apart, and momentarily his face.

He put the face back together. "That goddamned Vanca. He thought he was Sage's father. Belle told him that, to keep him off me. We couldn't let him know where Sage was. He would've—"

"He would have what?"

"How do I know? He was crazy. He would've . . . whatever it was, it would've ruined her life. Think of growing up Vanca's daughter, what that could do to a kid."

I'd seen what it could do. "What about Sybil?"

"It was just a deal we made, Jack. A deal your grandfather set up. You want to hear the story? It's a dilly."

I didn't want to hear the story. "Vanca's dead."

His hate and fear of Hiram Vanca were so old and strong that he didn't believe me. "Are you sure? Did you kill him?"

"I disposed of the body. Tom Pardun is dead too."

He looked at me, saw what I knew, didn't seem to care. "Then it's . . . finally over."

"No. Natty's still got his hold on you, Lanky. Now it's not his knowing who Sage is, it's his knowing what you've done for and with him for the last thirty years."

He shook his head. "It was nothin', Jack. A few favors here and there, a little percentage. Less than taxes."

"And James Bacigalupilaga? How much did he bleed from you?"

"It wasn't like that. You see everything ugly. . . . He did some legal work for me, every once in a while, that's all."

"You thought it was all in the file, didn't you, Lanky? The file that never existed?"

He sat up straighter. His eyes cleared. "It's over, Jack. Belle, Vanca, everybody's dead. None of it matters now."

"It won't be over until you tell Sage, Lanky. Maybe not even then, not if you tell her all of it."

He looked at me, looked away, looked into the mirror of the bar.

"No. They don't have anything on her. Everybody's dead. I'll be dead too, pretty soon. Maybe sooner."

He was serious, deadly. He'd kill himself before he told Sage the truth.

"She needs to know, Lanky."

He looked at his reflection, turned to look at me.

"There are things some people should never know. I— even you, Jack. There are things people haven't told you. For your own good."

"You mean who my father is? It doesn't matter anymore."

He shook his head, looked at me with what seemed to be real sympathy. "I mean, about your mother and your grandfather, why Celeste ran away from home, why he . . . did what he did."

I thought about it.

There had always been something very wrong at the bottom of it, at the bottom of his silences. There had always been a darkness lurking in the depths of the desert look.

But it didn't matter. It was just another story. I didn't want to hear it.

It was another locked door.

My mother and my grandfather were dead.

It didn't matter. I wasn't going to open that door either.

Nor would I tell Lanky Chandler that he wasn't Sage's father, that he'd lived a dream for thirty years, a dream as artificial as the legend he'd created.

"All right, Lanky," I said, "I won't—"

From the television screen, Miranda Santee smiled at us through her silently speaking lips. I nudged Lanky, called to the bartender to turn up the sound.

"It may not make any difference, Lanky."

He looked up at Miranda. "What? What's she—"

"I don't know," I said.

But I did know. She was going to tell a story. I didn't know what story she would tell. I didn't know what story she knew. But she would tell a story, and then maybe Lanky would have to tell a story and maybe I would have to tell a story. Stories and more stories.

I caught the scent of the desert after rain. Sage slipped onto a stool beside me.

". . . first story of our series is rather strange, but in Nevada the strange is the typical," Miranda was saying.

The smile on her face was the smile that she'd said she

hated, the smile that she'd said Nevada made every woman wear.

Her face vanished, and the screen filled with a shot of an aspen grove on a mountain in the interior of Nevada.

"It began, if stories can ever be said to begin, in the shade of trees carved by the knives of lonely young men. . . ."

The shot changed, the meadow appeared, the ranch house.

"Sixty years ago a woman named Mabel Margaret Madigan was born in this house," Miranda's disembodied voice said.

"Jesus," Lanky whispered, "what's she doing?"

I shrugged, watched the screen.

Sage Chandler leaned toward me, her damp dusty desert scent like a caress, and put her lips next to my ear. "Is Tom dead?"

I nodded, watched the screen.

"She died as Belle Smith in this house two weeks ago," Miranda's voice said.

The camera panned over the meadow, the house.

Sage whispered again. "Did you kill him?"

I nodded again, watched the screen.

The scent of the desert dissipated, dissolved, disappeared.

The camera panned slowly over the escarpment behind the house. Rocky ledge, dark trees, dark shadows of trees.

One of the shadows of one of the trees moved, wasn't a shadow and wasn't a tree.

Sunlight flashed on metal. The metal was a rifle barrel.

George Smith hadn't fired the first rifle shot on the mountain that afternoon.

Single John Smith had found something of consequence.

"This is the story of how Nevada transformed Mabel Madigan into Belle Smith. It's also the story of how Nevada killed her."

I rose, left Lanky Chandler at the bar listening to Miranda Santee tell a story.

Western Literature Series